Bachelor Doctor

Chapter 1

This is a story written by a woman about a man. It is, as well, a story written by a mother about her son. To me, that mother, this is an important thing to do, and I have made formal preparations for doing it. I have assembled an array of pencils and pens. I have a stack of large notebooks such as the children used to buy for their schoolwork. I can use a typewriter, and have one in the small sitting room that adjoins our bedroom, but somehow I feel that I can do more thinking and remembering if I write by pencil.

I have chosen to begin the task, and perhaps continue it, here in the smaller, brighter parlor of our stately old house. I shall write on this small table where there is a good lamp, and between writing sessions I shall put my material away into one of the cupboards in the wainscoting. No one would bother to read or disturb the papers should I leave them out, but the maids dusting, or Jason needing a scrap of paper on which to make a reminder note, would not respect the requirements of an author.

An author?

I suppose I shall be one if I really write Grady's story. I want to do it, and I shall try to finish it.

This small parlor is a pleasant room in a pleasant house. Necessarily a large house, it is of gray brick, ivy hung. It is an old house, built in the middle years of the last century. I was born in this house, as was my father before me. Jason and I have lived here all our married years, and have raised our family here.

Through the years there have been changes. Now a bay window in the front of the house extends from the second floor. In my girlhood, a high flight of double stairs led to the entrance there, but the stairs have been removed and a more suitable entrance at street level has been substituted.

Within the house there have been changes, too, but the French wallpaper still glows upon the walls of the two parlors, and wide-planked hardwood floors gleam with more than a hundred years of wax and rubbing muscles.

My name is Helen Shields McCord, and now, into my first sixties, my blonde hair is more gray than golden. As a girl I learned to sit erect and stand erect, so to do that now is the natural thing. My voice was modulated, my manner restrained — I remember no pain attached to such schooling. I regret that more is not done along those lines for our present young people.

The story I would tell is one which I know first-hand by intimately sharing in it. Some of the things I have heard by shamelessly eavesdropping. I am a quiet person and can stand at an open window, or sit in a chair unobtrusively enough that others in the room forget I am present. Perhaps, knowing that I am discreet, they consider me no obstacle to free talk. Some of the parts of this story were told me by my husband Jason, who talked things over with me; he talks to me. Especially when he is troubled.

And Grady often has troubled him.

I am Helen McCord, and I am the mother of six sons. I have heard myself called a good mother. I claim only to have loved my sons dearly, with the reward of believing that they love me.

My husband, Jason, is a doctor. A surgeon. I loved him at nineteen, I married him, and the excitement of our marriage has changed, of course, but not lessened through the years. I was proud of my tall, earnest young bridegroom; I am even more proud of my tall, gray-haired doctor now.

I was an only child, though Jason himself

9

comes from a large family. The McCords — I have never quite had time or courage to count all of them. There are the five brothers, their wives, their children . . .

The brothers — Jason is the next to oldest — are all doctors. The boys' uncles, this means. Though, truthfully, Abraham — Uncle A.B. — is a biochemist with a Ph.D degree. There was a time when Grady became rather a pest about this title, and the use of it. But then, Grady always liked to be pesty; he still does. I personally feel that Grady has been good for the family pomposity.

The boys' uncles, then, are doctors, as was their grandfather McCord. I remember him well. He lived in the house where his youngest son, Bishop, now lives — because Bish never married, and was living in the home when the old gentleman died. It was the natural thing for him to stay on, the other sons having established their households. Grandfather McCord is given credit for establishing the excellence of our medical school and its affiliated hospitals.

He was a tall, lean man with bushy gray eyebrows and a shock of gray hair. He was a very strong man; I don't suppose any one of his sons would have dared been anything but a doctor.

His father had been one of the developers of Southshire Place, a community of fifty large homes all built between 1835 and 1900. At the time of its establishment, the Place was considered suburban, almost rural. Several families kept a cow, or even two. All had horses. The parkway featured a pond which has now dwindled into a splashing fountain.

It is family fiction that the Medical Center was established three blocks down the Boulevard because of the McCord family and their homes in Southshire Place. Now and then, Jason or his oldest brother, Lucian, will say dryly that it is a great convenience to have the Center so close.

The Center, of course, is an ever-growing institution — in its physical size, its prestige, its accomplishments, its service to the community and the world. In the first World War, and in the second one, it sent a complete hospital unit into service. The Center is big in all senses of that word. At the time of my writing it consists of eleven hospitals, nine clinics, and the University Medical School for which it serves as a teaching hospital. The latest development is a high white tower, a city block square, which affords everything from diagnostic services, intensive care units, doctors' offices, to a restaurant and swimming pool on the roof.

The Center is often spoken of as the McCord hospitals, and the new tower is called that, officially. The McCords work in these hospitals, the McCords live in Southshire Place. The Boulevard — Sherwood Boulevard — connects the two institutions. On Sherwood there are fine hotels, the Junior League clubrooms, and their tearoom where old-city mothers present their daughters to society. There is a fine food store, and fine specialty shops of all sorts, linens, clothing, a jeweler, a decorator, a bookstore . . .

Southshire Place was conceived as a semirural community, and it has resisted the modern trend to country suburban living. It extends for three city blocks, from Sherwood Boulevard to Waterford Avenue, with no cross streets. There are wrought-iron gates set into massive stone at either end of the Place. These gates are locked at night. Residents must unlock them, and lock them behind their cars — or answer to the watchman, hired by the association and given police powers by the city. The doctors sometimes complain about this locking and unlocking, but their complaints dwindle as they grow older and as privacy becomes more of a treasure.

Within the Place are fifty homes. Every possible style of architecture can be seen. Our square brick, three stories tall, every window shuttered. Joe — Dr. Joseph McCord — has taken the shutters from his pink house, but it runs excessively to balustrades, along the sidewalk edge of his lawn, around each of the three front porches, even around the roof. There is Lucian's white brick mansion with its magnificent Corinthian portico, Henry Tibbs' three-story frame with its fine Palladian front, though the family friend and lawyer lived in two rooms to the rear of the first floor. There is Abraham's — A.B. we call him. His columned red brick house might have been moved bodily from Charleston. Bish McCord's long, low white stone house, the Falks' pink stucco, a couple of half-timbered Tudors . . .

The houses seem to lessen in size toward Waterford Avenue, and I think they actually do — which isn't bad, these days. Nowhere else does one find so many large and, often, largely empty homes. But we cling to them.

The city flows past its gates, with its noise and dust and bustle. Within there are tall trees, well-kept lawns, sprinklers flashing in the sun, carriage houses now become garages, with cars of all sorts — sleek modern cars, low sports cars, little foreign-made bugs, and almost as many old, classic cars kept sleek and pridefully functioning.

There are children of all sorts, too, in the Place. Ponies are ridden down the center parkway, servants who have, many of them, been inherited along with the homes. Their family lines go back as far as our own. Today, shutters do not suffice for protection. Most of us have iron grillwork at our windows and doors. The Falks put in this sort of ornamentation sixty years ago, for beauty's sake. Today it is a necessity.

I have lived in the Place for more than sixty years. I can testify that the effort has been toward comfort rather than ostentation, but sometimes it seems that the one has necessarily enfolded the other. The Place seems to have had a generative quality of its own. A modest, square house would need a wing for a growing family. That wing could demand a second one, perhaps to balance the architectural effect, perhaps to house grandchildren, or an aunt. A small herb garden at the kitchen door encouraged larger flower beds. Water should be piped conveniently to these plantings; one might as well put a small fountain against a wall, or build a small swimming pool – for summers when the family could not get to Wisconsin or to the coast. Shrubbery and a gigantic privet hedge would screen the pool. A bit of statuary adorned it.

And so, as the years passed, we found ourselves living in, and maintaining, a place of dignity, of richness, or what often has been called awesome pomposity by kids like my sons Grady and June.

14

The McCords all live close to each other — with Joe down a block away from the rest of us. Jason and I stayed on in my parents' home, Lucian, the oldest McCord brother, lives in the one formerly belonging to another Dr. McCord — an uncle. The brothers, Joe and A.B., both bought their homes, which involved a deal of red tape. Southshire Place is a private corporation. A piece of property there cannot be bought or sold without Board approval. There are no stated restrictions as to race or creed, but congenial people started the project, congenial people maintain it. Our city runs to such privately owned units, some less luxurious than Southshire; one, at least, is more so.

Some of the big houses on the Place are full, lively with children and dogs and friends. Some are almost empty — Henry Tibbs' and the Falks' across the street from us. Taylor was an only child, though a lovely, auburn-haired little girl, younger than the youngest of my sons. Not many houses are sold. Most of them are inherited, as are the servants and the family friends. This results in a unit of many parts, but a unit nevertheless. We have surprises, we share griefs, we share our joys with each other. Our children attend private schools together; frequently there are marriages within the gates. Jason and I were one of those marriages.

All this, of course, requires money. The very

rich live in Southshire, as do the once-rich. The money possessed is that of solid fortune. The Place is built along a single pattern, elegance being its style — a style which has become a little worn in spots, but is elegant nevertheless. We tend to be clannish, we build our own pools, our own tennis courts — and flood them in the winter to afford a skating surface. On such courts Grady learned to skate so wonderfully well.

Grady and his brothers — there are six boys. Abe, named for his Uncle A.B., born within the first year of our marriage, then Shields, and Grady. David, and Humphrey, and finally Jason, Jr. — June, the youngest. A gang of boys, their father called them. Each one precious, each one different from his brothers, all McCords.

Naturally, with the McCords following their fixed path of medicine, there are several doctor's wives to be included in this account. I am such a wife, and I feel myself privileged. With Jason a popular surgeon, Chief of Staff, Chief of Surgical Services — he has always been a busy man. I could consider myself neglected, but I do not. I am busy, too, caring for my husband, his home, his family — his lively family.

Now Mary feels that she should have a certain place in Lucian's life, that his plans for her should be as complete as his plans for his work as a famous heart specialist. Four children do not fill her time and interests.

And Eve – well, Joe doesn't always walk the straight and narrow either. If a man marries a great beauty, one whom men admire extravagantly, and desire openly, he should attend to his hearthside better than Joe sometimes does.

But this is to be my son Grady's story. He, of all the McCords, and of all the people who live in Southshire, did not fit into the pattern. I once saw a beautiful, silky Oriental rug – a tapestry, really, it was so beautiful. The colors were ivory, rose, soft blue and green – except for a single thread of brilliant red that slashed across the pattern. Was the rug spoiled by it? No. Rather, that one thread fascinated the beholder and made him look more closely at the whole rug, see it more clearly.

Grady . . . I am writing this, thinking that perhaps, if I put his story down on paper, I shall come to an understanding of my son.

I love Grady. I love him very dearly. The family – we all admire him. We have admired him when he was shocking us most. During the past months, during the past years –

Oh, he has shocked us many, many times.

I suppose the first real shock came when he ran away from home. He was sixteen, and – Of

17

course the boys all took their turns at "running away," leaving home. I remember Abe's first doing it when he was five, announcing his project to me. I asked him to wait until I could have Orlie, the houseman, pack a lunch for him. His eyes got very big, and he set his stack of books and his bow and arrow on the stairs. He wandered out through the front door and never missed a meal afterward.

When Shields ran away — one of the times — he was discovered hidden on the tiled roof of the carriage house, somewhat concealed by the branches and leaves of the gingko tree. No one spoke to him, or called to him, and after several hours he came down on his own and went about for days, quiet, thoughtful.

Grady — that was different. He was sixteen; he disappeared. We did not know where he had gone, we could not find him — we were shocked that such a thing could happen. When, years later, he finally returned, hungry for the love and security of our home, we were uneasy and shocked all over again.

We were very shocked, exceedingly shocked, when he decided to study medicine. His father asked him why, and Grady's answer shook him up for days.

Now medicine was a tradition in the family. When Shields made his decision and entered pre-medical school, there was a feeling of satisfaction in all concerned. That boy was exactly the right sort. Even as a child he had said he would be a doctor. He was a steady lad, unswerving in his purposes. But Grady?

Volatile, impulsive – even ruthless at times – perhaps he was the least probable of our six boys to study medicine.

But he did study it. And even as he began to study, to frequent the halls of the hospitals as a student, he began to write. Magazine articles, newspaper articles, about the things he was seeing, about the things he was being taught. I myself was proud to see his name, Grady McCord, in print.

But that name, so displayed, was a red rag to his father and to his uncles.

And finally . . .

Of course, apart from Grady, there had been other shocking events and intervals in Southshire Place, and in the McCord family.

There was Joe and Eve. That Joe should marry an actress startled us all. She was beautiful; and famous. It did not surprise us that the woman – any woman – should be attracted to Joe. He was a charming rascal, and clever, a slender, lithe man, with golden skin, black hair close to his skull, fine eyes, and a smile that crinkled the corners of those eyes and flashed his teeth. He could speak softly – gaily – noisily outrageous. Men liked him, and he was

19

exceedingly popular with women, especially those who were his patients.

Jason and I told each other that we had not really expected Joe to marry at all. He was thirty-four; he lived at the Racquet Club — we just did not see him as a family man.

But that summer he went to California for a medical convocation of some sort; he stayed on to conduct some seminars in his specialty, which was obstetrics and therapeutic abortions. I suppose, as always, his social life burgeoned. At any rate, we had word that he was marrying Eve Bernsen, that he would bring her home within the month; we should try to get the Guinn home for him.

Now! We all knew who Eve Bernsen was. An Austrian movie star, we had seen her face on the screen, in the newspapers, and in slick magazines. She was beautiful! She was famous! She was a great actress! But could she be the wife of a McCord? Could she be a doctor's wife? Live in our charming, but Midwestern city? Could she live in Southshire Place?

She learned to do all of those things, and we came to love Eve, though we never were as close to her as we were to A.B.'s wife, or to Mary, Lucian's wife. In quick succession after their marriage Eve produced four daughters, the first two twins. She traveled some, going to Europe at least once a year. There frequently were rumors that she would return to her career. She never quite did.

The marriage was not a calm one. Eve had a temper, Joe could act without conscience. Several family gatherings were marked by what we came to call Joe and Eve's troubles.

Joe continued to be a popular o.b. man, and Eve, after her fourth child was born — she did have beautiful children! — began to take a big part in the city and county's social life. Again her picture would be seen in newspapers and magazines. The beautiful Eve McCord at the Symphony opening program. The beautiful Mrs. Joseph McCord riding in one of the Hunts. The beautiful . . .

When the youngest little girl was five or so, Eve became pregnant again, and that time she was rebellious, and Joe was downright absurd. He claimed from the first that the child was not his. Oh, during those months there were many, many family conferences! The brothers did all they could to hush the man. Even the children of the family began to ask particular questions.

When the child was born, and was a son, Joe said that proved it! He sired only daughters. Eve had found another father — He accused various ones, even Bish.

I don't know if the family, or perhaps Eve herself, finally silenced Joe. At any rate, he did simmer down. He became very proud of his boy, who looked like most of the McCords, dark-haired, slender, and bright-faced. Joe's little girls were all blonde, like Eve.

Of course that interlude was shocking. We put in a bad two years, not helped at all by Eve's decision, after things seemed to have settled, to divorce Joe.

She did not. But we went through some more anxious months.

Through it all, however, Joe had never let his profession be compromised. He could fight his brother Bishop with his fists in the rose garden of his home, but he continued amicably to share offices and a staff with him.

While Grady . . . He opened every door that faced him without consideration or regret.

Then, though not in chronological sequence, there was the really heartbreaking time when Ann, Lucian's daughter, decided that she was in love with our oldest son, and Abe was sure that he loved her.

I think they did love each other, the lovely, dark-haired girl, and the serious young man, ten years older. But they were first cousins, and the doctors in the family could not approve of such a marriage. There were endless discussions and arguments about genes, both dominant and recessive. The church was brought in, and finally Ann told Abe that the thing just could not be. "We have too much family to oppose and give up."

He accepted her decision, but went East to live and work away from us. That was one of my greater sorrows. There were others. The way June consistently failed in every school he attended. David's illness —

And Grady.

Grady struck at the fundamentals of our family establishment.

Bish says we were shocked by the things Grady did mostly because he was so often *right*. He pointed out that to walk into a mirror disturbs anyone.

Chapter 2

All right then. Where does one start to tell Grady's story? At the beginning, I suppose.

Though not with his birth. A mother who is not writing her own story can skip that. This is to be Grady's story, and I shall try to keep it that.

Grady? Could I describe him? Fairly? Or not. He was a handsome child. Sturdy, compact. Grady's dark hair had a life to it, not quite a wave. It was brown rather than black, and he had very blue eyes. His features were regular, and early his smile developed an upward lift at the left corner of his mouth. In his cradle, he began to swagger. He was a mischievous little boy, and delighted in being so. Punishment slid from him like oil. He liked to tease, he liked to break rules in a small way, and would laugh about it when caught — his gay, rippling laughter.

All of the McCord men were — are — slender, dark-haired, compactly built, strong and tall, without one being too aware of their strength. David, of course, was blond, and the only one of the boys who was. He was "my child." He was also the only "pretty" baby I had. And he stayed handsome, as different from distinguished-looking. His hair had a tendency to curl, he had a handsome chin, his cheekbones were good, his blue eyes dark-lashed.

But, except for his blue eyes, Grady stayed with the McCord pattern of appearance. No hips, straight back, wide shoulders, quick-moving – a slender little boy, mischievous, dear, and talented. As a child, his dark hair needed cutting more often than the other boys'; he was impatient with clothes, hating to wrap up in the winter, discarding all he dared in the summer. He was like a sleek, graceful animal, an otter, or some such.

He loved to run, and he did run – gracefully, with long, straight thrusts of his brown limbs, along the beach on vacations, up one side of the parkway, back along the other, when we were at home. To think of Grady as a child, is to see him running, head back, dark hair bouncing, his face filled with ecstatic joy.

Grady had many talents. He learned to read by the time he was four; he could play almost any game – and all the games he attempted. He had no fear. No sense, his father said, patching him up after a rough session of touch football.

Grady could sing. He had a fine natural voice. At six, his voice would ring out in church, and he was quickly deposited in the junior choir. He loved to sing, but when voice lessons and training were suggested, he refused. "I wouldn't practice," he told me. And I believed him. I couldn't imagine him doing scales or vocalizing. So I said that he need not take lessons.

Grady was an exciting child, and a disturbing one. He would show interest in the most unexpected things, and attempt any sort of exploration and adventure. Of course, being a child, he often found himself in difficulty, or even in peril. At those times, being a child, he would become frightened, and when he was frightened, it was his way to become very noisy – to detract notice from his self-made predicament, I thought – and he would do outrageous things to avoid anyone's talking about his mistake or his foolishness. That was Grady, as a child.

His whole life, I have concluded, has been a struggle. It need not have been, perhaps, but Grady thought the struggle was demanded. He was the third in a family of six boys; he had no prestige as an older son, and he did not have the indulgence, the spoiling, accorded the babies of the family. Grady's struggle was to be noticed, to be an individualist in a situation

26

where it was hard to achieve such recognition.

When he was born — "Another boy," his father announced. When David came, he said, "Of course it's a boy." But Grady —

He never was willing to be another anything.

He came into, and grew up in, a strict household, a disciplined one. Jason, their father, had known such strict discipline. Loving, kind, but firm, too. The boys, from their earliest days, learned to address the older men of the family as "Sir." "Sir, may I have a two-wheel bicycle?" "Sir, may I use a car?" "Sir, may I have the drumstick?" It was always that, and no one minded. They still speak so.

If corrected, if chewed out, to use their term, their answer could be only a firm, brisk "Sir!" Even Grady accepted that mandate and obeyed it.

Bishop says we live in a compound, and I suppose we do. He is referring to the Place, and our group of households. I suppose the grandfather instituted the standards which prevail in that compound, and the grandmother, too, possibly. Their sons, the five doctors, survived, and even flourished, under such a regime, and so the standards continue to be maintained. A little boy is taught to eat his soup, scooping the spoon away from him, and to sit erectly at the table, one hand in his lap.

One hears, at church, in the theater, that

"things are changing. This is a new world."

"What is new about it?" some McCord is sure to reply to such a statement. "We move faster? There are more people? We have learned a few things? So we have. But the same basics prevail. It is still a sin to lie and to steal. A father loves his son, and expects obedience from that son. We ride on nylon tires, we fly in airplanes — but a gentleman does not abuse a woman or neglect her. A gentleman can fight with his fists, or a sword, or a gun. He does not lie or betray his country. No matter that his country is a hundred times greater than his grandfather's country."

These standards were no longer the world's. But they were the standards of our "compound." And they were maintained. The whole family wanted them to be maintained, and were stern about keeping them in effect. It did give one a strong, firm core on which to count, a mighty oak on which to lean. An uncle had authority over the children almost equaling that of the father. He could issue orders and punish disobedience.

"Humphrey, don't leave your tricycle on the sidewalk."

And when Humphrey's trike turned up missing, he knew he must go to his Uncle A.B. to reclaim it.

When there was an infraction, punishment

28

came swiftly, justly.

"Uncle Joe spanked me," June would tell me.
"Did you do something you shouldn't?"
"Sure," said June cheerfully.

In the compound, of course, there was great love. And the children knew that it was there. It made for a happy, secure childhood; it kept the older folk in line, too.

David was fifteen months younger than Grady, and the two boys were great pals. Then – when Grady was fifteen, and the boys were looking forward to a summer of tennis, swimming, sailboating, David was stricken with polio. Paralyzed. This was before Salk or Sabin.

We were at our summer home on the lake. A dozen McCords were there, mothers and children. Jason, home at last from the war, would spend two week ends a month with us.

Those summer vacations were happy interludes in our lives. The rambling frame house, the straw rugs, sand gritty on the floor. Shorts, and sunburn, cookouts on the beach, the old friends who also had been coming to that section for the past thirty years and more. We brought the children, the dogs, a servant or two. We lived simply and happily.

The children became as brown as Indians, their hair sun-bleached and dry. They would soak up enough sun to last through the winter. We liked that sort of summer better than camps for the children, or exhausting trips, though we did provide some experience in such things.

The day David became ill – late Sunday evening I had driven Jason to the station. For Monday, it had been arranged for the teen-agers to go on a hike along the lake shore to the next settlement of beach houses, no different, no more interesting than our own neighborhood, but the five-mile hike would be fun.

The youngsters were to take picnic supplies in back packs. A young college boy, Greg Sommers – one of the neighbors – was to be in charge of the kids. David and Grady went, and their cousin Ann. They wore T-shirts over their bathing suits, and sneakers. Ann had a canvas hat beneath which her dark braids bobbed against her shoulders. I watched them start out, and consoled the two little boys who could not go along. Shields asked if I thought he should go.

"If you'd like to . . ."

"Not if you think Greg can handle eight of them."

We decided that he could, and Shields went back to his boat caulking; I went inside to attend to my household duties. When next I came to the veranda, the eight youngsters, and Greg Sommers, had disappeared behind the dunes.

Afterward he told us, step by step, of their progress. They walked, he said; Grady ran – and David had tried to keep up with him. He couldn't. He should have known that he could not. They waded in the lake – the water was cold that morning, so they didn't swim. They reached the Harbor clubhouse; they bought Cokes and candy bars and ate the sandwiches which they had brought from home. They mingled with their friends there. Some of the children swam. Yes, Greg thought David had gone into the water, but right after lunch he seemed a bit upset. When, at three, they started for home, David suddenly became sick at his stomach.

With the other children present, this was a distressing event. He must really have been sick. But then he thought he felt better and could go on. Except that he could not; his legs felt funny.

By then they were a mile from the clubhouse and the road. Grady offered to go back for help, and Greg let him go – alone, because he could run faster. And it was all right, because Grady could handle such a situation. He was fifteen, and a resourceful boy. He reached the Harbor clubhouse and within minutes someone was starting by boat to help the sick boy. Another man hitched a horse to a small sand wagon such as we used for dune picnics. Someone else telephoned to me, and Grady talked to me.

"I think David's got appendicitis or something critical," he told me.

Of course I was panicky. Mary, Lucian's wife, took over the household, and I started by car and road for Harbor.

I reached the club before David was brought in, a very sick boy, only semiconscious, his skin blue; his limbs were rigid. I shall never lose the picture Greg made carrying that boy up from the dock. By then Grady had decided that his brother had had a stroke.

We all agreed that whatever it was, things were critical. Poor Greg was overwhelmed with remorse and guilt; I questioned him sharply.

"This didn't come on all at once," an older woman told us sensibly.

We took David to the nearest hospital; we sent for his father, and thanked God that he had returned from Europe in June.

Within twenty-four hours almost complete paralysis had set in. A plane was chartered; Grady begged to go with us, with David. We couldn't let him. David and I and his father went back to the city, to the hospital there. It was polio, and the word was like a death sentence to us.

I can't remember the rest of that summer too clearly. My whole life was confined to David's hospital room, the gown and mask we had to wear, the pulleys, the sandbags, the iron lung – the pain the boy suffered. Someone brought the family home from Wisconsin, someone closed the lake house. Someone cared for my children, and my home. I was not allowed to stay continuously at the hospital, but my mind and heart never left it.

My other children – it hurt to hear them call out in clear voices, to hear their running feet. Our oldest son, Abe, came home from his Navy service, and no one paid any attention to him. I don't know if that bothered him.

I do remember a shadow which haunted the doorway of my room when I was at home. A shadow which I knew was Grady, but at the time . . . The servants and the rest of the family took care of my children.

I went to the hospital at nine each morning, I stayed as close to David as I could until Jason brought me home at night. It was not that I loved only David; he was the one who needed me just then. He was paralyzed, he would be crippled – that was the only thing that mattered.

In August the war was entirely over, the uncle-doctors were all at home again; those important things made no impression on me.

I could think only of the great tragedy which had come to us, engulfing one of our sons. My whole interest and consciousness was confined to David's sickroom, to David himself, that big-eyed, golden-haired boy who was so very, very sick; who would, I knew, never walk again. I went nowhere, not to church, nor to see my friends, for an evening at one of the family homes . . . Jason, of course, had his work, and attended to it. I truly don't think he fully realized what was happening in our home. The uncles began to. I remember being angry when Eve and Joe offered to take over the family so that Jason and I could get away for a week's rest. I felt the suggestion of my leaving was outrageous.

Life went on, of course. I knew that the children went regularly to school, that Abe had come home only in time to resume his University studies. Food was cooked and served and eaten in the home. If asked at that time, I would have said I was attending to my usual family duties. But I did not attend to them.

In fact, I know now, the whole family, the uncles, the cousins, our other boys, were involved in our tragedy – at the hospital, and then at home. It was Joe and A.B. who suggested that we convert the third-floor ballroom of our house into quarters for David and his nurse. The idea horrified me at first, it seemed an acceptance of doom. But gradually my husband's patience won me over, and the work began, turning the whole house into a turmoil for a couple of months. An elevator was installed – and the little boys were punished for using it as a lark. I remember that. . . .

The rooms were pleasant up there on the third floor. At the back, wide windows were set into the brick wall to provide sunlight and air. They looked out across trees to the Park. David was brought home, and nurses employed. Three women a day at first. I hated them. I wanted to do for my own son, and resented the doctors in the family who vetoed such an idea. After a few months, a male nurse was found – a strong, good man who would stay night and day, sleep in one of the rooms we had made, drive David in the car when he was ready for that. This worked better.

The family settled down for the long siege we knew was ahead of us. The third floor became the most important part of our big house. There was the sunroom, Schmitt's room – like a monk's cell, and no one, maid or family, ever set foot in it. There was the therapy room, and David's own room, which we had endeavored to make bright and cheerful. But the hospital bed dominated it, the frame above it, the pulleys, and the very thin, big-eyed boy on the pillow. David could talk, he could use his arms – for that first year he spent his nights in the lung, and its thumping could be heard all over the house.

That was a very bad year for us, and we started a second one almost as bad.

Bad for David, of course. For his mother, and father — for his brothers. Poor kids. Like the uncles, they knew that nothing like this had ever happened before to the McCords. The doctors in the family were bound in a sense of guilt that all their medical training and experience could not have prevented this dreadful thing or helped its effects. David's illness took our time and our attention; we had little of either to give to other things, to give to Grady or to the other boys.

Except when it became a matter of discipline, the boys had to accept life as it was then lived in our home. Shields and Abe were older, and busy with their college work. The two little boys, I knew even then, spent a lot of time with Lucian's children, and Joe's. Grady, for a time, was very hard to handle. "He's stubborn," Jason told me. "Insubordinate." And I believe he was.

Later we were to know that those qualities which annoyed us in the boy were the self-confidence, the determination and initiative which he was to have and need as a man.

But then —

There were no vacations for the Jason Mc-Cords. I don't think the lake house was opened at all the next summer. Grady was naughty for the first six months of David's illness, then he seemed to settle down. He studied and read a lot. He had "projects." He worked on these out in the carriage house. He asked if he could have the tack room, which he could lock up for his own. I laughed, but his father agreed that he could. "If you have rats, keep their cages tight." I didn't even wonder about the rats.

I got used to Grady's wandering about the house. One evening I caught him as he stood watching David in his lung. I was sitting beside David, and in the mirror I caught sight of the other boy. I remember being shocked and surprised at the genuine grief that was in Grady's young face.

He was only fifteen, that first year. And then he was sixteen. A boy of that age has questions to ask, things to talk about. And there was no one in our house who would bother with him.

We vaguely knew then — Jason spoke of it — that Grady was spending a lot of time with Henry Tibbs. Now, Henry was an institution in the Place and among our family members. He owned, and lived in, a magnificent, tall, white frame house down the street from our home. Henry's ancestors first built the mansion, and I suppose that families lived in it. Henry was fifteen years older than I was. When I first became aware of him, he was already a practicing lawyer. I don't know that he always specialized in forensic law, but that is my only knowledge of him and his profession. He was a small man, almost birdlike, with a narrow, lantern-jawed face, and a way of grinning at one without speaking, just looking wise.

I have heard him called brilliant, and I have always believed that he was. In Grady's childhood, he lived alone in the big house; he had his office on the first floor. I suppose clients came to him there. It was too far down the street for me to observe it closely, though I never was too much aware of Henry Tibbs. Sometimes Jason would ask me to invite him to a dinner party; he never came, but always sent wine or flowers.

I don't know why Grady liked him. He was the only child of Southshire Place allowed to come into the Tibbs house. During those long months after David became ill, he seemed to have spent a lot of time with Henry Tibbs.

"He read all my lawbooks on medical jurisprudence," Henry later told Jason. "I don't know if he understood them. He'd talk about things pretty intelligently. Grady was a smart boy."

Henry warned Jason about Grady, about what was happening. When Jason later told me that he had, he said bitterly, "He shouldn't have had to warn me about the kid. I should have known that one of our sons was in trouble."

"And me?"

"I'm afraid so, Helen."

This of course added to our grief when we realized that Grady had left home.

Do you know? It took us a couple of days to realize that he was gone! Orlie had to ask me where Grady was sleeping. For two nights, he said, his bed had not been disturbed; the boy had not shown up for meals. . . .

At first, I was provoked at Grady. Didn't I have enough, with David? But – if Grady had left home . . . He was only sixteen! What had *happened?* I asked Shields.

"I think he just walked out, Mother," Shields told me.

"But where would he *go?* How . . . ?"

I called Jason at the hospital, a terrible thing to do to a surgeon. He was in the operating room, but the message would be given him. "Is it about your son, Mrs. McCord?"

"Yes," I said tensely. "Oh, not David. This is about another son. Grady . . ."

I waited for Jason to call me. I went to Grady's room; he had used to share it with David, and David's clothes still hung in the closet, filled the drawers of one chest.

I was just about as hysterical as I ever want to get when, finally, Jason came plunging into the house. He had a dozen questions. Some without answers. What had happened to Grady? Where had he gone? Why had he gone? When . . . ?

We both were shocked, grief-stricken, and contrite. That boy — He had taken a few clothes, we thought. A small canvas bag. Money? He got an allowance and could have been saving some of it.

Jason went out to the tack room, and broke into it. I followed him, wondering, fearfully, if he expected to find Grady there. The room was empty, and warm, with dust motes floating about. It was in some disorder, though not bad. There were apples and a box of graham crackers, some of Jason's old medical books on a shelf. A big, sliding stack of medical journals. There were two fencing foils — they had belonged to Bishop, Jason thought. The boy, laboriously, clumsily, had made a plastron out of an old tarp.

But Grady was not there.

We didn't know what to do, where to start. Should we tell David? The other children? We had to tell the family, of course.

And that evening, equally of course, the men of the family gathered in our home for one of their frequent conferences. I was in and out of the room, listening, not talking. I was sure that David suspected trouble. I had been away from him a lot that day. My face must have shown what I was feeling. At his bedtime I went up to him and told him that there were people downstairs. I kissed him.

"Don't be worried, Mother," he told me. Yes, he knew.

In their conference, the men explored every possibility. Yes, the police should be told, we hoped without publicity. Could Henry Tibbs take care of this? That would be determined. They talked about everything – everything they knew of Grady's summer. They called in Abe and Shields. Jason told about the tack room and what Grady had stored there. He told about Henry Tibbs' warning. "He said Helen and I were neglecting the rest of our family."

"I don't think," said A.B., the lines deep in his face, "that you should blame yourselves too much, and certainly not David."

Jason said gruffly that he would have to develop that line.

"I can," said his brother. "David surely did not choose to get polio. *He* did not dictate the amount of care and attention you and Helen have given him. He deserved and needed everything you did give him. All right!"

The brothers nodded agreement. I remember the scene, there was a great bouquet of red roses on the candlestand beside the chair where our son, young Abraham, sat. "Grady was fond of Davy," he said gruffly.

A.B. glanced at him and nodded. "My second point: No one should ever blame parents for feeling and acting as Jase and Helen have done this past year. They were pulled across a rough bit of country. Their behavior is only what we should expect from parents."

"All right," said Jason hoarsely, "but that still leaves a kid out in the night somewhere. Here in the city, or along a highway . . ."

"Grady can take care of himself," said Shields.

"Agggh!" cried Grady's father.

"I think he may have had plans," said Abe. "He talked to me . . ."

"About *leaving?*" We all turned on him.

"No. Not that. But about school and stuff. This summer, you see, he was bored. Here at home, with nothing special to do, and school was coming up pretty soon again. You see, last year, he did two years of high school work. He went through both forms. . . ."

Jason and I gaped at each other. We hadn't known. "There was something about extra courses," said Jason, shaking his head. "I paid the bills —"

"Well, he did that," Abe repeated. "Got his diploma, in fact. It wasn't too hard for Grady. He has that kind of brains. But this summer, he realized that the next step was college; he'd passed the Boards. I think he could get in anywhere — but he knew he was only sixteen, and he and I agreed that going to college at that age would be grim. So — I suppose — there wasn't anything to do around here, and he left."

"Don't talk like a fool!" cried Jason.

"Sir!" said the oldest son.

His Uncle Bishop laughed.

That was only the first of many, many conferences. I would see the brothers talking together, on the walk leading to our front door, on the terrace at Bish's house — Jason didn't go far from me except for his hospital duties. I suppose there were conferences there, too.

He and I talked and talked. There was panic — mine. At first I was like a crazed person. Even David's illness had not been bad in this particular way. There we had known what to do for the boy, where he was. But with Grady —

His father was panicky, too, but he covered that with anger — at himself, and at Grady. Both should have been smarter, both should have talked about things. He was angry at the school for not telling him what Grady was doing.

And our panic, our anger, was all a part of the great fear which engulfed us — which froze us, and smothered us, and kept us awake at nights.

There were so many new things to come up.

When Abe must make arrangements to go back to his eastern university, we were swamped with dismay about what would happen to Grady and his education! These young years were too precious to be wasted. If we could just find the boy!

The police could not locate him in the city; at their suggestion, and that of Henry Tibbs, it was decided to have professionals seek to trace Grady.

"And bring him home," I said.

"We'll trace him," said Lucian, "though quietly. The boy has committed no crime. As for bringing him back . . ."

"That's nonsense," said Joe. "Grady is a smart boy. Give him a little rope."

"But he is only sixteen."

"Seventeen now, Mother," Shields reminded me.

"Yes," I agreed. "But even then — what if he is sick? Or hungry?"

"He would know where to find a doctor," said Bish.

"And food, too," Shields agreed. "I can't feature Grady going without food. Good food."

I thought they were heartless. "He could be killed," I insisted.

"Yes," A.B. agreed. "There is that chance. He could have been killed, crossing the Boulevard, had he stayed here at home."

44

"Oh, that's not the same, and you know it!"

A.B. came to me and stroked my cheek. "I do know it," he said. "And it is not the same."

I was at the end of my resources. "Will you locate him?" I asked the men.

"Yes." They agreed that they would, and I believed that they would. They would use every means, and they would find Grady.

"But," they decided, "unless he's sick, we should let him come back on his own, when he is ready."

"Do you think he will come back?"

"We think so."

And Grady's mother must content herself with that.

Chapter 3

It seems incredible now; it was a nightmare then; but it took two years to locate Grady. I have not the words to tell what that long time was to me in the living of it. I would wake at night and realize — I would stop short in whatever I was doing to think about that boy. And I would despair.

I did do one thing because of Grady's disappearance. I paid more attention to my other sons, and to my home. David still took a lot of my time and attention, and his progress, such as it was, was agonizingly slow. There was rest, and then there was therapy. A tutor came in for lessons. We found ways to entertain the boy — music, movies, the other children of the family.

He too became sixteen, but any sick child is only half his age. Of course he asked about Grady, and his father told him what had happened. David's eyes lit up. "I'll bet he's having fun!" he cried.

"I hope you are right," I said limply.

Repeatedly we were told not to worry. If

things got too tough, Grady would telephone. Yes, with that smile of his, he could always get a coin to use.

And then he was located.

He was safe, I was told, and well. The men made quite a ceremony of telling me. He had been found in Canada, and had moved since, but it was thought he could be watched.

I wanted his father to go immediately to him, to bring him home. I wanted to go myself. He would come if I asked him. I wanted at least to have him telephone me. If I could hear his voice . . .

I gazed at the men seated about the room. "He doesn't know you've found him!" I accused them.

"No, Helen," said Lucian gravely.

I turned to Jason. "Don't let them tell you what to do!" I cried. "He is our son, not theirs."

"He is our son," Jason agreed. "But I think they are right, my dear. We should let the boy work out his problem."

"And what problem is that?" I demanded. "We neglected him, but we loved him. We must tell him that."

"He knows it, darling. And at his age — he is almost nineteen, you know."

"To me," I said, "he is six, and defenseless."

The men were kind to me. Everyone was kind. But I had only one thought. I wanted to see my son! To touch him!

And then – right after Christmas – a picture of my Grady showed up in the newspaper. I don't know what hand of fortune guided me to look at that section of the Sunday newspaper. I was, I remember vividly, picking up the scatter of newsprint which the men always made on Sunday. I would never read the sports section. But as I picked up the papers and straightened them to make a tidy stack, there, on top, was Grady's face smiling up at me – his dark hair, his eyes, his smile. *Grady!* For a moment I felt faint. I sat down in a chair and looked at the picture.

Oh, it *was* Grady! No mistaking that.

My first instinct was to hide the picture, to find out where he was, and then go to him. If I said nothing to anyone – just walked out – they couldn't stop me.

In that brief second some understanding of my son came to me. He too had said nothing – he had walked out – no one had stopped him.

For minutes I sat in that chair and held the newspaper in my hands. They were shaking, and I rested them against my knee. I read the article that pertained to the picture. It was about Grady; the rascal was playing professional hockey! He was using his own name, for there it was – Grady McCord – with no connection made at all to the famous McCord

48

family of doctors. He was an American, playing on a Canadian team. The writer said that Grady was very good. "Possibly the coming wing of the future." That meant nothing to me. The writer said that he was very young, too. Strong and fearless. "When he fills out and gets all the muscles he will need, I expect great things of McCord."

I folded the paper. I took a deep breath. I would find some of the men —

I took a sweater out of the closet in the hall. It was January, but a pleasant, sunny day. Jason had said he was going to see Lucian. . . . My sweater was the amethyst-colored one which Mary had brought me from Scotland — hand-knitted, a warm and glowing color. Afterward I wore it constantly, until it was threadbare. I loved it because of the pleasant things I connected to it.

I went out through the side door and I heard men's voices. Yes. In the bricked courtyard, under the gingko tree, Jason was talking to Lucian and A.B.

There must have been that in my face — Jason came to me quickly. "Helen?" he asked anxiously.

I held out the folded newspaper. "Read that!" I said. I walked a few feet away from him. The three men bent their dark heads over the sports page.

"Helen . . ." said Lucian finally.

I whirled. "You knew where he was!" I accused them.

"We told you that we knew."

I took the newspaper. I looked again at Grady's picture. "If you had told me . . ."

"He's doing well, Helen. He —"

"I am going to see him."

"Oh, now, Helen . . ."

They argued; the teams, they said, moved about. I said I could get a schedule.

Grady would have no time to see me, they said.

"I'll take a chance."

"I can't get away just now, dear," said Jason. "The College of Surgeons Board exams are this week."

"I'll go alone."

They argued. It would be better to let Grady come to us.

I walked away from them.

I took my newspaper up to David's rooms. He was sitting in the big, upholstered wheel-chair playing checkers with Humphrey. Schmitt was close by, I was sure, but not in evidence.

"I have something to show you," I told the boys.

They took the newspaper and were excited about it. "Good old Grady!" cried Humphrey.

50

"I wonder if he's had his nose broken." They assured their shocked mother that all hockey players got broken noses.

They were excited and envious. "I'll have to practice my skating," Humphrey decided. David –

He was seventeen then. In three years he had strengthened his arms, his back. He could not stand on his feet or walk. He was a slender, golden-haired boy, with sharply chiseled features. He was sweet and patient – and sad. But Jason told me often that David had taken his "circumstances" very well.

He had, I supposed. Better than I had taken them. I could see only his withered, helpless limbs, the question which so often came into his blue eyes.

"I'm going to see Grady," I told the boys.

"Take me with you," said Humphrey.

"When will you go?" asked David.

The matter seemed quite simple to them.

"Do you think he'll want to see me?" I asked.

"Oh, sure," said Humphrey. "If you don't act too much like a mother."

We laughed quite a bit over the definition I demanded of him.

When I went downstairs, Jason had come into the house, and he tried to persuade me not to go to Grady.

"I'm going," I told him flatly. "I don't often

disobey you, Jason . . ."

"I am not forbidding you. This was advice — to save you, Helen."

The rest of the family tried to persuade me. I would not listen to them, either. I bought a new suit — since David's illness I had had little interest in clothes. The suit was blue, as was my small turban hat. I would wear my fur coat — I needed to go only to St. Paul. I would stay only a day or two.

I left on Thursday, and Jason took me to the plane. Yes, he confirmed, their promise had been kept. No one had sent word to Grady that I was coming. "But I did get you a good ticket for the game. It will be waiting at your hotel. Helen — my dear —"

He looked so distressed, a line deep between his eyes, his usually firm mouth threatening to tremble. I put my hand on his arm.

"Let me go with you," he begged.

I shook my head. "This is mother-business, Jason," I told him "I know I've been too much mother, not enough wife, these past few years. But if you'll let me do this . . ."

He kissed me, and I walked up the steps into the plane.

I had never seen a hockey game, I had never been to a large ice rink. I wore my fur coat, and wished I had worn fur boots. I came into the place early; my seat was right on the ice — or almost. Just a waist-high partition separated the seats from the surface. Now, I understand, there is glass and warmth for the spectators.

I watched the people assemble. I looked at the program. I looked at the pictures of Grady — one singly, one with the team. He did look young. . . .

All sorts of people came to see the game. A lot of men, some of them rough. Some of the women were rough-speaking, too. A few looked curiously at me.

I watched men in coveralls sweep the ice. There were lines, and circles marked out, a netted box arrangement at either end. When the teams came out, my chief interest was in finding Grady. Did he wear a red sweater or a white one? The program said his number was 6. I watched in a daze of excitement. And I found him! I watched him. I think I may have screamed a time or two when I thought he was in danger. As he was! Hockey is a dangerous game.

"Take it easy, lady," said the big man in the seat next to mine.

"My son . . ." I gasped.

"You not kiddin'? You got a boy in there? Which one?"

"Grady McCord."

"Oh, boy!" said the man. The teams swept up the ice, they swept back. They came close to me. My eyes clung to Grady, padded and unfamiliar. His head looked small above the big white sweater.

"Looka him take that puck up the ice," cried my neighbor. "He'll circle round the goal – to get momentum, you see – there he *goes!*"

And there he did go, his skates flashing, the stick in his big-gloved hand like an extension of his arm.

I didn't understand a thing. I was conscious of grace, and strength – and a fighting spirit. There were fights. A surging of big men in red jerseys, and in white ones, referees in striped shirts. There was one time when the big gloves were thrown on the ice, and two men went at each other with bare knuckles. One of these men was Grady. When he went to the penalty box – my neighbor told me about that – he saw me. I knew that he saw me; his eyes lit up, his jaw dropped, and he laughed. He actually *laughed!*

He had to go back into the game then, and I watched him.

Can a mother fall in love with her son? If so, I did that night. I watched Grady, I yearned for him. I knew that I must speak to him.

There was an intermission and an usher brought me a note – from Grady. I was to wait for him in the lobby lounge.

I looked at his handwriting. It had tightened, and improved, since he had left home. I trembled to think . . .

The other part of the game was a blur. Grady fell, he played the dangerous game — of course it was dangerous! If you put knives on men's feet and clubs into their hands . . .

Grady made another goal. "That's two he's slammed in," said my neighbor.

"I'm glad," I said, and the man laughed. "You're O.K., sister," he told me. "You gonna see the kid?"

"He's meeting me in the lobby."

"That's good. He's quite a hockey player."

I had to wait. The crowd took forever to leave the arena. I had to show my note to the head usher, who led me to a couch. The place began to echo with emptiness — and finally there was Grady coming along the corridor, even then stopping to sign a score card for a boy, to speak to some man —

I watched him, happy just to be able to see his crest of dark hair, his crooked smile, the jaunty way he walked. He wore a camel's-hair coat over a dark suit. He came to me as swiftly as he could. And he hugged me closely, hungrily, in his arms. I wept a little, and he wiped the tears away with his thumb. "Oh, Lady Vere de Vere," he said huskily. "Imagine seeing you at a hockey game!"

"Grady, Grady – " I put my fingertips to his nose. "Don't let them break it," I said.

This made him laugh.

He was lovely to me. He said he had not eaten dinner – would I go with him? Of course I did. To a beautiful restaurant, we sat in a silk-upholstered banquette, and there was an orchid beside my plate. He ate a huge steak – and talked to me. I talked to him. There were no reproaches, no apologies. He asked about David, he wanted to know all about him. And I told him. He asked about everyone. He loved us all, that was plain. But he would not promise to come home at any fixed time. Now, of course he couldn't go with me. He had a contract.

He took me to my hotel and told me that I had better go home the next day. I was needed there.

I had to take him at his word. He was young, but much, much older, too. He left me to hold his orchid in my hands and remember him. The next day I did go home, telephoning to Jason that I was coming. I was somewhat satisfied. I had seen Grady. He was all right.

He had not promised to write, and he did not.

I became an avid reader of the sports pages,

and sometimes I would see his name – for a short time. With summer, his name disappeared. And the next winter I did not find it at all.

I knew there was a war going on. A "police engagement." The men talked and argued about it constantly. Shields, a young medic, was doing his residency in the Air Force. Some young men of Southshire Place were in Korea.

I don't know why I didn't worry about Grady. I just didn't. And the messages which came to us that early spring were shocking. They came in the form of telegrams; Lieutenant Grady McCord, the telegrams said, was reported to be missing in action over some strange-sounding place in North Korea. On the other side of the world. My son. Lieutenant Grady McCord, USNAF.

It was the first we knew that Grady was in the Navy, that he had learned to fly, that he was flying a combat plane. . . .

The whole concept was strange to us, to me. Shields could fly an airplane. He had learned right out at our city's airport. Shields was in uniform, an Air Force medic – not a pilot. But that was different, somehow. Shields was five years older, and as steady as a rock.

Grady – we had to adjust all our mental pictures of him. After my trip to St. Paul, Jason had told me that he was no longer keeping a tracer on the "boy." Grady was on his own.

To me, even at twenty-two, he was young. Too young to be flying an airplane, too young to be shot down – much, much too young to be missing behind enemy lines.

Within days the newspapers became full of him. Grady was, it seemed, a hero. He had been making secret reconnaissance flights; we were told that he had been the source of invaluable information to the intelligence forces. But we, all of the family, were put under censorship. We were not to say one word to the newspapers about Grady, except that we had been notified, and we knew nothing further. This was a strict rule, strictly enforced.

Pictures of our home, old news pictures of Jason and me, appeared. Grady was called a fabulous hero. David collected these news accounts. Mention was made of awarding the Congressional Medal. I saw David's clippings.

All that mattered to me was the telegram which said that Grady was missing and in enemy territory. I felt again all the pangs of losing my son – of not knowing where he was, how he was.

This was an exceedingly dry desert to travel so often, and for so long. He had been shot down behind enemy lines, and this time I could have no hope, his father had no hope, that Grady, catlike, would land on his feet.

This time nothing of that sort seemed to have happened. He was just gone. Hurt, surely. And — gone.

Gradually the stories about him stopped appearing in the press. No one had heard from him, or about him. He was "presumed lost."

I would not give up all hope, though even Jason told me it would be easier to accept what had come.

"Have you lost hope?" I asked him.

"Well," said my husband, "I try to be reasonable."

The desert leveled off before us, and we made our way across it. Weeks went by, a month, another month. It was a warm day, I remember, when the telephone call came. I took it in the hall, and I immediately called Jason.

That night there were again black newspaper headlines, TV announcements; reporters, cameras, besieged our home — to get our reaction, we were told. Dear God.

I trembled for hours. I wept. The men of the family took turns talking to people. Stern, blank-faced doctors, they could do it. I got, as June said, sloppy about my other sons. Jason walked, walked, and walked, slapping his hands together, taking deep breaths, coming often to touch me.

What sort of reaction could we be expected to

have? The father and the mother of a son we had thought dead — we knew then that we had thought him dead! A Navy Commander came in person to tell us what they knew.

I remember how he sat here in this small drawing room. This beautifully uniformed man, his white-topped cap clamped under his arm, ribbons on his breast, anxiety in his eyes — anxiety that I not make a fool of myself. There were other people in the larger room, some of the family, a friend or two, one reporter, chosen by lot.

The Commander told Jason and me that it seemed Grady had crashed in a wooded, mountain area; he had begun to make his way, painfully, down the mountain — I could see him doing it. Grady had never been a boy to know when he was licked.

"Was he hurt?" asked Jason, his voice harsh.

"Yes, doctor, he seems to have been. Rather badly hurt, we think. His plane crashed, you know. A woman — a native woman — found him. He had been burned . . ."

Jason bit his lip.

"Where is Grady now?" I asked.

"Let the Commander tell his story," Jason advised me. I sighed.

"Where he crashed," said the man in blue, "was not too far from a town. In enemy territory, it was. This woman — one account says her little boy found Lieutenant McCord. He told his mother; she came out and brought him back to her house; she kept him there for a time, and cared for him, at a risk to herself, I imagine. Then she managed to bring him down through the valley and across the line, claiming amnesty because of the care she gave him."

"Was she a North Korean?" I asked.

"She was an Eurasian. Chinese-white or Japanese-white. She and her son brought him to their house. It was, really, a brothel, but . . ."

Jason looked at the man angrily. He felt that I need not have been told that.

I was shocked. I knew what a brothel was. But it was also shelter.

The men of the family were hysterically amused at this last revelation. Even that day I heard one of them laugh. Later I would hear them, or see them, laughing as they gathered in their little knots to talk about this wonderful news that Grady was alive.

"Is he still there?" I asked the Commander. The men laughed about that, too, and repeated my question. I was angry at them. It still angers me.

Then — that day — I rather collapsed, I am ashamed to say. I wept, and I shook with a chill which was not entirely emotional. For it developed that I was coming down with the flu.

I think Jason was relieved to have me con-

61

fined to bed. When he took off for Honolulu, and the naval hospital where Grady had been brought, there was no argument about my going with him.

"Be good to him!" I begged. "Bring him home."

"I'll be good to him," Jason promised. "As for bringing him back, I'll have little status, I'm afraid. These service hospitals . . ."

"They'll take care of him?"

"They will take excellent care of him, Helen."

I had to be content. And I was, really. I was sure Jason would come home, with Grady.

But when he came back, within the week, he was alone. He looked tired, and he was very quiet. I was up and out of bed, but one of the brothers met his plane and brought him to the house. The whole family gathered – all except Bishop, who had a case at the hospital.

I was bitterly disappointed that Jason had not brought Grady with him. "I couldn't, Helen," he told me. "He was in no condition to travel."

I stared at him blankly.

"He's all right," he said quickly. "He will live, and he will be home. But for now –" He turned to his brothers, to the doctors. "He was burned," he said. "He had not had proper initial care. There is much work to be done." He turned back to me and held me close. "But he will be all right," he promised.

He said nothing then. It was much, much later that I found that Grady had been tortured – by that awful woman. She had tried to get information which she could sell, either to the North Koreans, or to us – maybe even to both.

But I declared from the first that she was an awful woman. Then Jason said my feeling about her was unreasonable. He said I was jealous. And I was, of course, of the woman who could care for my son and comfort him.

In a daze, I heard Jason telling the men about Grady's burns. His face . . . ? Yes, it was bad.

And I thought about that woman, who had not given him proper care. Who . . .

"It's over now, Helen," Lucian told me in concern.

I shook my head. "It will never be over," I said. Even then I was sure that woman would always be in Grady's life. In our lives. "Why didn't you bring him home?" I screamed at Jason. "If he can walk . . ."

Jason sat down beside me. His face was terrible – broken, and sad.

"I'm sorry," I told him.

He held my hand in his. "I couldn't bring him home, my dear," he told me.

"But – why?"

"Well – for one thing, he belongs to the Navy still. Then – he needs doctoring. Lots of doctoring. In that hospital. They are set up to give him the plastic surgery he will need."

"Jason . . ."

"His face was dreadfully burned, my darling. His eye . . ."

But the woman still bothered me more than Grady's injuries. Jason tried not to tell me that this woman, this Kim Bacquillon, had come out with Grady, but I guessed that she had. The Government forces may have thought she could be of use to them; she must have had information which they needed. They took her with Grady to Honolulu. And having saved Grady, she felt that she had a claim upon him; she clung to him. Yes, the Navy, the authorities, had "handled" her, but Jason told that she had made some "sticky" scenes.

"She seems to have an exaggerated idea of Grady's importance and the McCord wealth," he said.

"I wish I could have gone with you," I mourned.

"I am glad you could not," Jason said flatly. "One woman fighting over that kid was enough."

It hurt me to have him say this. I had a right to fight for my son. For a time I behaved very badly. I am ashamed of having done so, but I would do it again, I am sure.

I tried to become familiar with the thought that Grady's handsome face would be scarred. I

64

thought I was ready to handle that thought, but I could not accept the fact that this Eurasian woman still was in Honolulu, and after my husband was at home again, she had made some sort of contact with Jason. He never told me just how she did this, or what she wanted. But at the time, when I challenged him, he said that, yes, he had heard from her.

And again I was in a frenzy. I was sure that she would harm Grady; I was certain that she already had harmed him. I wanted desperately to go to him, to see for myself that he was all right. I thought perhaps I would stay with him until he could come home. I wanted to put my body, my presence, between my child and this evil thing.

Jason said that he could not go again to Honolulu. In fact, he didn't think he should even try to go. Nor should I. He would, and did, telephone. I talked to my son, his voice muffled, distorted by the squeals and sound-waves of radio-telephone.

It was not enough. I wanted to see for myself that he was safe.

"You'd be no match for that woman, Helen," Jason told me. "You have no training for that sort of dirty combat. I don't want you to think of going."

"I just want to be sure that Grady's safe."

"The Navy will see to that."

"The Navy!" I cried in scorn.

Again the men laughed, kindly, sorrowing with me. "We should let the mothers fight our wars," drawled Joe.

"We'd do things differently!" I assured him.

I still wanted to go to my son. I wrote and suggested that he ask me to come.

But before he could do this, if he would have, Henry Tibbs came to our house. I can see him yet as he was that evening. Of course he was a most familiar figure to all of us. Jason greeted him, as the doctors usually did greet Henry. "What have I done now, Counselor?"

The little man – he wore a brown suit – a color of brown which men were not using for suits those days. His was out of style, his tie was an old one, carelessly knotted. He smiled at us in that long-jawed way of his, his eyes puckish.

"I thought I'd tell you," he said, sitting on the front edge of his chair, "that I am going to Honolulu tomorrow. To see Grady."

Jason and I – Humphrey was there with us – we couldn't think of anything to say.

Henry nodded. "I know Helen has been fretting to go have a look for herself. I thought, myself, that someone should do this. Not medically, Jase. I'll leave all that to you and the Navy doctors. But if the boy is in any other sort of trouble – I know quite a bit about

66

blackmail and stuff — so if the family wants me to go — Oh, well!" He rubbed his bony hands together. "Even if they don't want me, I'm going! On my own! Just to see what goes on out there."

"Hula skirts and fresh pineapple goes on out there, Mr. Tibbs," said Humphrey impudently.

"So I've heard, boy. So I've heard."

And the next day, the funny little man did go to Honolulu. He agreed to let Orlie drive him to the plane. I could go along for the ride. . . .

I stood on the wide stretch of concrete apron, with my skirts and hair blowing in the wind which the propellers kicked up, and I watched Henry go where I so wanted to go!

But he could do more than I could for Grady. My going would have been to do things for *me!* And Henry must have "handled" matters in Honolulu. I've always thought the McCords gave him a sum of money to use if needed. I think he must have used it, or some means, to handle that woman.

It probably was not an easy thing to do. Or, just as probably, the sight of Grady, hurt so dreadfully —

In any case, Henry suffered his first heart attack while he still was in Honolulu. It was Grady who sent word to his Uncle Lucian, who was a heart specialist — a famous heart specialist.

Lucian was the oldest of the brothers, and, I suppose, the most handsome. He was — is — a large man, flat-waisted, but tall, with massive shoulders, and great strength. He has a rugged, square-jawed face, heavy dark eyebrows that overhang his dark eyes. His hair is thick and dark. I have always been just a little afraid of Lucian, though certainly he has always been kind to me — beautifully courteous and considerate. However, he takes his position as head of the family quite seriously, and is stern not only with the children, but with the brothers. The laws and rules of his family, his household, Southshire Place, his profession — one does not break those laws around Lucian McCord.

We — a dozen of us, that Saturday afternoon — were out on the bricks in front of A.B.'s home. The family was well into one of its talk-talks about nothing when I saw Lucian coming across the parkway at the fountain. The expression on his face — I touched Jason's arm warningly.

Jason started toward his brother. "What's happened?" he asked.

"I am leaving for Hawaii in an hour," Lucian said. He drew the telegram from his pocket. "I've wired Grady."

We were all shocked, and sorry, and we were agreed that Lucian should go, that he must go.

He got a bit huffy, explaining to the other

doctors that such a trip was not easy for him to make.

"I'll drive you out," A.B. offered.

"I just wish," fumed Lucian, "that Grady had not felt it necessary to be such a blooming hero!"

At that, Jason flared. It is a man's way, when frightened, to get mad and place blame. I have come to recognize the reaction, and usually I then become calm.

I said that Jason and I would drive Lucian — I'd go change my dress and arrange for dinner, speak to David. . . .

"Don't tell him I'm an old grouch," Lucian called after me.

"He knows what he knows," I said over my shoulder.

We all felt bad about Henry. We hoped he would be all right. And of course Grady *was* the cause of all these trips out to the airport and across the ocean.

"I wish I were going with you," I told Lucian when I kissed him good-by.

"Why didn't we think of that?" he asked.

"Give Grady my love. . . ."

I would certainly have been a nuisance to Lucian. After a week, he brought Henry back on a stretcher to our hospital; he forbade us to talk to him about Grady.

The heart attack was not too bad, except for Henry's age. When Lucian said the old man could go home, if he had someone to care for him, I said, "He won't let anyone in that house."

"Then he stays at the hospital."

"If he's able to go home, you certainly can talk to him," I said. "Did you find out if he was able to do anything for Grady?"

"Oh, yes. I think so. He hasn't talked much."

"All he'll say," said Jason, "is that this Kim person certainly used all the wrong medicines on Grady's burns."

"You mean . . . ?" I was furious at the men. I'd been holding back, wondering — dreading — hoping. "Did Henry *do* anything for Grady?" I demanded.

"He didn't shoot Madame Bacquillon," drawled Lucian, "if that's what you mean."

I was disgusted. "I don't know what I mean," I said. "You told me not to ask questions."

"I told you to stay away from Henry with your questions."

"But you talked to him. And Jason has!"

"Yes —"

"Did you see Grady?"

"Oh, yes. Several times. I've told you that."

"Did Henry . . . ?" I asked faintly. Those men could defeat me.

"He did various things for Grady's interests,

Helen. That woman . . ."

"Did you see *her?*"

"Yes, I did."

This the family had not known. We were up in David's rooms, a half dozen of us. It was a rainy night, with water streaming down the windows and pounding on the skylight. There was a little fire on the marble hearth of the old ballroom; its light flickered upon our faces as dusk folded in, gleamed upon the polished floor, and struck sparks from a crystal vase, a framed picture, the diamond on my hand.

"This woman," said Lucian, speaking slowly. His voice is very deep. "Henry warned me not to talk to her. But I saw her. She is —" He glanced at me. "She is pretty awful, as we judge things. Grady, incidentally, calls her Baggy."

"Does he see her?"

"Some, I believe. You see, Helen, she is in a position to give our people intelligence which they need. About enemy build-ups, and troop locations, fortifications . . ."

"And they are using Grady."

"Not against his knowledge and will, my dear. And if you have any notion that she has some personal claim on him, get rid of it. She is not young, nor physically attractive in any way. She is French-Chinese, a large woman, a cruel woman. She is clever, of course. She knew what she had when Grady fell into her hands. She knows what we want of her."

"The family, you mean?"

"I meant the United States. But, of course, the family has become important to her, too."

"Sure," I said bitterly. "If Henry went over there and showed that money was available. It will only mean — that woman is going to mean trouble for us, I am sure of that! I'd put her in jail and keep her there."

"And what would you do with Grady?" asked Lucian, his tone cold.

"Now, what do you mean by that?"

"I meant that Grady can mean trouble, too. And perhaps now is not quite soon enough for us to decide what we are going to do with the boy."

"Sir?" It was David who spoke. We all turned to look at him.

Lucian nodded to him.

"I was going to remind you — and the rest of us — that this is a matter of what Grady has already done to the family."

"I don't understand," said Lucian.

"I was thinking of the sense of guilt Grady has put upon us. I don't think we should feel guilty. Certainly not for the scars Grady has acquired in this war. He would have gone to war, had he been living right here at home. And if he had gone, he would have been shot down — and we would have felt terrible, but

72

not guilty. As things are, you think you can decide what to do to Grady and about him. But you cannot."

"Do you have any suggestions about what we can or should do?"

David shifted his shoulders against the pillow of his chair. "Not me," he said cheerfully. "No, I'd just be glad to have the guy come home, if only to see what he'd think up next. I wouldn't, to any extent, try to anticipate him and try to prevent that next thing."

"If only he would come home," I agreed sadly.

"He's coming," said Lucian.

We all jumped.

Lucian nodded to us. "I talked to him," he said. "He plans to come home."

I could feel the tension of years relaxing its hold on me. Jason reached for my hand and held it. "How does he look now?" he asked Lucian, his voice shaking.

"Pretty good, except for the bandages. I think we'd all do better to wait and see how he is going to look."

"When will he come?"

Lucian shrugged.

"But he wants to come?" I persisted.

"He told me that he did."

"I wonder if he really will come," said June. "You know — things can get pretty tight

73

around here. And Grady now — He's a hero, you see. He's made a big name for himself. Bigger, I guess, than all the Dr. McCords have made."

There was a little silence. June had an unfortunate way of saying the wrong thing.

"If he comes, when he comes," said Lucian deeply, "it will be because he wants what we have around here. Call it being tight, if you like. He knows what's here. If he comes home, it will be to get what we have for him."

I sat hugging my joy close and warm. Grady was coming home! I believed Lucian when he said that Grady would come, and I was glad. I didn't think he would come home and want to stir things up. I didn't think the hero-name he had made for himself was going to matter too much to Grady.

Chapter 4

It did not.

Of course, matters did not move too quickly. It took months and months for the necessary plastic surgery to be done. Grady was brought back to the States, and I went to see him. The bandages, and then the eye patch, did not bother me too much. This was Grady; his crooked smile was the same. He talked to me and told me that having only one eye took getting used to. One didn't have depth perception. He would have to learn to drive a car all over.

"But you won't fly?" I said anxiously.

He laughed at me. "Don't tell me what I won't do, Lady Vere de Vere!"

"That's what David says. That we are not to tell you things."

"Well, you just jolly well better tell me!" cried Grady. "Or I'll not come home. Here I've been practicing my 'sirs,' and all the rest of the routine . . ."

But after a time — after two years — he did come home. He looked well, and his strength was good. One must forget the blankness where one of his blue eyes had used to be.

He came home quietly, and quietly took his place among us. For days there was no word in the newspapers, and no parties — he was just there. He explored every inch of home — our home, and the others in the compound. He checked on the age of each cousin; there were two new ones, Joe's boy and Lucian's youngest. He noted the hair-do of each aunt, our hats, and our shoes, each servant, new and old. Everything must be located and identified. It was as if he had made lists of things at home. He knew where a change had been made.

"What happened to that old blue lamp?" he would ask.

"What happened to Myrtle?" Myrtle had been a second-floor maid at Lucian's home. She'd lasted only a year or so.

He still had his key to the tack room — after all that had happened to him!

"That kid's been homesick!" Jason told me in an awed tone.

"I could cry," I agreed.

"Well, don't. He's back. That's what counts. And, you know, David was right. He's setting the pace. As he should."

"He's a good boy, Jason."

"He's no longer a boy, Helen. But, yes, he is good. Or I hope so."

Grady came home in the summer – in June. In August he told us that he had enrolled at the University. No, he didn't need tuition. He had saved his pay. . . .

"I pay for my son's education," Jason told him sternly.

Grady looked up at him. We were at dinner. Then – "Sir!" he said crisply. And that was that.

Grady bought himself a car, and he told David that he was to go to the U. with him. This startled everyone.

But Grady insisted that it could be done. All right; Schmitt could go along. Though there were motorized wheelchairs, Grady was going to get David "checked out" on swinging his weight between crutches. Could he pass the entrance exams? "I've my credits from Country Day, but you've been goofing off here at home."

That was the way he talked to David. He stayed with his younger brother, he bullied him, he made the crutch mishaps seem like fun. And he took David to school, Schmitt riding sternly, largely, in the back seat of the low-slung car.

Grady took David to many places, to the Zoo, to see the brightly decorated windows of the stores at Christmastime, and to restaurants for dinner, telling us that "Davy in his wheelchair is better than a cute dog to attract the girls."

This was good for David; we all felt that it was. Even his occasional times of being tired – Grady had helped David become a person again, a man. He didn't stay up in his rooms all the time; he ate dinner with the family; his chair could be seen tooling along the sidewalks of Southshire Place.

Grady didn't need his cute dog to attract the girls. He went about – to church, to the ball games, to the Symphony. Joe told us of the evening when he went up on the stage of a night club to dance with the singer appearing there.

"His attitude seems to be, 'Isn't everybody one-eyed?' "

I didn't let myself worry about Grady. He was at home; he seemed content – and even gay. He came in and out of the house, he was invited around; he was just as happy running the length of the parkway with Bish's Great Dane. That was a sight to see. The tawny dog and the laughing, dark-haired man. He made the newsreels doing that. He was, occasionally, also pictured at the University, dancing with some debutante at a party, or –

But gradually people let him alone. The best sight of all, I thought, was to see him jumping rope with Taylor Falk who lived across the street. She was an enchanting nine-year-old, with green eyes, freckles, and bobbing auburn braids. But that picture never made the newspapers.

Grady worked hard, he studied hard. "I'm late starting," he told us. "I have to make this thing in three years."

Even his Uncle Lucian could find no fault with Grady's behavior. He seemed to lean on the discipline of the home and the family. He liked the order there was in his life. He asked permission before he moved up to the third floor with David.

He was pushing himself with the books, but he would not let David take on too much. "You're younger than I am," he told his brother. At first, Schmitt resented Grady's interference. But within months, he was working toward the same purposes. It was Schmitt who suggested a car of his own for David. "He doesn't put in as long hours on the campus as Mr. Grady does," he told Jason. "English classes don't require as much as the laboratory courses."

This was true. David got his own car. And I never knew more delight in the family than the evening David offered to drive Jason's secretary back to her apartment. Jason had come home to dress before going on a surgery consultation in Denver. Miss Hallowell had brought him his plane tickets, along with some papers for him to sign. Orlie could have driven her home. . . .

But David offered, and everyone was pleased. Before Grady's return, the boy had shown almost no initiative.

"Isabelle's a good-looking girl," Jason reminded me.

"Now, don't expect too much."

"Me? Fathers my age just go along for the ride, Helen. Didn't you know that?"

"It can't be too romantic," I pointed out, "with Schmitt at the wheel of that car."

"No," laughed Jason. "It certainly can't be. But there are cars which David could drive. . . ."

"Now who's pushing things? When does your plane leave?"

After he had been home for a time, Grady began to talk about the years he had been away. The first time he did it was at a family dinner in A.B.'s home.

A.B.'s daughter, Christine, was thirteen. In our family, we make an event of a child's entering his, or her, teens. The irreverent speak of these celebrations as our bar mitzvahs, but we go right on celebrating the events, and this party was especially important for Christine. Her mother had died at her birth, and A.B., very much in love with his beautiful wife, had done a conscientious, and good, thing of raising his daughter alone.

This evening, when Christine would be thirteen, was to be marked fittingly. The family dressed in their very best for the dinner, the men in black ties, the women in floor-length gowns; the children under twelve did not attend. This was the welcoming of another daughter into adolescence, an introduction of her to maturity and responsibility. Not that we got that pompous about it. We brought gifts, we were very gay – and Christine was a happy, dark-haired young girl as she sat beside her father in A.B.'s lovely dining room. The furniture was English Hepplewhite, and the silken draperies of that room were of pale yellow Chinese silk.

"I used to remember that armchair beside the fireplace here in Uncle A.B.'s dining room," said Grady unexpectedly. "Where else do you find such a chair in a dining room? Not of course that I did much congregating in dining rooms as such in those days of my independence."

I suppose everyone in that room was immediately careful of his expression, and gave thought to what he might say. Even the youngsters. It was the very first time . . .

"What kind of dining rooms did you see?" asked Christine, and we all blessed her for being thirteen and able to say what was in all our minds.

Grady laughed. "Coffee shops," he told her. "Hamburger stands. I knocked around those places at first. Did you know what my first paying job was?" he asked us, leaning forward to look down the long table. "I sang in a church choir for pay."

"Oh, Grady!" cried his father.

"I know it," said Grady. "I'm not good, but I am loud. And I'd heard enough orders from our choirmaster to know the lingo. I got a job. Ten dollars a week. Five extra for weddings and funerals."

"Why don't you sing in the choir here?" asked Shields forthrightly.

"For free?"

"Well, yes, I'd think so. That would be a good place for you. You could put your evil eye on the whole congregation."

I was shocked. All of us were, a little.

Not Grady. "I still don't know how to sing," he said cheerfully.

"But you'll do it anyway," said Shields.

"Singing at that church wasn't a bad job," Grady went on. "Of course I couldn't live on the ten dollars, so I got me another job, as night clerk in a motel. You grow up fast in a place like that."

I wanted to ask him where this had been. Instead, I took asparagus spears from the silver dish being held at my left shoulder.

"I got into playing hockey by being a rink attendant," Grady told us. "You know? I think the hardest work in the world must be putting shoes on fat women's feet."

"Oh, Grady!" protested his father.

"You ever try it?"

"Not me," said Jason crisply.

"I liked playing hockey," Grady told us.

"But you joined the Navy . . ." drawled Shields.

"Well, I did that because I liked the uniform. I had the figure for it, and I'd learned to fly a plane when I was doing the hockey bit."

"Only the Navy unlearned you."

"They sure did," Grady agreed good-naturedly. "But I still was good at it."

"Modesty has always been a family trait," Bish reminded us.

Grady didn't talk further than that about his Navy duty — that night, or any night, at any time. If any mention ever was made of his crash, his rescue, the Eurasian woman or her son, a spasm would cross Grady's face, and he would get up and walk away from whatever group he was with. At the edge of the swimming pool, or out in the country, skeet shooting — he would not talk about those things. I don't believe he let himself think about them either, though Schmitt had told us that, sometimes, Mr. Grady dreamed.

"It don't pay to go in an' touch him," the nurse said. "One time I did. He climbed all over me. Good thing I'm big."

Well, Schmitt was big. Like a boulder.

That night, at A.B.'s dinner party, over the game hen and asparagus, the stuffed mushrooms, Grady didn't talk about Korea, but he did talk.

He said he'd learned other things fast, ever since he first left home. "When I tried to get a job – I thought I knew it all, of course. And I got by with the choir singing –"

"Because you're loud," said Shields.

Grady laughed. "That's right. But it didn't take me six months to know that I'd closed more doors on myself than I had opened, by leaving home. Education was the first thing. I had some idea I could work myself through a college – and maybe some guys can and do. It didn't work for me. And I soon knew that you just plain had to have more education than I'd had. Unless you were going to play hockey. . . ."

"Why didn't you come home?" asked Bish bluntly.

Grady smiled at him – his engaging, patient smile. "I couldn't, sir," he said. "You see – what had happened . . . Oh, I know you people thought I left home, that I had dropped you. But what really happened, you see, I was finding – or ready to find – that you, that my family, had dropped me."

Everyone said something. "Oh, Grady, Grady!" I whispered.

"Never!" his father said loudly.

Grady carefully cut into the little brown bird on his plate. "I don't think you should say 'never,' sir," he told his father respectfully. "I was wrong in thinking what I did when I took off. But you know that you *should* drop a guy, after a certain point. . . ."

"I can't imagine what that point would be," said Jason stubbornly.

The uncles and the older boys argued about this a little. Grady let them, cleaning his plate, listening, now and then smiling across at me. There were candles on the table, and the other light in the room was soft. Except for the eye patch, one could scarcely see Grady's scars.

Then someone attracted his attention – it was Mary, Lucian's wife, I am pretty sure – by saying that the reason he had left his family was because he had suffered an identity crisis – because of David's illness, and the seeming indifference of his big family. He was struggling for his own identification. . . .

"Oh, baloney!" said Grady loudly and roughly.

"Grady!" Mary protested, looking shocked.

The men grumbled an agreement.

"I'm sorry," Grady said to them quickly. "But what you said was nonsense. There wasn't a thing wrong with me when I left except that I was a spoiled kid. Of course, when I *was* a kid — three years old or so, I mean — and would have a temper tantrum, you would let me scream it out. You —" He broke off and sat thoughtful for a long minute, while we all looked at him, silent too, and watchful. Then he lifted his head, a smile brightening his face. "But that's what you *did!*" he cried excitedly. "All those years, you let me — and now, here I am! Oh, I do love you all!"

We laughed then, happily. The birthday cake was brought in, twinkling beautifully.

That was a very happy evening. I am glad we all had it together.

After it, things went along in our homes, and in our families. Our son Abe and Lucian's daughter Ann had their troubled love affair, and Abe went to New York. Humphrey went off to Annapolis. Hero-worship of Grady had turned him toward a career in the Navy, I felt sure, and that was all right, too. June, for a year, attended a school in the Southwest.

With only three of my boys at home, our big house seemed empty. "I've nothing to do," I told Jason.

"You've earned a rest."

"It really isn't a rest, my dear. I worry about the boys who are away more than I do about those here with us."

"Grady has taken some of that pressure off."

"Ye-es," I agreed. "It is wonderful to have him at home."

Jason said nothing, and I looked at him where he sat in the big armchair beside the bed. Ours is not a frilly bedroom. Its color – blue – is a concession to my femininity, but there is this big chair for my husband, the window draperies are tailored, the furniture is on a man-sized scale. We like our big bedroom and its little sitting room. Jason does a lot of reading there, I attend to my household affairs at the satinwood desk.

"Did I tell you?" I asked, "about going upstairs to kiss David good night last week . . . ?"

Jason put his finger between the pages of his thick magazine and smiled at me.

I was sure I had told him, but I told him again. "I went up," I said happily, "as I've done every night since he's been up there. Grady's room is that small one, you know, off to one side. And as I went through, I heard his voice, very quiet, but very clear. I stopped to listen. And that boy was praying, Jason! He actually was. David could see me. I could see him; he already was in bed. He put his finger to his lips, and I went to him. He held

87

my hand, and we listened."

"What sort of prayers . . . ?" Jason asked, his voice gruff.

"Oh — that one from Evening Prayer. 'Lighten the darkness, Lord . . .' Then he said the Twenty-third Psalm, making it sound like a prayer. He has a fine voice, Jason!"

Jason nodded.

"And finally he said something that I think is from Compline. I won't get it right, but it goes something like, 'Preserve us, Lord, while we are waking, and guard us while asleep. That waking we may watch with Christ, and sleeping, rest in peace.' "

"Humph!" said Grady's father.

"Yes," I agreed. "It hurt. That quiet voice — I kissed David and started to leave, still being quiet. But Grady called to me, and I went to his little room and kissed him.

" 'I started to do that,' he told me, 'when I was alone.' " Playing hockey, flying his fast spy plane, in the hospital, hurt and in pain. . . .

" 'Were you often lonely, Grady?' " I asked him.

" 'Oh . . .' he began to say, in that way he has of throwing off sentiment. Then his hand tightened on mine. 'Yes,' he said. 'I was lonely. Often.' "

From his first coming home, Grady had seen

a lot of Henry Tibbs. I don't think many days went by that he didn't go down there to speak to the old man, to do some small chore for him, or, sometimes, to sit for hours with him. Henry was able to attend to his practice, but he didn't get out much beyond the requirements of his profession. Grady, I am sure, ran many errands for him. What they talked about is anybody's guess.

What Grady talked about to Henry's neighbor, Lizzie Paradis, would need further speculation, though, I feared, in a different direction. Lizzie was getting to be an old woman, and she had always been a foolish one. Her mother was foolish before her, a large, florid woman given to wearing fluttery clothes, ruffles, lace, scarves and veils. A lot of jewelry.

Lizzie did the same, though on a muted scale. She still dyed her hair to the blonde it had been in her girlhood. She talked in a thin, high voice and was "cute." She accepted every invitation issued to her, and paid her social obligations by giving an "open house" reception once a year where she served eggnog and fruit cake, and talked endlessly about how good each person, especially the doctors, had been to poor Mamma.

Her home was at once the plainest, and perhaps the most handsome, on the Place. It stood on a corner, across from Henry Tibbs'.

Two stories high, built of white painted bricks, with green shutters, it was a square house with two or three dormers protruding from the roof, and an enormous chimney at either end of it.

We all thought money had lately become scarce for Lizzie Paradis. She could have sold the house for a good sum. When we went into it, we noticed that there was a scarcity of the bric-a-brac which had used to crowd every mantel and table-top, every shelf and cupboard. Dresden, Lalique, Steuben . . .

But the two white Wedgwood vases on the mantel, the single silver pitcher on a little round table — even the widely spaced paintings on the walls — gave the house an elegance which it had not known before. The furnishings were magnificent — Sheraton, American Chippendale — everything was kept spotlessly clean, though Lizzie's only servant was a woman who had, fifty years ago, come, a country girl, to work for her mother.

What Lizzie talked to Grady about, what he said to her, we could only guess. Theirs was another strange friendship. Grady spoke of her as Baggie, which was the nickname he had for the Eurasian woman he had known in Korea. This troubled all the family to varying degrees. It troubled me very much, and I decided that, while he didn't like the old woman, he gave her some of his time and attention because she was old, lonely, and queer. The name, subconsciously, would reveal his basic dislike. Jason said I was searching for hidden significance.

In any case, I thought Grady should seek companionship among younger people, and he did, of course. The girls certainly afforded him every opportunity. Debutante daughters of our friends, and some we had never heard of except through their pictures in the paper, fellow students at the University, these girls called Grady on the phone, some drove to the house. Grady was nice to them all, and talked to them, sometimes he would get in a car and go off, sometimes he would accept a more formal invitation – he seemed to like girls, but there was no single one.

David had selected his girl. His father's young British secretary, Isabelle Hallowell, a truly lovely young woman with an exquisite complexion, large, dark eyes, and dark hair which she wore to her shoulders, brushed smooth and shining. David recognized his limitations, but there should have been no reason why Grady – He just did not select a girl. When pressed about this – and I heard various ones so press him – he would say that he didn't plan to marry.

"Because of your banged-up face?" Shields demanded.

"Sure. What else? And since that's the situation, it's best not to let myself fall in love with a girl."

I told myself that this phase too would pass for Grady. Let the right girl come along. . . .

It was the second summer after Grady came home that June began really to trouble him and the rest of us. Now one must make a real effort to understand June without becoming angry at the boy. One liked him on sight. He was that sort. Handsome, with deep creases in his brown cheeks, a flashing white-toothed smile, tousled dark hair. He was the youngest of our six boys, and as such perhaps he had been spoiled. He never, even as a little boy, learned to stick with any task or talent and see it through. He had always admired Grady, and had tagged his older brother unmercifully. Grady had shown patience beyond what is usual from one brother to another seven years younger. That summer, when June was nineteen, Grady seemed to understand that June was at the point where he thought he must determine himself as a man, and chart his life.

June sang very well, and had let his voice be trained. He had made his only good reports at school through his interest in music. That summer, he offered to go with Grady to the church for choir rehearsals, and sing there on Sundays. He was, it developed, or as he developed, very religious. Exceedingly so. He talked about his convictions to the associate rector, to the curate, and most of all, to Grady. He seemed to expect Grady to share this passion.

I thought it was one of June's phases. He had had others; his interests, his passions, had gone, alphabetically, from astronomy to zoology. Now, he was, it seemed, head, neck, and heels, pious. Religious.

I wondered what Grady would say, how he would handle his brother. I know that he talked to the boy — and let him talk. They went to choir practice, and to the services where a choir was required. June went to other services, too, but Grady did not. He respected June's interests, but they were not, particularly, his own.

And then, that summer, other things took such attention as Grady could spare from his summer courses at the University. Because, that summer, Henry Tibbs had his second heart attack.

It was Grady who found the little man fallen to the floor of his cluttered office. He had the sense, to quote his uncles, to call an ambulance, though since Henry was no bigger than a jockey, Grady could have carried him to the hospital in his arms.

But he called the ambulance; he sat beside the stretcher and followed it into the hospital receiving room, then down along the shining corridors and through the tiled tunnels, and finally up to a room in the cardiac ward where Lucian told Grady he could go on home. "You did a good job, son."

"Sir?"

"What is it?"

"I'd like to stay."

"You cannot. This is a major attack, I'm pretty sure. Henry is going to be on the strictest sort of regime."

For a minute, Grady stood uncertain. "When I can be with him . . . ?"

"I'll tell you. That's a promise."

Grady accepted it.

I suppose the hospital made its impact on the young man that summer. The size, the shining cleanness, the busy people, all privileged to help the sick.

The other men in the family told that he came almost every day to inquire at the floor desk about Henry, to send the old man little messages. "Tell him I've been here." "Tell him to quit goofing off and get on home." "Tell him the big toad's back in the lavender bed." He would sit out in the hall and watch things.

And finally, one evening, Lucian told Grady that he could go in to see Henry sometime, for fifteen minutes.

Grady was so pleased that he considered cutting a class. "You may go at any time,"

Lucian told him gruffly. "I'll leave orders at the desk."

"Is Henry going to be all right?"

Lucian snorted. "That's a fine thing to ask! You were raised in a family of doctors. You should know that only a fool or a quack makes that sort of prediction."

"Sir!" said Grady meekly.

When Grady did go to see the old man, and many times after, Henry asked him to take him home and stay with him there. It was through overhearing these discussions that we got some knowledge of how Grady talked to Henry.

"Certainly I won't live with you in that house!" he said brusquely. "It's a pigpen. Filthy dirty. It needs burning down."

So Grady, we knew, talked to his brothers, to the children of the family, to Taylor Falk, the pretty little girl across the street.

Henry liked being talked to in that way. And for reasons that were his own, but which took us years to understand, Grady continued to visit the old man every day, to run errands for him.

It was during this time that Grady first spoke to us about Henry's house out in the country. That night, rather late, he knocked on our bedroom door and came in, saying he had something to ask us. Earlier that evening Grady had paid his usual call on the old man and had come home to study with David. Now, his hair tousled, his shirt open at the throat, he came in and sat on the foot of our bed.

"Has he got a house out in the country?" he asked. "Or is his mind wandering again?"

"It's out there," Jason told him.

"But what the dickens does he want with another house? He uses only a tenth of the one he has."

"I take it you haven't seen it."

"Well, he told me where it was supposed to be, and I drove out there before coming home this evening. I didn't get out of the car. But what gives with Henry?"

His father laughed, and Grady grinned — sheepishly. "I know he's a kook," he muttered. "But he's a man, Dad. Something makes him the way he is."

"Have you determined what that way is?" asked Jason, busy at his chest of drawers, laying out clothing for the morning, or against a night emergency call. This was a habit which he had established when a resident surgeon. He set everything in precise order, and ready. The boys said he should have a fireman's pole.

Grady watched him. "Well, sir," he said thoughtfully, "I know Henry is a lonely old man . . ."

"You're sure he is lonely?"

"He lets me hang around. He must be hard

up for companionship."

Both Jason and I laughed. "We let you hang around here," said his father.

Grady scratched his head. "Yes, you do. I'll have to do some work on that question, too, maybe. But tell me about that house of Henry's. Did he ever live there?"

"Perhaps you could get him to talk to you about it?"

Grady considered this. "He gave me some keys tonight. He wanted me to get him some papers from his files."

Jason's head lifted warningly.

"Uncle Lucian said I could do it," said Grady hastily.

"All right, then."

"Henry told me which key was which, and he mentioned the house. 'That's the house in the country,' he told me. I asked about it, and he told me where it was. But he didn't say any more, and I guess I won't bring up the matter." Grady stood up and stretched his arms toward the ceiling. "I suppose a guy should be allowed to have his inner rooms. 'Night, folks. See you in the morning."

Sometimes it is difficult for me to stick to Grady's story and not give in to the temptation to digress, to insert a few chapters, at least, giving some mention to the stories of other family members. The McCords are a lively group of people. They do interesting things. They have their problems and their triumphs. And it is a temptation to speak of such things. Still – I started to write Grady's story, and I'll not bring in other lines of development except where those lines tangle or touch Grady's life.

Sometimes it is difficult, as well, to place incidents correctly and chronologically in the account of what Grady did, and of what happened to him.

But I think this scene fits in just about here. It is a scene which I shall always remember, and vividly.

It happened on one of those tender spring evenings we sometimes get in late March or early April. The trees are coming into leaf, the bulbs planted last fall are blooming gloriously. I decided I would take a walk down the length of the Place to see the flowers and talk to anyone I met.

I had done those things, and was on my way home when I realized that the saucer magnolia behind A.B.'s house was in full bloom. I walked around to look at it. The tree was like a giant bouquet; I stood for as much as ten minutes gazing at its beauty.

When I decided that it was time to go home, instead of walking along the drive, I went through the arched and colonnaded portico that encircles A.B.'s brick home. This is one of my favorite places; it has a cloistered, peaceful atmosphere which I like. Within it, the walls of the house are whitewashed, here and there are set oak benches, or a great earthenware jar. The bricks underfoot are mossy. As I came around to the front side of the house, I was aware of voices — rather loud ones. I began to hear what was being said before I realized that I already had begun to understand what was happening.

I stopped where I was, undecided as to what I should do. I could go on, of course, and reveal myself to the young people. I could turn, softly, go back — cut through Bishop's rose garden, and on to the back of our place.

And I could stand where I was, hidden behind the supporting pillar of the colonnade, and listen to what Grady and Isabelle Hallowell were quarreling about.

Because they were quarreling, and loudly enough for anyone in that block who had his window open, or who came along the street, to hear them. If A.B. or Christine were at home, they must be able to hear.

So, I assured myself, I was not really eavesdropping. I just happened to be where I could hear; to walk out and reveal myself would be most embarrassing — to me, certainly.

I had at once heard David's name. I had immediately been aware of the tone of the voices. Where I was by then, I could see Isabelle in a gold-colored skirt, a gold and white striped blouse. I could see Grady in the dark trousers, white shirt, and flannel blazer which he had worn to dinner.

For a year, we had watched, with mixed feelings, David's apparent capitulation to Jason's pretty, darkhaired secretary. I thought the situation could mean heartbreak for the young man, but I could not say a cautioning word to him. As clever as he was, he must know his handicaps much more exactly than anyone else.

I don't know just how or why Grady and Isabelle were where they were. Perhaps Grady had fetched Isabelle for an evening with him and David. This often happened; the young people played cards, read, listened to music — talked. The sitting room up in David's quarters was an attractive place. Or perhaps Grady, having gone to see Henry, had come upon Isabelle in the hospital area. She often worked late, I knew.

In any case, there they were, on A.B.'s front lawn, angry with each other, and loudly saying so.

Grady leaned against the trunk of the big wineglass elm, his hands playing with a small stick which he had picked up. Isabelle confronted him, her slender body shaken with the passion of what she had to say. Her dark hair gleamed in the light from the street lamps which were beginning to take over in the dusk.

"I am like everyone else, Grady McCord," she was saying, in her clipped way of speaking. The words fell clearly in the evening quiet. "I think you are a wonderful person. I have especially admired the way you have managed to take your brother out of his invalidism. The way you have taken him out of his self-absorption and made him aware of the world. I have watched you as you made him learn to manipulate crutches; I hear you argue with him, and I see you even roughhouse with David, a thing no one else would dare to do."

Grady murmured something, and Isabelle answered him. "I know you don't do it to be wonderful. Certainly not! You are fond of your brother, and you like to be with him. You like to have him going to classes at the University. You want him to have the freedom of getting a car which he can drive without feet, able to go places away from Schmitt or, to be honest, away from you."

"Oh, now look here, Belle," cried Grady, straightening.

Isabelle's hand brushed her hair away from her face. "Maybe you don't get tired of David, maybe he doesn't get tired of you – and I hope he gets his car and enjoys using it. I think you will have done a good, therapeutic thing for him. He deserves to live more widely than he has done in the past. He is a wonderful person, handsome, sweet-natured — and he has a fine mind. Like you, I think he will do something with his writing."

Again, Grady said something.

"I'll tell you what my 'beef' is," cried the girl. "And I'll tell you specifically . . ."

By then, wild horses could not have pulled me away from my listening post. I was only afraid that the two combatants would move away, or that someone might interrupt them, before Isabelle spoke "specifically."

". . . I'll even agree that you are correct to tell David he has a right to marry. Of course he can do it, and should do it sometime. But, Grady, why must you bring *me* into that discussion? What right have you . . . ?"

Grady stood very straight then, and he too spoke loudly. "Because you are the girl he is in love with," he said roughly. "You are the one he will want to marry badly enough to think he can marry!"

I knew that Isabelle must be dreadfully upset, or she would never have raised her voice as she did that evening. Grady wouldn't have cared that he was shouting, but he probably had forgotten where they were and what they were doing.

"Good Lord in *heaven*, Belle!" he cried.

"David – that guy is so in love with you – and you surely must know it!"

"And you think, knowing it, I should prepare myself to marry him, regardless of how I feel?"

"I think it would be a wonderful thing," said Grady firmly, "for you to marry David."

Isabelle threw out her hands in a gesture of despair. "And what about yourself, Grady McCord?" she demanded. "What about the wonderful thing that could happen to *you?*"

I knew what she was saying, and why; my heart ached for her, and for David. But Grady was only furious. He shouted at Isabelle, he even put his hands on her arms, and shook her. He was no John Alden, he cried angrily. He wouldn't be, he was not – And what was the use of trying to talk sensibly to a girl, anyway?

"Come along," he said roughly. "I'll take you home."

That scene worried me, and for some time to come. I didn't think Isabelle should consider marriage to David without loving him, but I just as certainly did not think she should dream of marrying Grady, because he did not love her. I hoped that each of the young people could find interests and mates elsewhere.

Before warm weather settled in, Henry Tibbs was fitted with a pacemaker. These were new at that time, even somewhat experimental, as Lucian admitted. But he thought Henry was a proper subject for the little battery-powered gadget which could be inserted into his body, and which would offer an electric stimulus for the lagging heart.

Lucian talked with his brothers about doing this, and Grady listened, fascinated. He asked dozens of questions and wanted to watch the minor surgery involved in its implantation. He was brusquely refused, but he lost no time in seeing Henry afterward, and he questioned the old man endlessly.

"He takes Henry's pulse!" Jason told me. "Really, Helen, that boy . . . You know what he reminds me of? Do you remember the Christmas when we gave him his first gasoline engine airplane?"

"I remember," I said, seeing the picture of Grady and his father out on the bricks, a stiff wind fanning their hair, getting the little red airplane into the air, hearing it whine, watching it circle and pitch — and crash. But Grady said he could fix it!

"He wore it out," I said, "examining it, working with it."

"That's what I mean. I am going to have to tell him to give Tibbs a chance."

I presume he did tell Grady, and probably Grady stopped getting Henry stirred up, though his interest in the pacemaker did not abate. "That's real hand-of-God stuff," he told me seriously. "I'm proud of Uncle Lucy."

"Grady . . ."

"I know, I know. It slipped out. He's a prime doctor, Lady Vere de Vere. He's going to let Henry come home before long."

"If Henry will let someone be there to help him."

"He will. I'll work on him. I'm going to clean up his house first, too."

"You'll be the one to need help."

"I'll get it."

"You must tell Henry about your plan."

"I shall. Cripes, Mother, that guy acts as if he had loose diamonds all over the place."

"Maybe he does."

"Loose everything else. No diamonds."

Grady did clean Henry's house – the lower floor – enlisting the help of practically everyone in the family. Lucian's boys, and Joe's small son, an assortment of maids, yardmen, and even his Uncle Bishop. They hauled junk away in loaded station wagons, or in trailers hitched to Grady's sports car. They swept, dusted, washed windows. . . .

"Now I'll get the upstairs," planned Grady.

"You must ask Henry."

"He let me do the first floor. The second won't be as bad. He never goes up there, does he?"

"You know the man better than I do."

"Yeah. And he might – Lord, we found stacks of magazines from nineteen twenty-six."

Henry would not let Grady go upstairs. "There's nothing there," he said.

"But cobwebs and dust, you mean."

"Don't go up there," said Henry.

"O.K. What about that house out in the country?"

"No," said Henry. "No."

When a man had been found willing to live in Henry's house and care for the old man, Lucian said he could go home.

"I'll bring him home in David's wheelchair," said Grady, who had been reading in the adjoining room. "I've planned this. . . ."

"What's happened to all the automobiles?" asked Lucian coldly. "Including Henry's ancient, but serviceable, Buick?"

"Wait a minute," said Grady, running out of the room, up the stairs, coming back with some papers in his hands. They looked like pages of books, or magazines, torn out, clipped with identifying blue tabs.

"Sir," he said to his Uncle Lucian, "have you read this material on the effect of electromagnetism on pacemakers?"

Lucian frowned. "Henry's pacemaker is synchronous. . . ."

106

"Yes, sir, but look here. Read this — it's the best I could find on the subject."

Lucian groaned.

"It's just this one article . . ." Grady reassured him.

Lucian stood there, his dark face like a thundercloud. Jason was more amused than anything else. But he had had more experience with Grady's enthusiasms. I didn't know what to expect. I still was happy, and grateful, to have my son home with us, and apparently content.

"This article says," Grady told us, waving the sheet of glossy paper at us, "that an automobile may be a killer for people wearing certain types of artificial pacemakers. It cites here the case of a woman in California, who became pulseless while the automobile's motor was running."

"How could that happen?" I asks

"Helen!" protested Lucian.

"But I want to know."

"The automobile's ignition system produces broad-band radio frequency signals," Grady told me.

I smiled at him. "Thanks a lot."

"You asked. But that's why I think . . ."

"We could test pacemakers like Henry's, I suppose," said Jason.

"I am not convinced that he should go through the streets in a wheelchair," Lucian retorted. "And I understand the synchronous type pacemaker . . ."

"If it's fixed-rate," said Grady, picking up another sheet of paper, "you'd have to check it rather exhaustively, Uncle Lucian, to be sure it wouldn't shut down during a nonpacing mode. I think using the chair would be simpler, for now at any rate. Later, having checked the thing, Henry could ride in a car." He spoke with authority.

"What about the motor on David's chair?" Lucian asked sourly. He did not appreciate this young man's advice.

"Oh, I'd push him," said Grady.

"Then we'll get a chair for Henry," Lucian told him. "No need to borrow David's."

Jason and I, privately, thought the whole episode was rather amusing. But we agreed that Grady should not be encouraged in the confounding of his elders. "We might be next," said Jason grimly.

Two weeks later, Henry came home, Grady pushing his chair for the three-block journey, making the move early in the morning when traffic was light on the side-walks. Crossing the Boulevard is always an adventure. But Henry enjoyed the trip, and afterward could often be seen going up and down Southshire Place, with his houseman, Grady — or someone — pushing his chair.

★

It was that winter that Grady moved downstairs to his old room and left the third floor to David and Isabelle, who were married at Christmastime.

Why? Troubled, I asked myself why that beautiful girl should have entered such a difficult marriage. And the best answer I could find was that David loved and needed her, and Grady did not.

Chapter 5

The next June, Grady graduated from the University, with honors, though he refused to wear a cap and gown and march in "any procession." David, he said, would finish the next year and we could all attend. Meanwhile, he had been helping David, encouraging him, to write, and that summer marked his brother's first sale of a story to a magazine. Grady was more excited and proud than David was. But the whole family made a fuss over the event.

Not exactly the same sort of "fuss" as was made over Grady's announcement that he meant to study medicine.

He told his father and Shields and me at lunch on Sunday. We had come home from church, and Orlie was serving us. We sat in the small dining room; there were roses in a blue pitcher, and we had slices of cold meat, a salad of fresh tomatoes and lettuce on the Wedgwood plates. I remember the way Grady looked, with the light slanting across his face through the stained-glass squares around the window. He spoke quietly, and as if this was a development which could have been expected.

I was ready to agree with him on that.

I could, quite easily, see Grady, early each morning — before eight — joining the doctors on the Place, well-dressed, closely shaven gentlemen, most of them middle-aged, coming out of their homes, getting into their cars, or, if the weather favored, walking briskly along, picking up a brother, striding, shoulder to shoulder, on toward the Boulevard, turning the corner, talking to each other, interested in each other's work. The Doctors McCord, a phalanx, crossing the Boulevard at the light, going into the various hospitals — speaking to those whom they met, being spoken to.

"Good morning, doctor."

"Good morning, Jason. How are things?"

And Jason's answering, not slowing his step. He would check in at the front desk, go up to the locker room and change from his cordovan shoes, tweed suit, shirt and tie into the shapeless, baggy scrub suit; he would put a long white coat over it, and go out to check on the surgical schedule. Then up to the surgery floor, busy already with residents, interns, orderlies, and nurses — even a cart or two. Again he would check the schedule, and go on to the scrub room, to o.r. or to the theater. Again it would be, "Good morning, Dr. McCord."

Capped, gowned, masked, he would stand beside the table and begin to work silently on the problem which he had already studied and solved, doing the work he had previously planned, his hand sure, his voice clear — a doctor. And only a doctor.

It would be much the same with Joe, and Bishop, though their going to the hospital could be more irregular than Jason's, for babies are born at all hours, and emergencies develop. But still they usually made the morning parade, Joe the gay, debonair obstetrician, the gynecologist whose specialty, to my continuing amazement, was abortion. He lectured, he consulted, he practiced. He cared for diabetic women, those with t.b. He was an authority, and he took his profession seriously.

As did Bishop McCord. He was a gynecological surgeon, and was what Jason called a great clinician. The two brothers shared an office and worked together.

A.B. could go along with the others; he could go to his lab earlier, or later.

Lucian, of course. And Shields, lately, also. . . .

It had seemed the most natural thing in the world for Shields to study medicine, to become another Dr. McCord. But — Grady?

We were surprised. I couldn't think of a thing to say. I shivered a little and sat gazing at him.

Shields coughed quickly, spasmodically, and reached for his iced-tea glass.

Jason listened to his son; he carefully cut a piece of meat and put it into his mouth.

"Just why," he asked then, "have you decided on medicine?"

Grady took a minute to answer. I was looking at him, and Shields lifted his head and rested his knife and fork.

"I decided about three years ago," said Grady, "that if you are in the health field, you never have to get up in the morning and ask yourself if what you are doing is worthwhile."

I looked at Jason. He touched his napkin to his lips. He had nothing to say.

But that afternoon, the men of the family held their usual conference and had a great deal to say. This meeting was held at poolside, behind Bishop's house. There were others around the pool; Isabelle had come down with David. There were several children, in and out of the water. Eve, Joe's wife, was on a chaise soaking up sun. I sat in the shade with Lucian's wife, Mary. The girl cousins, Ann and Christine, were swimming; there was a dog or two about.

But the men, all five brothers and my son Shields, were seated beyond me, in the glider and a couple of chairs; Bishop sat on the flagstones and clasped his hands around his

113

bare knees. He was as brown as walnut from the sun. His shoulders and his black hair still glistened with beaded water. Lucian had pulled a white shirt over his shoulders. Jason wore Bermudas and a striped shirt. Shields had on a yellow shirt, with a figured scarf in the throat of it.

Jason made his announcement and looked from one brother's face to another's, gauging their reactions. It was shock, largely. And in varying degrees. Joe laughed and shook his head. A.B. and Lucian both frowned. Bishop whispered softly and scrubbed his knuckles down the ridge of his fine nose.

"I don't think you should be surprised," Shields told his father and his uncles. "He's been taking pre-med courses at the U. for three years. He took his degree in Science."

"That's true," said Grady's father.

Grady was not present. He probably had anticipated this conference, and the shock.

"Grady's not the temperament," said A.B. lamely. He knew it was a poor thing to say, and he smiled wryly. "I suppose Grady can do almost anything he really wants to do," he conceded. "Maybe that's what worries me."

"I suppose he means to get at it immediately," said Lucian.

"He should," Jason agreed. "He's a bit over-age, as it is."

"Where does he plan . . . ?" Two brothers spoke at once.

Jason repeated what had been said at the luncheon table. "He told me he planned to study medicine, I asked him why — and he answered me. He said . . ."

Grady's answer silenced the brothers, too.

"He meant it," said Shields softly.

"Where . . . ?" asked Bishop, tracing a damp finger across a flat red stone.

"Shields went East . . ." said Lucian. "But Grady — I imagine you'd rather he would stay at home, Jase?"

Jason shook his head. "I don't know," he said. "Shields, do you know where Grady — Where is he now, by the way? Or *do* you know where he plans to go to school?"

Shields shrugged. "He's not talked to me either," he said.

I tipped my head back and looked up at the leaf-shadowed white walls of Bishop's house. In this big, spreading house, the McCord brothers had lived and grown from children to manhood. Had any one of them ever caused the stirred emotions which my son Grady could produce?

It was established that Grady was playing golf that afternoon. The men must discuss his future plans without him.

He should stay at home.

No, it would be better if he studied at another school. There already were too many — too damn many — McCords at this one.

The men guessed at the specialty which Grady would elect to follow. . . .

Once Shields looked across at me and winked. And I felt better. Of course! Grady would already have made his plans.

And he had.

Months earlier he had applied at the University Medical School and been accepted. He was enrolled, and that summer he served a clerkship in the hospital laboratories.

As a result of the work he did, that winter he published his article on "Danger in the Laboratory."

It first appeared in the slick-paged magazine published by one of the large pharmaceutical companies; it was picked up and quoted in our local newspapers, then in newspapers all over the country.

Grady had been paid a thousand dollars for the article, which had to do with the too-many errors made in hospital and commercial laboratories. He told of transfusions given disastrously because of the wrong blood type being recorded on a patient's chart. He told of the failure to double-check a tissue test, and the amputation of a young woman's breast for a cancer which did not exist. He told of what he

116

called many avoidable laboratory factors – and urged, in rather fervid language, that lab work be considered as important, as vital, as that done by any surgeon or internist.

I was shocked by what he wrote and revealed. It was not a long article. It was well-written, I thought, easily readable, and convincing. The uncles were shocked that he had written anything at all, and immediately assembled to discuss the matter.

That meeting took place in the Chinese parlor of Joe's big, pink brick house, and I was not present. But Jason told me about it when he came home that night.

"They were upset?" I asked. I was already in bed, propped up on the big pillows which I like.

Jason grinned at me and rattled his loose change and his keys into the tray on his chest of drawers. "I can't help but be proud of the kid," he said gruffly.

"Were the others . . . ?"

"Lucian is as mad as hell!" said Lucian's brother. "The others – Well, I suppose we all are somewhat concerned. Lucian demanded to know where Grady got his information and the figures he quoted."

"Did anyone know?"

"I told them, and I could tell you, Helen, to ask Grady. He'd tell us. But I am pretty sure he had his facts straight or a trade magazine like that would not have printed his stuff. David said . . ."

"David?"

"Yes. He was there. He and Isabelle had had dinner at Joe's house. I think Isabelle and Eve are quite friendly."

"Yes, they are. What did David say?"

"Oh, he sat there in his chair watching us get all hot and bothered, and then he asked us quietly if any one of us knew where Grady goes on his week ends, or on the vacation-type trips he takes."

"He went to Washington in August," I said. "I thought for a check-up at Bethesda."

"That's right, he did go. And had his check-up. David told us – all of us older men, and presumably wiser ones than he – that Grady would tell us where he went on those trips. And then, do you know what?" Jason came to sit on the foot of the bed and look earnestly at me. "My oldest brother had the gall to ask me if I was giving him money to make these so-called research journeys."

"Why, Jason . . ."

"I told him it was none of his damn business, but then I reminded him that Grady lived at home. I paid his tuition at any school he felt necessary for his education, as I had paid it for all my sons. About there Bish told me not to get hot. And I told him I didn't need to *get* anything! I was hot.

"I reminded my brothers that Grady had saved the money he had earned in the Navy, and while he was convalescing. The Government sent his disability check each month. I knew he bought his clothes and car with that money. I *supposed* he used it for the trips which he took. And they'd better do as David suggested, question Grady. I could predict they would get an answer.

"As for myself, I told them, I was proud of my son. I reminded them that the things he had said in his article were true, as they all knew."

"And who answered that?"

"A.B. He said such an article was not for a McCord to write."

I waited.

"Yes!" said Jason. "I asked him why not? And he had the grace to back down a little. He said that such material belonged in a noncommercial journal. Then I really jumped on him. I asked him how many articles he had read lately in journals, written by first-year medical students."

"Was he mad, Jason?" I liked A.B.

"He backed down, and of course we all laughed at the notion." Jason resumed his task of setting out the next day's clothes. "We all hope," he said, as he went into the bathroom, "that this will end Grady's literary career."

But of course it did not.

That fall, Grady had entered medical school, five years older than most of the other students. He had asked for permission to try to do the four-year course in three years, and was brusquely denied. He made excellent grades, Jason told me. Won some awards. . . .

"And on his own, Helen. We McCords never heard of this student medic."

"He's a smart boy."

"I sometimes think matters would be simpler if he were not so smart."

Grady continued to spend his short vacations traveling — at Thanksgiving, during Christmas week — the spring break. He would punctiliously tell me that he would be away. "For a couple of days, Lady Vere de Vere. You won't worry?"

"I worry about you when you're upstairs in your bed."

He touched my cheek "Just a born mother," he said, smiling at me.

"Grady — Could I ask you where you go on these trips, what you do?"

He set his small canvas bag on the floor and straddled a chair, his chin on his folded forearms. "You can ask me anything in the world," he told me. "As for my answer — You'll be surprised to know that I ride buses, generally. I go from here to there, and back again. I talk to people." His forefinger touched his eye patch. "This makes people talk to me. And so I carry on from there." He gazed at me for a moment, then his lips quirked. "Specifically, dear, I go to see hospitals and medical schools – other med schools than our tight one here. I see big hospitals and little ones. I look at records where I can. I see all manner of med schools and their records. I visit clinics, huge ones with staffs of four hundred doctors, little ones that have only two or three. But let me tell you about a nice one I visited at Christmastime. It is really nice. I wouldn't mind working there, or being sick there, either. They'd take care of me, in either case.

"It's in the Middle West, Mother, in a somewhat small town. Twenty thousand people. There are eight doctors, all Board-certified as qualified in their specialties, and a couple of them are diplomates. That means . . ."

"I know what it means, Grady. The men in our family studied for, took, and passed the Board exams. Your father and Joe are *on* Boards."

"Yes, that's true. I remember when Uncle Bishop – Well, anyway, this clinic is a good place." He stood up, set the chair back against the wall, and picked up his bag. He stooped to kiss my cheek. "Remember, now. Don't worry."

I didn't — much. He came home in time to resume his schedule at the school; he studied long and late. All med students did, Jason told me. And I expected Grady to write and publish something about his nice little clinic.

He did not — not then, at any rate. The articles which he wrote, and did publish, had to do with medical schools, and the changes that were needed in them.

He criticized the small amount of clinical training afforded in medical colleges, and said there should be a way to force students to attend clinical classes, to learn from them. In one article he asked a provocative question: Were the medical schools to blame for the faults too often found in doctors? This matter, he said, should be looked into.

He wrote about the high rate of failure in medical schools, and said it accounted for some of the doctor scarcity. This could be prevented by more careful screening of student admissions. He thought medical students who failed should be removed, and at once. The schools could admit more students, and afford to force out the inept. Good doctors taught and made new good doctors. Inept ones . . .

He challenged the medical schools to establish two, or perhaps three, curricula. One to deal with science, one to teach the clinical arts, a third to teach the humanities of medicine.

He wrote that medical students should have sooner contact with patients, that, upon admission, they should immediately begin to live their new profession. He deplored the trend away from patient care to research, asserting that many of the doctors on the faculties of medical schools could not actually care for patients. They were scientists, researchers — the clinicians were downgraded, and so only poor clinicians survived; they in turn taught and graduated still poorer ones. . . .

He wrote that university medical schools were the best, but that there should be many improvements to them. Acceleration and shorter terms of training were not the answers. Any student had youth, immaturity — and a great amount of things to learn. Closer time and attention, some new programs to integrate science with the human being, would produce better doctors of human beings.

I read every article he wrote, which I could find. Jason began to put the magazines on the leaf of my desk, without any comment from him. During this time, the McCords had nothing to say, that I heard.

I asked Shields about Grady's performance at school, and he told me that he was a good student and was making a fine record. Shields himself had begun to work with the burn center that was to bring another eminent Dr. McCord to the profession.

In his last year of medical school, Grady applied for an internship, stating our hospital center as his first choice of a service. And this was granted to him, without, I was told, benefit of any family member's influence.

The following year he did his second internship, and published two articles on intern training.

ARE INTERNS CHEAP LABOR?
WHY DON'T INTERNS WORK AT THEIR JOBS?

Such titles attracted attention, readers, and comment. Again I read each word, and longed to talk with Grady about the points he raised, and with the other doctors of the family. I thought what he said was provocative. When I said that to Jason, he nodded and told me that Grady had one sure and certain talent. He could arouse instant interest.

In his articles on intern training, Grady again found fault with the teaching afforded young doctors. He said again that the emphasis was on science rather than on doctor-patient relationship. That institutionally trained doctors dealt with crisis cases rather than the average, day-to-day illnesses met in general practice. Doctors graduating from large medical schools, and interning in large hospital centers, were poorly prepared to open an office and handle ambulatory sick people. He cited the great amount of tests ordered in big hospitals, many of them for research purposes rather than to promote individual patient care. "And no one tells the learning doctor when *not* to order an electrocardiogram."

Again and again, Grady came back to the human side of medicine. He called intern training hit-and-miss, without proper standards of performance or excellence. He called for the instant dismissal of poor interns. Hospitals, afraid to acknowledge poor judgment in their admission of interns, would let the men continue, to become poor residents, and then poor doctors, prepared to train unsuspecting medical school graduates. . . . He said the intern and resident training programs needed a system of teaching and examinations, rather than the present system of "expecting the young doctors to attend lectures and to learn." He said talented, dedicated doctors did manage to learn, but the uncaring, the unable, did not, and they survived anyway. He said intern and resident training should be a part of the medical school, and M.D.'s should not be awarded until stiff requirements were met.

He said a lot. He said it well.

In Grady's second year of internship — at

that time he was away from home more than he was with us — David published his first novel. This, we decided, was a big event in the family. The book got good reviews, and we were all proud of David.

"Grady should get some of the credit," Jason frequently said. "He's bullied that boy into doing things, being somebody."

And finally, inevitably, someone asked Jason if David was writing Grady's stuff. It may have been a member of the family, though at the time, I rather thought it was a staff member at the hospital.

"The things Grady does . . ." said my husband. We were driving to church, and he kept his attention on the street before us. "Grady's articles are bright, interesting — and the patients read them —"

"Do they do any harm, Jason?" I asked.

"Well," said my husband, "let's say they are disturbing. Change is always disturbing, Helen, or the promise of it."

"Yes, I know. In the church — in the home —"

"That's it. And in the hospitals. Do you know if David *is* doing Grady's writing?"

"Why don't you ask Grady? Or even David? You see your sons occasionally."

Jason only grinned. He was absorbed in parking the car without hitting one, or six, of the racing and running Sunday school pupils just released from class.

But that evening he asked me why we didn't go upstairs to see David and Isabelle. There was no reason, so we did go up to the third floor, and were warmly welcomed.

Schmitt and Isabelle had amicably worked out each other's duties and privileges. Isabelle had made some good changes in the rooms. . . .

She suggested tea; we agreed and, basking in the glow of a small fire on the hearth, enjoying the fragrant contents of the cup in his hand, Jason asked David if he was writing Grady's articles for him.

David laughed. "Medicine, hospitals, doctors, would not be my subject of choice, sir," he said.

"I didn't mean the subject matter. But the wording, the polish, the style . . ."

David leaned forward. "Look, sir," he said earnestly, "make no mistake. Grady is your smart son. There isn't a thing he can't do."

I don't know why — I didn't know then — but on that quiet evening, I again felt the tug of loss. I had only barely survived the loss of the boy who was my son. Now, to face the loss of the man he had become . . .

Chapter 6

The brother-doctors talked together about Grady's published writings, and came to an agreement on the matter, as they had done at other times of strain and crisis – during the war, during Joe's difficulties with Eve – over Grady's spectacular injury and the resultant publicity – and at times of more intimate testing of our solidarity, like Joe's unthinking decision to build his own swimming pool . . .

"Going to set up competition against me, eh?" Bish had challenged him.

"I've got a big batch of kids. . . ."

"My pool's to be for bachelors and old folk, I suppose?"

It was a little funny, it could have meant hard feeling – the family managed the matter, and closed their ranks against all threats. They did the same about the annoyance which Grady's writings must surely have caused. As one man, the doctors refused to make any comment, either for or against, his declarations. The family front, its integrity, was impenetrable.

"If a McCord says it, it has to be true," Shields explained to me when I talked to him a little about the situation.

"Does everybody think that?" I asked.

"No, but the McCords sure do. And they have weight, Mother. They have weight."

I leaned heavily upon my good, solid son, who was Shields. Because I — and the whole family — had to give a good deal of thought and feeling that year to June, our youngest, who was neither solid nor always good.

June had always been a boy to vacillate, to go from one enthusiasm to another. He had never actually graduated from the University — he attended three — he had even spent a year in Europe "trying to find himself."

"If he ever does," growled Bish, "it will scare him to death."

There was little Jason, or I, could say to defend June.

"He's never brought scandal to us," Jason reminded me.

No, he had not. But that year . . .

June had stayed with his idea of entering the religious life and had enrolled in the Episcopal seminary with a view toward becoming a priest. Everybody had his doubts about his doing this except June. I don't know if I was relieved, or not, to have him decide to attend the seminary in our city. He was admitted without difficulty, so I told Jason it must be all right.

"Mother's intuition?"

I laughed. "I don't seem to have any."

"I'll admit that boy bugs me."

"Now that doesn't sound like the dignified surgeon."

"Your dignified surgeon's own vocabulary has been exhausted long ago."

We were going to a football game. Our University makes little or nothing of its sports program, but the city, a year before, had branched out into professional football. The men thought the effort should be supported; they bought two boxes for the season, and that afternoon two cars full of McCords, all ages, departed for the converted baseball park where the game would be held. Supported by plaid lap robes, chrysanthemums, thermos bottles of what Lucian called "decent" coffee, we would watch the football game. It was a good day for it, sunny, cold, but not bitter. The younger folk, and a friend or two of theirs, occupied one box. We older ones – Jason and I, Joe, Lucian and Mary, Bish and A.B. – occupied the other. I watched the young folk more than I did the game, I will admit. I used to understand football, but this new game was a mystery to me. The substitutions, the multiple teams, the specialists –

Still, I liked the people, watching them.

130

The men talked rather a lot, even as the game progressed. And during half time . . .

"I could have sworn that was June," said Bish unexpectedly, dropping his binoculars. "Only of course he would not be at a place like this on Sunday afternoon."

"You ready to bet on that?" asked June's father.

"Well, the guy was with what I'd certainly call a dame."

"Then I hope it wasn't June," said Jason firmly. "Celibacy is cheaper."

The men laughed and began to speculate upon the incidence of double pneumonia among baton twirlers.

When the younger members of the family began to return from whatever hot dog stand they had been patronizing, Christine leaned across the rail to ask us if we had seen June.

"I did," said Bishop, "but I was outvoted."

"D'you see his date?" she persisted.

"Well —"

"You saw her," she decided. "Our cousin likes to live dangerously, doesn't he?" She sat down, ready to give her attention to her own date, a nice-looking boy with thick auburn hair.

"Now what did she mean by that?" asked Jason.

I thought he should not have asked.

"Did you ever hear of a Dodie Mulvihill?"

asked Mary in that cool way she has of dropping gritty little stones into the family machin-
ery.

"I've heard of Roger Mulvihill," said Jason.
"He's in the architectural firm that's building
the Tower."

"That's the one," said Mary. "Only I don't
suppose Roger is here this afternoon."

"Why not?" asked Joe, his eyes glinting.

I wished the game would start. But some dull
man was making a dull speech out on the field.

Mary shrugged the fur collar of her coat up
around her blonde hair. "Dodie almost never
goes to football games with Roger," she said.
"She likes younger men."

"And June's younger?" asked Jason, his voice
grating.

"Oh, yes. Dodie admits to thirty-five."

"She's good-looking," said Bish.

"Very," agreed Lucian's wife. "And she
dresses well."

"That means expensively," Lucian instructed
us, perhaps hoping to change the trend of the
conversation.

He did change it a little. While I considered
my youngest and a married woman who
dressed expensively, the men said various
things about boys all going through a phase
of being interested in older women.
Yes, and those same women often had

132

their fling with the boys. . . .

I didn't like that conversation, but it wasn't any help when Grady's name came up.

How did it happen, someone asked, that he'd kept himself unentangled?

"Ask Bish. He knows that answer."

Grady, they decided, had been too busy doing his hospital work and writing about it.

"The kid's got some real ideas," drawled Bishop.

"That's legitimate. If he keeps them under control."

"And joins the McCord brothers, you mean?"

"We're not too bad."

"We're not bad at all. Maybe Grady will let us join him."

"Just so he stays friendly," said Joe, turning to watch the kickoff.

That summer Grady had started his first residency, and under his father. I didn't know if I was happy about that, or if Jason was. He talked about it a little — that is, if I would bring up the subject, he would reply.

I asked him first, if he meant to put some of Grady's ideas to work on him. The past year he'd had a lot to say about what residents should do and be.

Jason had peered at me over his Ben Franklin half-glasses. He was reading. "Grady," he said firmly, "is to be one of my boys. I train them all as best I can. And I do it myself, not leaving too much to the second and third residents."

Another time I asked Jason if it meant anything for Grady to be on his father's service.

That time, Jason chuckled. "He says I hustle him more than I do the other chaps."

"Do you?"

"Perhaps I do."

"Do you suppose the other residents suspect him of getting preference?"

"They may *say* they suspect it, and needle Grady. But the truth is – and I honestly believe this, Helen – Dr. Grady McCord is good or bad, and his record will so read, strictly by his own determination."

I thought this was eminently fair, and I hoped Grady knew his father's position. But, womanlike, I had to inquire.

My son was no less patient with me than his father had been. "Don't worry," he told me. "Dad and I should have no trouble. I'm good."

"Modesty, Grady?"

He laughed. "I really am good, Lady Vere de Vere. I studied. I made a nuisance of myself, asking questions, and demanding to be taught. In that way, I've learned my trade. I think all interns should be forced to do as I did."

"It would mean more work for the staff doctors."

"Oh, yes! And some — the majority — would fight it tooth and nail. They will fight it."

By then Grady was being solicited to write articles about the medical situation. I knew this from the mail which came to him. Various journal editors wrote to him on engraved, pebbled-bond stationery. He got stacks of mail, and on his free days, his typewriter would click busily.

He wrote articles on the way the obstetrical training program was conducted in big hospitals, and he trod many, many toes when he attacked the stranglehold which the AMA had upon hospital accreditation and its required stamp of approval upon residency and internship training programs. He published still another one, which appeared in a popular magazine, on the AMA as opposed to organized medicine.

This stirred up a tempest in the McCord family because it had created such a storm within the hospital staff.

"That boy's just asking for trouble!" cried Jason. "He's a glutton for punishment!"

I had been wondering . . . "Do they persecute him, Jason?" I asked.

He turned to look at me. "What — how do you mean 'persecute'?"

"Well — the other doctors, the teachers, the staff men who don't like what he tells, do they . . . ?"

"I see," said Jason. He had had a long day, and he should have been able to come home, change into loose, old clothes and relax. "There's a row going on just now," he told me. "But there's been no official stand taken against Grady about the things he writes and publishes. I suspect some men have asked for action. I suspect there's been some singling out. When he was an intern, I know he did more than his share of scut work."

I was familiar with the term. Scut work was a comprehensive name for all manner of grubby, unpleasant tasks which an intern could be asked to perform.

"How did Grady take that?" I asked. "Did he know he was being singled out?"

"He knew," said Jason, grinning. "And Grady — well, he takes what comes, and thinks a lot."

"Then, when the time is right, he does something about it." So the boy Grady had survived the bullying of his older brothers and his young uncles.

"He sure does do something about it," Jason agreed. "But, you know, Helen, I still wish . . ."

"Does he make your life difficult, Jason?"

He thought about his reply. "It isn't so much that he does make things difficult for me, as that I am on the defensive. I get some ragging, of course. Lucian hates the whole situation. He thinks I should take my belt to Grady, or something of that sort."

"Do you talk to him? Grady, I mean."

"Occasionally. Yes, I do. When he brings up the subject."

I thought Jason was unduly tired that night. I've been a surgeon's wife for a long time, and Jason was one to be concerned about his patients. But that night, his tiredness was somewhat different. There was a worried quality to it. Worry about himself, and his own ability to handle things.

I was prepared to ask Grady, when next he was at home for his thirty-six-hour break, just how upset the hospital staff was about his articles.

And then Eve told me. . . .

I do my turn at serving as a hospital volunteer. Eve and Mary do, too. I like the work, and am always ready to be assigned wherever I am needed. This can be behind a desk in admissions, or in the convalescents' nursery over at Children's, where I read to, and cuddle, the youngsters. I can be assigned to hold and feed newborns at Maternity, or, as on that day, to sit beside the red telephone in the Poison Center.

This can be a hair-raising, exciting post, or one can get in hours of uninterrupted reading or needlepoint. The duty is to sit beside that red telephone, kept free of all but emergency calls, and when it rings — a child has got some of a perfume stick in her mouth, a woman has taken some pills in a suicide attempt, a little boy has a burned mouth from tasting turpentine — the job is to tell the caller where the nearest hospital is, and sometimes to call the police or fire department, or an ambulance, for the panic-stricken caller.

Sometimes I can feel I have saved a life. Sometimes we can't do anything in time.

The Poison Center has a grim display case containing souvenirs of our emergency calls. A jar of hair-straightening preparation, which is sold as a cosmetic and which contains one simple thing — lye. We have a half-unwound golf ball; the center exploded, squirting its liquid into a child's eye. We have cigarettes; a child can die from eating one and its filter. We keep a display of pesticides, soaps — lilies of the valley — rhubarb leaves. . . .

That particular morning had been only somewhat busy. A child had eaten match heads — the whole matches, as a matter of fact. That was a new one to me, so I found a book of matches and put it in the display case.

I was glad when, at noon, Eve came around and suggested that we eat lunch together. "I've something to tell you," she said. Her voice is throaty and she has a fascinating accent. "I hope we can get a table. . . ."

We just barely did. We shook our heads at a

dozen invitations to join larger groups. But there was a small table against the far wall. We went straight to it; I put my sewing bag upon it, and then we tackled the line at the counter. I chose soup, an English muffin, a baked pear. Eve got a fruit plate and a package of crackers. There are reasons for her fine figure, though weight is no real problem for me.

I was prepared for Eve to tell me some gossip about our friends, or even about someone at the hospital; I braced myself for that. But I did not expect what she did tell me.

She glanced around to see who was sitting close, though even I would have difficulty hearing her in that noisy room. I felt sure every one of the five thousand hospital personnel was attempting to eat lunch at that minute, and were all talking about it. The place smelled of salmon croquettes and coffee; it roared with noise.

Eve leaned close. "Did you know it had been decided not to name the Tower *McCord*, Helen?"

I had not heard that. "Who decided?" I asked faintly.

"Oh, the Board, I suppose. Or the Staff. Maybe both." She leaned back. "It is all because of Grady and those articles he writes."

I didn't believe her. I knew she was probably right, but I wouldn't talk about it to Eve, or believe what she said. "I'll ask Jason," was all she could get me to say.

I suppose she studied my face, and I suppose she saw plenty there. Shock, indignation — a mother's concern for a son who might be a little wayward — a mother's defense of that same son. A wife's loyalty and distress.

That evening I did ask Jason about the story, and he immediately charged off down the street to Joe's house to ask his brother, "Where in hell does Eve get such information?"

And Joe, his face like a rock, answered him. "She got *this* information when she overheard me telling the Board what it could do with its . . . Tower!"

Jason would not repeat to me the profanity which Joe had used. He did not come home for a couple of hours. The men had held a gathering right there and then. They had talked, and then they had drafted a letter to the Board Chairman. If I had been there, I would have stopped them — or tried to. I know it is always unwise to write any kind of letter when one is angry or emotional.

But the men wrote it — somebody went inside — perhaps they all did, and it was written by hand. They signed it and sent it off by hand.

And the next day there was another meeting of all the Doctors McCord with the Center's

Board of Trustees. Shields told me about it. He was included, because he has staff status. But Grady was not there. Shields said the meeting was very stiff and formal.

"All the Board, and all the McCords, had pokers down their coats," he told me. "Me, too. We went into the room together, and that's rather formidable, Mother. Such a parade of McCords. I suspect the Board trembled a little in their chairs."

I smiled faintly.

Shields nodded. "O.K. The Board Chairman had the letter which Dad and the uncles had written. He read it and asked Uncle Lucian if he had any additional thing to say. And of course Uncle Lucy – I mean Lucian – said the letter spoke for itself. Then the Chairman ran his finger around inside his collar and said the McCords had put them in a difficult situation. And you *should* have heard Dad snort!"

I sighed. I had heard Jason snort on other occasions.

Shields' hazel eyes were shining. "Then the Chairman said the letter deserved consideration, but it had come too late. Now that threw our side for a loop. But nobody said anything; we just waited.

"And the Board Chairman got downright affable. He leaned across the table and smiled at us. He said that of course we would remember that, months ago, we had given our consent to the Tower's being named McCord. Now, I hadn't even been asked, but it seemed certain that the family had consented. And probably in writing. 'Yes,' said the Chairman. And Uncle Joe said something about reconsidering. 'You can't reconsider,' said the Chairman. 'It is too late for that. We have the stone carved with the name. We have the name on all the furnishings, stationery, towels, furniture, equipment. Even the menus for the restaurant and the doormats downstairs.' "

"What did they find to say? Our men?"

"Well, really not much of anything. Uncle A.B. asked if it were true that consideration had been given to naming the Tower something besides McCord, and the Chairman said, yes, he had heard that suggestion. But he had used the same arguments as he had used to us. McCord Tower it would be, and had to be. So we all got up and filed out. It was kind of funny, Mother, but really it was not funny at all."

No, it was not funny. When Jason told me about the meeting, he said only that he was glad the matter had been settled. "We couldn't have stayed on. . . ."

Then I was really shocked. For the McCords to leave the Center? To abandon the services which they had built up? To leave their big

142

homes in the Place? Not to live close to one another . . . ?

"Oh, Jason!" I cried.

He patted my shoulder. "That's why I wish Grady would stop writing the things he does."

"Perhaps if you would ask him . . . ?"

"You know I wouldn't do that. But it makes it hard for him to work with us. I am about convinced it would be better if he worked elsewhere."

"Oh, no!" I cried. "Oh, no!"

The family had been shaken, and they worried about what might happen next, though they all agreed that it would not be their usual way of doing things to tell Grady to stop writing.

"It wouldn't do any good, either," said Bishop.

He was right.

But something could be done, or should be. . . .

Get him interested in something else.

What "something else" would compete?

A girl, maybe. Girls. One very special girl. If that guy would ever fall in love and marry . . .

So for months, those men produced girls and arranged ways for Grady's interest and enticement. Sometimes they were clumsy, sometimes clever. I was sure Grady knew what was going

143

on, and he seemed to enjoy his position. He went happily on the ski trip which Bishop arranged for the younger people of the Place. His hospital duties considered, Grady accepted some of the dinner invitations, and was charming, I was sure, to the girls invited as his partners. He went to Bachelor Club parties, and double-dated with his Uncle Bishop, who knew every attractive young woman in the city.

"But that's no good," Shields told me. "Uncle Bish is too firmly the bachelor. He sets Grade the wrong example."

"Bish is very attractive, Shields."

"He knows it. Grady, too. That Grady's attractive, I mean."

"Now, Shields . . ."

Shields shrugged. "I'm not envious. I'm busy enough just now. When I get around to it, I'll pick me a girl."

"You'll get her too. How does it happen that you aren't working to divert Grady?"

Shields laughed. "I did introduce him to the new woman doctor we have up on Burns. She's got the brains and the looks to appeal to Grady."

But not to Shields. "Did Grady . . . ?"

"Oh, he was nice to her. He even took her on a date. She's quite a looker. They went skating. Her name is Laubert. Gussie Laubert."

"Such a name . . ."

"It's no handicap. Men fall for her."

"But not my sons."

"Well, Mother . . . And Grady just isn't ready to settle down yet."

I sighed.

Henry Tibbs had been watching all this turmoil, and he had smiled about it. "Don't they know Grady is too busy trying to catch up on his living, Helen?" he asked me. "That boy's five years behind."

"I don't suppose fathers, or mothers, ever come to consider their children as grown-up individuals, Henry."

"That's all right," Henry told me. "But you did know that, even as a little boy, Grady could take care of himself. What's more, he did!"

"You think we should let Grady alone?" I asked him.

"Oh, no. He'd miss your interest in him."

"And he enjoys it, I suppose."

Henry shrugged. "Now if you old folk really want something to smoke and fume about, why don't you take a look at your younger son?"

I stared at Henry. That morning I had met him at the gates as I was coming back from the Boulevard where I'd gone to make some purchase or other. I joined Henry in his walk back to his house. He took that walk every pretty day. He said it kept him in touch with what went on in Southshire. He knew all the children by name, the nursemaids, and all the dogs.

"What's June done now?" I asked our old friend.

He punctiliously offered his arm to help me across a driveway. I am a tall woman, but not heavy or muscular. Still, I could have picked little Henry up and carried him. I put my fingers on his sleeve.

"I don't know what he's done," Henry said. "Tell Jason to come down and talk to me about this. It's no business for the ladies."

I stopped where we were. A black cocker spaniel puppy raced and capered about my ankles. I paid no attention to it. "It's business for this lady," I told the lawyer.

He stood away and looked at me. I couldn't have seemed too impressive. I was wearing a white-monogrammed blue linen dress, and my hair was blowing in the gentle wind. By that year my blonde hair was getting silvery. I clasped my purse and my package firmly with my white-gloved hands and waited for Henry to answer me.

"You tell Jason . . ." he said again.

"I'll tell him, but now you tell me."

"Well, all right, Helen, but I'd rather tell you both together. Suppose you bring Jason down if he gets home at a decent hour this evening."

"We'll phone you," I agreed.

Henry nodded and walked down the street. I crossed and went on to my own home. June . . .

He was living at home and attending classes at the seminary. He wore a round collar, and had seemed absorbed in his work. He'd been talking about doing some chaplain service at one of the city hospitals though I really did not know too much about what June was doing those days. It had been easier to watch the boys when they were little.

During the afternoon Jason called and said he thought he could get away later for a few holes of golf; did I want to ride out to the Club with him? I told him about Henry, and he said he'd rather play golf.

"If we come home by six . . ."

He laughed. "You're a glutton for punishment, my sweet."

"I know we won't gain much by putting this off."

"You're right. I'll pick you up about four."

I agreed. Jason came home, changed quickly into slacks and a pullover; I spent an hour on the clubhouse veranda with my knitting and a friend or two.

After we got home, while Jason was again changing his clothes, I phoned Henry. He said he would be right there, to come down.

We walked down the street hand in hand. We

147

had not speculated any further about what June had stirred up. But when we reached Henry's big white house and started up the driveway, I said, "We could have asked June . . ."

Jason said nothing.

"Or Grady," I said faintly.

Jason slowed his step. "Look, my dear," he said firmly. "You've made a fine wife. You gave me six healthy sons, and I have been proud of them. I suppose I still love them. . . ."

"But of course you do, Jason!"

"I'm glad you are sure," he said, going on to the side door.

Henry's office — we were used to it. It had been, I think, originally the library of that great house. Palatial in size, the room was walled with bookshelves crammed with books — all sorts of books, with one whole wall filled with the yellow leather of lawbooks. Once Jason had told me that Henry had a fortune tied up in his legal library. The room was large, and it was cluttered. There was Henry's big desk, his wheelchair, and a half dozen large leather chairs. There were all sorts of small tables — one held an ancient typewriter, another supported a modern electric machine. Henry had a clerk and a stenographer who came in each day. His office must have driven these people crazy.

The place smelled, not unpleasantly, of old

leather, old paper, the drying apples and oranges in a tarnished silver bowl.

Henry lived and worked in this room, like a dried-up brown spider, his bright eyes watching what went on about his web; he occasionally left the office to go into court, when he had to, or to attend to business of his own. But clients and friends had to come to him on their business.

That evening he greeted us quietly and suggested that we find comfortable chairs. The place wasn't really dusty, but both Jason and I acted as if we thought it was. We sat down gingerly and faced the attorney who, from behind his desk, watched us.

"What's June been up to now?" Jason blurted, having gone through the amenities of a doctor inquiring about a friend's health.

Henry put his fingertips together. "I'm not sure," he said slowly, "that June's done anything."

Jason frowned at him. "Get on with it, Henry," he begged. "I'm hungry, and I want my dinner."

Henry nodded. He shot a glance at me. "You won't like this," he warned.

"We didn't expect to," Jason told him.

"No, I suppose not. Well — is the name Mulvihill familiar to you folks?"

I had heard it — something to do with the

building of the Tower – and – Yes! The football game! That blonde woman, though I had not seen her.

Jason was saying that, yes, he had met Roger Mulvihill.

"Ah-hum!" said Henry. "How old is June now?"

Jason looked at me.

"He's twenty-five," I said, feeling my finger-tips go cold.

"Does he have any property, income . . . ?"

"What I give him," said Jason gruffly. "It is sometimes a handsome sum."

"Ill bet it is. But June himself doesn't –"

"Helen's father left each of the boys five thousand apiece. June spent his the day after he was twenty-one."

"Now, Jason . . ." I protested.

"Well, didn't he? He bought that expensive sports car – smashed it up, and there went the whole basket of turnips."

I sighed.

"Of course, now," said Henry, "I know he's still in school. . . ."

"Seminary," I corrected.

Both Jason and Henry gave me looks which made me blush. "I should have thrown him out years ago," Jason growled.

"Yes, you should," Henry agreed. "Though at his age, and if he has no assets . . ."

We waited. By then I was getting cold all over. And Jason was hot. He got up and went to stare at the backs of some books. Henry took up a blue-bound folder from a stack of such things on the side of his desk. He pushed books and other papers out of his way and opened the cover, leaning forward to read the top page within it. He straightened.

"Yes!" he said. "A day or two ago, this man – this Roger Mulvihill – he's a well-appearing chap, and looks as if he might have played football years ago – he's well-kept even now. Guess he'd be forty-five or so – fresh-complexioned . . ."

Jason growled. Henry winked at me. But I felt like growling, too.

"Yes!" said Henry again. "Well, this man came to me and said he was going to sue June for alienation of his wife's affections. He – You say something, Helen?"

I shook my head. I could not have made a sound. Jason strode over to the desk. "Did he want you to represent him?" he demanded.

Henry smiled at the folder before him. "Don't get hot, Jason," he said. "You know I don't conduct any sort of suit against my friends. It may have been in Mulvihill's mind. I told him I did only medical-connected law work. And then I told him, gratis, that his suit against June would be pure nonsense. I said

June was just a boy — I was thinking of him as about nineteen or so . . ."

"He's twenty-five," I said dully.

"I told this fella," Henry continued, "that few alienation suits ever came to court. That they were hard to win —"

"But," cried Jason, "there's the publicity, Henry!"

"Exactly. Their strength lies in that threat."

"I'll not buy this man off!" Jason declared.

"Good! I hope you'll stick to that!"

"But — could we?" I asked. "With June a student priest, and his father a prominent surgeon?"

Henry shrugged.

Jason was walking up and down the room and crashing his doubled fists together. "Blast that boy!" he said over and over.

"You had better simmer down, Jase," Henry told him.

"I should, should I?" cried Jason. "With this — Why, Henry, this is worse than anything Grady has *ever* done, or written, or said!"

"June's apt to get the McCords into the papers again," Henry admitted.

"Has he been — well — seeing that girl, Helen?" Jason demanded.

"I don't know . . ." I began.

"She's thirty-two," said Henry. "Not really a girl. Has three or four kids."

"But what's June been doing? Does he have any crazy notion of marrying such a woman?"

"That's implied in the alienation suit," Henry told us.

We talked some more, and got nowhere. As we left, Henry said to us, "Don't worry so much about Grady, you two. Try to understand that boy of yours, why he's doing what he does . . ."

We didn't listen to what he said in our angered worry about June.

"We're in a fine condition to eat dinner," Jason told me as we walked home.

"You'd better take Henry's advice and simmer down. Until we talk to June —"

"I'll talk to him all right. I wonder how much Grady knows of this. He said something this morning about seeing me at dinner. Maybe we could talk to him."

"Yes, we could," I agreed. "But after dinner, Jason?"

"All right. Though he's sure to know I'm in a state."

Grady did know it, but I managed to say to him that his father thought it would be better to talk about the matter later.

"Have I done something?" Grady asked.

"No, dear. No."

"Want to bet?" growled Jason, and then we all laughed. The men had their cocktails, and dinner went much better than we had expected. June didn't show up; David and Isabelle were out of town. We enjoyed our lamb chops and peas, the salad and the orange sherbet.

Bishop came in before we had had our coffee, and I knew Jason would include him in the talk with Grady. He did. With some thought of avoiding interruption, we took our coffee and brandy up to the Palladian room. This is a wide, open space at the head of the stairs on the second floor. Its chief feature is the large, arched window which overlooks our front doorway, and from there out across the trees and lawns of Southshire Place. I kept growing plants on shelves across the small side windows — ivy, ferns, things like that. Some old wicker furniture had been painted white and reupholstered in a bright green-on-white print. There was a long table, and a white-shaded lamp. Books and magazines invited one to sit there for a minute's rest. One Christmas, Grady had given me a large cane birdcage, with three canaries to fly about in it, and to sing. We all liked and used the Palladian room.

That evening we went up there for privacy, and the men sat fondling their brandy glasses. I poured coffee for them into Dresden cups, and waited for Jason to tell Bish and Grady what Henry had told us that afternoon.

"I realize," he said angrily, "that I have been a

complete fool to let June sponge on me this long! I should have made him get out and go to work!"

"You carried Shields and me through medical school," Grady pointed out to his father.

"You were working! You had a goal."

"June claims that he does."

It all spilled out then, the threatened lawsuit, June's irresponsibility. . . .

Grady whistled and shook his head. But he was smiling the way he does, with one corner of his mouth lifted.

"Mulvihill had a nerve to go to Henry," said Bishop. "And there's a good chance he meant to be impudent."

"Do you know these people, Bish?" Jason asked his brother.

"Not well. You know he's an architect. They go about. His wife is what is called well-stacked. I think she could be pretty, but she follows all the fads — white lipstick, unmade-up skin — her hair streaked gray-blonde and brown."

"Not your type," drawled Grady.

Bish laughed and lifted his coffee cup.

"Are they new people in town?" I asked.

"Oh, Mother — *New* to you means anyone coming to the city less than fifty years ago."

"That's not fair."

"It is wonderful, however. But, yes, the

155

Mulvihills are new, aren't they, Bish? Wasn't there something about memberships? The Country Club, the October ball —"

"He's building up business," said Bishop mildly. "Our city, like your mother, can be pretty clannish."

"Does he think involving our family in a lawsuit will help him?" asked Jason.

"Didn't you say Henry told you that alienation suits . . . ?"

"I am not paying them off."

"You could try telling June a few what-fors."

"I plan to. I plan to. This woman — What does she see in June?"

"He's a man, Dad. And I think he's attractive to women. I believe, too, there is an added fillip to his being a clergyman. You know, forbidden sin, or something."

Jason growled.

"There's supposed to be some sort of attraction for women to doctors," drawled Bishop.

"Isn't there?" Grady challenged him, his blue eye bright.

Bish laughed. "If so, it's a one-way street with you, boy. Why, Helen, we've put this budding doctor into contact with the best and most beautiful girls in this neighborhood —"

"Twenty-five-mile radius, that neighborhood," laughed Grady. "I've been enticed, Lady Vere de Vere. Temptation

156

has been put in my path."

I had watched the men's efforts to divert Grady. I had suspected that Grady knew what was going on. I had seen the parade of girls — and even speculated as to which ones I would welcome for a daughter-in-law. . . .

"Perhaps you should have shown him June's dame," said Jason bitterly. He was very angry at June.

"Oh, no!" I protested. "I couldn't take that sort of woman into the family."

The men stared at me; then they laughed.

"What sort of girl would you welcome into the family?" Grady asked me, his tone affectionate and patient.

"Well, a nice girl. Someone with our sort of background," I answered him seriously. This was a serious thing. "Someone like – well – Taylor Falk, across the street."

Grady chuckled. "That's the girl!" he cried. "Thank you, Lady Vere de Vere. I'm safe for the next ten years."

"Don't count on that," Bishop told him. "Taylor's growing up to be a most attractive young woman."

"She will be, in the ten years I'm giving her," said Grady. "And until then I warn all you matchmakers, she is the only girl I'm interested in."

Bish glanced at me. I smiled. "Taylor is

eighteen," I said softly. "I don't know if she will make her debut this year. If she does, I'll give a party for her and count on you to help me, Grady."

Grady's face was a study. It isn't often that we get him off-balance. But for that moment, he just stood there, his mouth open. He was startled. Stunned. "She can't be eighteen," he said.

"And she'd be all right for you, too," said Bishop; Jason nodded emphatically.

Grady glanced at me. "I wish you would help me keep my mouth shut," he told me plaintively.

"Yes, dear," I said. "That's what the men in the family have been wanting you to do."

He frowned. "Should I?" he asked anxiously.

"Oh, I'm not the one to tell you such a thing, Grady," I answered quickly. Then I added, "Nor is your father, or your uncles."

He nodded and dropped into the corner of the couch.

I wanted to ask him more about the Mulvihills. I wanted to know what to expect of June, and this woman. I wanted things to be resolved, right then and there. But of course they could not be. Bishop was called to the hospital, and Grady went to his room to get some sleep. He would go back on duty at midnight. Jason and I watched TV in the sitting room, not wanting to

158

talk any more, though when we were getting ready for bed, we did speak, amused again, about Grady's confusion over Taylor Falk.

"She really is a lovely girl," I told Grady's father. Taylor had beauty. Thick auburn hair, green eyes . . .

"I think the message Grady was trying to get through to us, Helen, was to let him do his own picking and choosing."

"But look where that method has got June!" I retorted.

"When will David get home?" Jason asked, by way of dismissing the unhappy subject.

"Tomorrow. Do you think he and Isabelle are happy, Jason?"

My husband groaned and told me to turn out the light. He had a full day for tomorrow.

I planned to talk to Grady further about this Dodie Mulvihill, but like Jason's, my "tomorrow" was a busy one. David and Isabelle, and Schmitt, of course, came home in the early afternoon, with all the confusion such a project made.

Besides, Grady was on duty that day, and the next, at the hospital. And before he was at home again, for more than an hour or so, June did the unforgivable; he brought Dodie to our house. "For protection," he explained.

I think I had gone to the dentist. At any rate, I was away. Of course Jason was.

And when I came home —

June had brought the woman to our house, and, failing to find me, he had brought Isabelle down to receive his guest, which she did, not knowing at all what was going on.

So when I returned, there was Mrs. Mulvihill, established in our best guest room, and June, grinning like a ten-year-old, ready to introduce us, to tell me that he'd had to bring Dodie there. She needed protection, he repeated to me, and since he planned to marry her —

I stood there in the hall, and I hoped I would not cry. Grady calls me Lady Vere de Vere because, he once explained to me, I can look so much like the invulnerable lady. At times, I glimpse this in myself.

But girls of my day were taught to conceal their emotions, not to raise their voices, and certainly not to be rude to a guest in the home.

So that afternoon I stood there in my tailored blue suit, my furs and my small hat, my white gloves, my pearls . . .

And this Dodie . . . She did get up off the bed when June took me into her room. She was not a young girl; I agreed to that description of her. And I did not find her pretty. Her hair looked unkempt to me, and her eyes seemed bold — challenging. Her whole attitude demanded of June's mother what that mother was going to do about the situation in hand.

And June's mother . . .

Though everything about this woman offended me, I was the lady Grady called me, and I had to avoid giving offense to my daughter-in-law, Isabelle.

But I could not be warm to Dodie Mulvihill. So I said something chilly like "I understand." And I went off to my own room, closed the door, and sank, trembling, into Jason's big chair.

What was I going to *do?*

It soon occurred to me that I must see Jason immediately on his arrival home, and prepare him for what was going on in our house. So I changed quickly into one of the silk dresses I use for an evening at home, and I went downstairs. There June hunted me out to ask if I had told Orlie we had a guest.

"Didn't you tell him?" I asked coolly.

"Should I have?" June was nervous, not able to stand still or look at me directly when he talked.

"June . . ." I began.

"Now, Mother, I don't want any pious lectures or mention made of Dodie's jealous husband. . . ."

I sighed. "Pious," I repeated "You said you planned to marry this woman."

"Don't call her . . ."

"Isn't she a woman?" I was beginning to feel a little on top of things.

"Well, yes," said June, "but —"

"What I am about to ask you is: what has happened to the clergyman you were due to become next summer?"

"Oh," said June. "That." He ran his hand through his curly black hair. He is the only one in the family with curly hair. "We are allowed to marry," he pointed out.

"Yes, and some priests go through a divorce. Not easily. And not ever seminarians, I think, June."

"Well," he cried desperately, "in that case, I'd be good and ready to sacrifice my career for Dodie. She's wonderful, Mother. She really is."

"No doubt," I said.

I managed to catch Jason as he came in the side door. He was more disgusted than angry at my word of our house guest and June's readiness to sacrifice his latest career.

"The only thing to do," he said firmly, "is to throw the woman out."

"Yes," I agreed. "Of course she must leave. Will you tell her, or shall I?"

Jason only growled at me and asked me if dinner wasn't ready.

It was, and we went to the dining room. This is not the prettiest room in our old home, but I imagine that evening it impressed our guest.

The walls of the room are covered with old, metallic tea-box paper. There is a formidable ancestor-portrait over the mantel. Shell cupboards in two corners hold chinoiserie. The long table is narrow, and that evening Orlie had chosen to set the heavy gold candelabra on it. I smiled a little at this touch of elegance, and glanced at my sons to see if they appreciated it. Jason did, I was sure.

And Grady, perhaps, though he gave no sign. He sat on the other side of Dodie Mulvihill and appeared to be entranced with the young woman in bright green.

Facing those three sat David and Isabelle. Dodie made some appropriate remarks to David. She thought it was wonderful how he managed, was one thing she said.

She had speculative eyes — for the men. She studied David, and even June's father. But she decided that Grady was the one on whom to concentrate. She hung on his words, she let him help her with the asparagus tongs, she laughed merrily at everything he said.

And the rascal played up to her. I wished I could have reached him to kick him, and I was apprehensive lest Jason say something. It is Grady's way to be charming to everyone, and of course he is attractive. Even with the eye patch — perhaps because of it — he is a very handsome man. He is quick in speech, and clever.

Little gestures of kindness and solicitude come naturally to Grady. I didn't suppose he cared two cents about this overly vivacious woman, but that was not significant. Dodie thought he was smitten.

Jason was shooting angry glances down the table to me, but what he expected me to do or say, I am not sure.

With the dessert – I have no memory of what we ate that night! – Dodie began to coo and speak confidentially to Grady. And June flared into anger. He said something to Dodie, and when she didn't answer him, he lifted his voice and told her that he was speaking to her and expected her to answer.

She turned to gaze at him, wide-eyed – eyes rimmed with gooey black stuff. . . .

June said something else, and Grady told him to "cool it a little, June-o."

June hates his nickname, and is always furious when one of the boys further corrupts it. So he shouted at Grady – and Grady laughed.

Then Jason stood up and told them all to shut up, and if they couldn't, to clear out.

June subsided sulkily and mumbled some sort of apology.

"Very well," said his father. "But I meant what I said. And I'll say this in addition. I don't think Mrs. Mulvihill, under the circumstances, makes an appropriate guest in our home."

"I thought it was my home," said June, belatedly adding the *sir*. Jason's face was ice-cold with anger.

"It is your home," he said coldly, "so long as you subscribe to its discipline. And I repeat . . ."

"Then," said June, "if I can't bring my friends here, I would say it was time I was moving my home elsewhere. I can get an apartment, and it seems that I should."

"I trust you are prepared to earn the money to pay for such an accommodation, if you do need it," said Jason.

"Well, of course I need it," said June. "And right now. Dodie has to go somewhere — her husband threw her out — she needs shelter and protection."

"So do you!" shouted Jason. "So do you!"

Shields had not eaten dinner with us, but when he came in, in time for coffee, he lost no time asking me who the "pussy cat" was.

"Oh, Shields . . ." I protested.

"Whose pussy cat is she, Mother?" he asked again, putting his warm, strong hand on my arm. "She looks June's type, but Grady seems to be making the play."

By then I was sure that Grady definitely was making a play. He would have his reasons, but I did not think — I didn't want to think — that he was smitten suddenly with June's young woman. I could just barely take bad taste in my youngest son, but Grady, I had always felt, had more discrimination.

But that evening — it was he who sat on the loveseat with Dodie, it was he who held her coffee cup while she did something to the fastening at the back of her dress — this caused her to strain her arms up and back, even more plainly displaying her feminine charms which I, for one, felt sure were enhanced artificially.

She smiled at Grady, she dropped her head to his shoulder when he said something which amused her. She talked frankly of her difficulties with her husband. She did not mention her children.

June stood off at one side of the room and sulked. I was, mostly, concerned lest, in her animation, she break one of the fragile coffee cups. And Isabelle . . .

I was amazed at Isabelle. Generally she is a poised, self-controlled young woman. She had made David a patient wife, as such an invalid requires a wife to be patient and understanding. She lived in our home without ever having become really a member of the family. For one thing, Isabelle had never made a confidante of me, which of course was her privilege. I should have liked to have had a daughter. She was always courteous and thoughtful; she would take on any duty asked of her. I had decided that she was not, essentially, a warm person, at least not one to speak easily of her feelings, nor, for that matter, to display them.

But that evening –

We had crossed the hall to have our coffee in the south parlor. Isabelle sat, as always, close to David's wheelchair, ready to assist him in any way she could. She had learned to do this unobtrusively, quickly, and often before he himself was aware that he needed help. I had, I thought quite happily, given over this care of my son to his wife.

I had no way of knowing if Isabelle was happy in the sort of marriage she had. I remembered the scene with Grady beneath the elm tree at A.B.'s house. But her appearance was always that of a solicitous and loving wife.

David, himself, seemed happy – content. He would watch Isabelle with eyes that showed only affection for her.

But that night he was disgusted with June and shocked at the woman whom his brother had ventured to bring into our home. I don't think he was giving Grady's behavior much thought until Isabelle said what she did, and did the things she did do.

Then, like me, he read her behavior as jealousy. Isabelle was jealous of Grady, and of the attention which he was paying to that — that woman!

Ten minutes before, Jason had been called to the telephone, and he had not returned to the drawing room. I was sure he had gone upstairs. Shields, too, melted out of the picture.

"Why don't you do something, June?" Isabelle asked unexpectedly, the syllables falling like raindrops into the murky waters of the mess this same June had produced for us. "If Mrs. Mulvihill is your girl — and I suppose she is —"

Dodie looked across at the pretty, brown-haired woman in pale yellow. "Are you English?" she asked, "or have you just learned to talk that way?"

I gasped. Grady laughed.

"No American *learns* to speak like an Englishman, Dodie," he told the woman beside him.

She tossed her head. "Oh, I think they could," she said.

"Well, don't you try it," June advised, walking toward the loveseat. "Come on, Dodie. I'll help you pack your bag. Dad thinks you shouldn't stay here, and I've decided he's right."

"Certainly he is right," said Isabelle.

"She can go to a hotel," Grady suggested. "Would you help June gather up her stuff, Belle?"

"I don't care to handle her things," said

Isabelle coldly. "In fact, I would not have supposed that I should ever have been asked to meet her."

David made some sound of protest. June told her to watch what she said to *his* guest.

Isabelle smiled at him. "I really had forgotten that she was *your* guest," she said sweetly. "Hadn't you?"

"Meow, meow," said Dodie Mulvihill. "What green eyes Grandma has! I'll go pack my own things." She flounced out of the room, her high heels tapping on the polished floors. June, glancing at Grady, followed her.

"Mother," said David quietly, "I don't think June is the one to take Mrs. Mulvihill to a hotel and register her there."

"Why not?" I asked inanely.

"He is in deep water enough, bringing her here."

"I'll take her," said Grady.

"Oh, *no!*" cried Isabelle. "That's no better!"

"Yes, it is," Grady told her. "Her irate husband isn't worrying about me."

"I think she should be sent home," said Isabelle. "Schmitt would drive her."

"June claims she has been threatened by Mulvihill. Now, Isabelle, you surely wouldn't want to be responsible . . ."

"No," said Isabelle coldly, "I should not want to be responsible at all for Mrs. Mulvihill."

It took a little talk to persuade June that Grady should be the one to take Dodie to the hotel — for safety's sake. Dodie had come downstairs and stood, smiling, during the discussion. "I'm a respectable doctor," said Grady. "Older, you know, and all that?" His eyebrow went up and I would not have blamed June for swinging at him.

Finally June agreed that Grady could, he guessed, take Dodie to the hotel. "Though I don't see why it is any better than here. . . ."

Grady looked across at me. "Mother, while I'm gone, will you please tell your youngest a few facts of life?"

I shook my head at him. And Grady departed with Dodie, her voice coming back to us, even with the front door closed.

"I'm going up to talk to Dad," June told us.

"Good!" said David. "But take that damn collar off first."

I don't know what Jason and his son had to say to each other. I was feeling bruised and soiled by the whole affair. We three left behind tried to talk, but we all were watching the clock, and it did seem a long time before Grady returned. Actually he was gone only half an hour.

He came in as casually as if he were returning from the hospital. He asked if the coffee was still hot. Isabelle picked up the pot and

170

said she would go get fresh. "Come and help me, Grady, if I need to make more. I understand the British cannot make decent coffee."

David and I exchanged glances. I asked him if he'd want to play cribbage, or perhaps go upstairs?

He shook his head. So we sat and listened, perforce, to Isabelle talking to Grady. They were in the pantry, across the hall and the width of the dining room, but we could hear every word that Isabelle was saying. Anyone in the house, I thought, could overhear.

Not that very much was said, or, I supposed, done. Isabelle talked a little about David. . . . "Of course I think about him, Grady! I do consider him. And he knows that I consider him, that I am sorry for him. I've been sorry for him since I first knew him. Being married to him only makes me sorrier. Not that that is a good basis for marriage.

"Don't you ever marry, Grady, or let a girl marry you, unless you love each other. And I mean everything you can imagine I mean by love."

We could hear Grady's voice, but not what he said. I am sure he was being nice to Isabelle — kind.

Dodie's name was not mentioned, though Isabelle did say something about the lengths to which one brother should, or should *not*, go to save another from a mess.

When finally they came back to us, David watched Isabelle as she moved about, filling our cups with fresh coffee. Grady sat in one of the black chairs and watched her, too. I wanted to slap someone. But I was not sure whom to slap first, Grady or Isabelle. I wanted to cradle David's head against my breast and put this woman, too, out of our house. David had been hurt enough.

But this, I remember, is to be Grady's story. I could, of course, write another about David.

Or any one of my sons. Each of my sons.

Now Grady — he was nice to all women — kind to them. He had a way with them, my father would have said. This amounted to genuine courtesy, and an interest in them. Of course this attitude was flattering, and women liked to have Grady around. They would have liked to have him center his interest and courtesy on them individually. Sometimes, perhaps, he did single out a particular girl or woman. Of course there was queer old Lizzie Paradis down the block — but that was different. I'm sure Lizzie knew that it was.

I remember his reaction when he found that his name was on the debutante lists. This began when he first came home from his years in the hospitals. I had to tell him why he was getting so many invitations, from girls he did not know, or whose families he did not know.

I told him about the women — we had two flourishing services in our city — who kept lists of debutantes, their balls, teas, dinners, and who also kept lists of eligible men. Four to a debutante was the proportion they strove to maintain.

Grady squinted his good eye at me. "What am I supposed to do?" he asked.

"Go to the parties, if you can and care to."

He stacked his sheaf of thick white envelopes. "And if not?"

"Regret. Perhaps send flowers. You send flowers if you accept, of course."

"Like hell I will!"

He was angry. He was white with anger. Couldn't, he demanded, a man live in a town and not be listed on the male side of the marriage stock quotations? Couldn't a man do the things he wanted to do, and be let alone? If he knew a girl, if he asked a girl for a date — sure, then her mother could invite him to a party for that girl. But he did not want nets put out for him, he declared.

"If you had stayed at home," I reminded him, "and gone to the fortnightlies . . ."

"I went to dancing school," he reminded me.

I smiled grimly. Yes, he had. Always rebelliously. Always needing to be hunted down, dressed, and *taken.*

173

He slapped his invitations against his other palm. Then he threw them all into the rubbish burner. "I won't use my time sending regrets — that would take cards, and envelopes and stamps, and sitting down to scratch out my message — and I won't send flowers either." He whirled to face me. "And you're not to fish those things out of there, Lady Vere de Vere! You're not to send flowers in my name."

"Oh, Grady . . ."

"Explain to the mothers who are your friends, remind them how queer your son has always been." He stood thinking about that. "Yes!" he said firmly. "You tell 'em, if you need to."

The invitations kept coming, and Grady came to be amused by them. "Don't they know how old I am?" he asked.

"You'd enjoy a party now and then."

"I go to one now and then. I went to Christine's bash."

He had gone to his cousin's debut party, and he'd been a great success. The telephone rang and invitations arrived in ever greater volume that winter. But now, he still —

"I don't have time for women just now, Lady V. de V.," he explained to me patiently. "I'm working my tail off at the hospital. And such free time as I have, I don't want to spend it with any of the women this family has been

174

shoving at me. Of course —"

He stood gazing at me. "If you all insist — it will of course divert me from my medical interests — and perhaps you will all be sorry."

Chapter 7

We were sorry.

Perhaps that next month was the most shocking time of all the hard times Grady gave us. It lasted only a month, but while it was going on, it seemed endless to us all.

June and his Dodie had precipitated the whole affair. I suppose June said certain things to Grady; we already had heard what Isabelle had said to him.

With those things in mind, not liking them at all, I thought I knew what Grady was doing, but as the days passed, I became less sure. He seemed so to enjoy himself! He went all-out. He gave all his time and energy to the project. He bought clothes. . . .

And I began to wonder about him. I had thought I knew my son. But the Grady I knew, and believed in, would never have engaged upon such a whirlwind campaign to take David's wife away from him.

"Isabelle wouldn't . . ." said Jason.

"Oh, yes, she would," I told my husband.

Grady, I thought, could get any woman he wanted. I had already heard Isabelle indicate that, in her case, the task would be simple.

"But why, after all these years . . . ?"

"She's young, she's attractive."

"It's not a very square thing to do, when the other man is an invalid."

"Being an invalid can carry its own appeal, Jason."

"You mean, that's why she married David?"

I did mean that.

Jason nodded. "It's a hard thing to ask of any girl, to push a wheelchair. But I thought Isabelle . . ."

It didn't seem to matter what we thought. Not to Grady. And not to Isabelle. She agreed to do anything, all the things, which Grady suggested to her. She too must have bought clothes. For what use had she had, previously, for golf shoes? For a slim white tennis dress?

Grady set out to do all the things with Isabelle which David could not do. Every sort of sport — they rode together, they played tennis, they swam. A white scarf tied about her hair, Isabelle spent part of every day driving with Grady in his low sports car, doing "fun things," they said; going to "fun places." On many nights they went dancing, Isabelle wearing long dresses of floating chiffon, incredibly printed in wild colors and designs — or slim, short dresses that showed off her lovely figure and her long slim legs. Grady in a dark blue brocade dinner jacket, Grady with a yellow scarf about his throat, Grady in formal black and white — they went off in his car, or Jason's, or Bish's; they came in late, waking that whole end of Southshire Place with their gay laughter. Evenings when they were at home, they danced, kicking the rugs out of the way; they danced into one parlor, out into the hall — with David sitting in his chair gravely watching them.

We were all shocked. But it took June to speak of his astonishment. And then he said only, and feebly, that he knew what Grady was up to.

"You mean he has a plan?" asked Jason acidly.

"Well, sure, Dad. Look. He disapproved of my interest in Dodie Mulvihill . . ."

"What happened to her, by the way?"

"Oh, she's back at home. Her children needed her."

Jason choked over his coffee.

"I still think she is a wonderful woman. That's why Grady is trying to show me that we shouldn't set our hearts on a married woman — that it isn't right, or something."

Jason looked at June. "If you only knew how much I wished you were right," he said gravely.

178

"But, Dad . . . ?"

"Let's not talk about it, June. I'd much rather worry in peace."

Later he said to me, "I don't know about sons, Helen. Our sons. If they'd just sow their oats when they were at an age when I could take a strap to them or stop their allowance. But Grady! I'm ready to give up on that boy. I'll confess I am."

The uncles sounded as if they were ready, too. None of the men liked what he was doing with Isabelle. And the doctors –

Jason became ever more furious. Grady was not performing his duties as surgical resident. He was late, he didn't show up at all, he disappeared at odd times – he didn't attend meetings or conduct the classes he was supposed to conduct. . . .

"I won't shield him, Helen!" he warned. "I'll send in the reports, just as I would do for any resident on my service."

I thought he should, but my heart was breaking – for Jason, for Grady – and for David.

My heart bled for that son of mine; I could feel him bound in the chains of his invalidism, helpless to defend himself and his household. From the first months of his illness, we had tried hard not to surround David with pity. He was certainly the victim of a tragic illness, a hurt. But he was to handle it much as a person learns to handle living in an inconvenient, uncomfortable home. To this point, David had done quite well. Grady had been a big help to him.

But now — He spent much time alone up in his rooms or out in the car, alone, with Schmitt.

Lucian was away part of this bad time. If he had been at home, I feel sure he would have put his foot down — or tried to. He thought that any family scandal was to be avoided at all costs. Besides, what Grady and Isabelle were doing was not right.

No, it was not.

Jason and I were well aware of that. Jason chose, first, to approach the situation from the medical side. And that was correct enough. If Grady was indeed "goofing off," he should and could be disciplined within his profession.

From the vantage which time gives one, I realize now that we were hoping that matters could be handled in this way.

Of course the family members saw what was going on, and the neighbors did. Taylor Falk — I had known the girl since her birth. The bushes and trees and flower beds of the mid-street parkway separated her home from ours. She was younger than my children, but she had, as a very little girl, liked to escape her

180

nursemaid and follow me about like a small puppy, talking guilelessly, happy to be given a cookie. She still would come across to visit with me if she saw me working with my flowers. One morning she came over and offered to help my attempts to curb the violet plants under the shrubbery.

"My dad says to pull 'em out; they'll grow back," she told me.

"I'm a softie, Taylor," I told the slender girl. "I can't bear to cut back or destroy anything that could be called a flower."

She laughed. "I myself think the violets are pretty," she confessed. That morning she wore yellow Bermuda shorts, a yellow and white plaid shirt. Her hair caught the sunlight in its auburn thickness. I thought she was a very pretty girl. I have never known anyone with such green eyes, dark-lashed, lovely.

She chattered about a Junior League luncheon, and about the hospital volunteer work she had just begun to do that summer. "I saw Grady yesterday," she told me shyly.

"Good," said I. "I'm glad he was at work."

"He has been pretty gay lately, hasn't he? You know, Mrs. McCord? I thought he had a girl. I'd see him – them – in his car, going to some party in the evening, or to play tennis or something in the daytime – all very gay and glamorous – with her scarf flying, and his hair blowing. I thought he was on vacation — and — had a girl." Thoughtfully she pulled a small weed from under the barberry bush.

"Then," she went on, brightly again, "I realized it was only Isabelle he was being nice to and taking around."

I said nothing.

Taylor jumped to her feet. She had nice, smooth, brown legs. "I guess I was glad he didn't have a girl," she told me. "I've always made a hero of Grady, you know. Prince Charming, and all that. I'll be jealous of any girl he'll ever get." She laughed and skipped off across the lawn, across the parkway.

I sighed. I wished Grady did have a girl — someone as nice and appropriate as Taylor Falk.

When all this nonsense had been going on for a couple of weeks, and each temper in the family was at the boiling point, someone in Joe's family had a birthday. We do not celebrate all the birthdays with a family gathering, but we did gather that Sunday afternoon at Joe's. I remember the cake, and the children's being present. His children were growing up fast. The twins, in fact, were contemporaries of Taylor Falk.

The grown-ups eventually went indoors, leaving the lawn and garden to the children and the balloons and the games. Champagne, or something, was served to us instead of the ice cream and punch outside.

While we were sitting about and deciding we could go to our respective homes, Henry Tibbs showed up. Perhaps he had been invited to the party, though we were all surprised to see him.

He came in, walking carefully, as he did those days, and grinned at our surprise. Someone offered him a chair, but he went over to look at the Chinese statue in the corner niche. Joe has always collected Chinese art, and the reception room of his house contains many of his rarities. The wallpaper . . . Well, anyway –

Henry looked at the statue, which is of a woman with jewels dangling from her head-dress, and then he walked back and sat down in the chair he had previously ignored.

"Well!" he said, looking around at us.

"What do you have on your mind, Henry?" Lucian asked the lawyer.

The little man crossed his bony knees. "The same thing you do, I'd think," he answered. "I saw you all gathered here – I saw you come inside, and I guessed it was a good time to come in and offer to straighten out the mess your family is in."

Nobody said a word. I didn't dare look at anyone, not even Jason.

"I figured," Henry continued, "that you'd

come to me sooner or later. If only to ask me to recommend a lawyer."

Lucian cleared his throat; Jason glanced at his older brother, frowning. This was *not* Lucian's affair, his frown said.

Henry put up a hand. "Now, let's not get hot and hostile," he advised. "I'd want the thing done quietly, too. And while it is not in my line, I think I'm adequate enough as a lawyer to handle David's divorce. . . ."

Joe tipped over his wineglass. Bishop dropped the mahjong tiles he'd been handling; there is an ivory set in an open chest on a small table.

Henry leaned farther back in his chair and smiled more deeply; his lantern jaw was about to touch his shirt front. "I've already said I would take care of the Mulvihill alienation suit June got you into. For that matter," he looked around at us brightly, "David's got material for an alienation suit of his own."

Jason snorted.

Henry looked up at him innocently. "I thought I'd tell you," he said, "that I'd take on the whole ball of wax. Not my line of work, of course, unless Grady brings in some malpractice trouble. . . ."

This time I did look at the others — at the men. And each one of them had gone as white as paper.

So we had not yet plumbed the depths. . . .

I don't remember that we stayed at Joe's very much later. Henry left quite soon. I walked home with Jason, not saying much of anything.

"He wanted to shock us," he told me.

"As if we needed that."

"We have to do something, Helen."

I had no suggestions, so I said nothing.

For the next day or two, the brothers would gather, two of them, three. They went from house to house, and they talked. I suppose they talked at the hospital.

They — we — all were worried and angry, Grady, we felt, had got us into a real mess. We were all dismayed at what could happen. Now and then, someone — Jason, for instance — would say mournfully, "The boy showed such promise! I thought he meant it when he worked so hard. . . ."

It was Bish and Joe who brought up what they called Grady's "holier than thou" articles.

"You wanted him to stop writing them!" I defended my son.

The men glared at me.

And Grady? All of us, at one time or another, must have said things to him. Jason, I knew, had jumped on him about his work. But Grady went blithely on his way, as if he were doing everything he should. He seemed to be having a wonderful time, too. It became fascinating to watch him.

He blossomed out in all sorts of new clothes — gay ones. "Far-out," June called his raiment.

And wherever he went, whatever he did, Isabelle was with him. I don't think anyone tried to talk to Isabelle. I thought she was acting like a snake, fascinated by the music which Grady was playing.

Grady — he knew what he was doing, I felt sure. I told his father that he did.

"All right!" said Jason angrily. "Does he know when to stop?"

I had no answer to that. I was frightened for my son.

I am sure the men, individually, had all spoken to Jason on the subject before, but the next Sunday afternoon, the brothers descended on him in a body, and told my husband that he had the power to stop Grady.

It was a rainy day; we had a small fire going, Jason had been reading the Sunday papers and had dozed a little in his deep chair. I had some knitting with which to busy my fingers.

The men came in a group; they must have gathered elsewhere first. The doorbell rang, and I answered.

I was dismayed at the onslaught of McCords, but of course I could not have stopped them on our doorstep, even if I had wanted to. Jason had heard their arrival and was on his feet to greet them.

"Now what?" he asked his visitors.

A.B. told him.

"Hmmmmn," said Jason. "Power, eh?" He rubbed his pipe bowl along the seam of his trousers. He was still standing. "I could remind you," he said slowly, "that Grady is not fifteen. And I could tell you that I no longer use, nor possess, a razor strop."

"He's a resident on your surgical service," said Lucian. "There are orders you can give."

"And need to give," said Joe.

Jason nodded. "That's right," he agreed.

"The boy can't be doing his job."

Jason nodded again. "No, he is not. All right. I'll give the orders."

The men looked at each other. I suppose they had thought they would need to handle some argument. Jason glanced at me. And his eyes almost smiled.

"He'll be confined to the hospital for a good week," he said to his brothers. "He has quite a bit of time to make up. Helen, could we have some coffee?"

I suppose Dr. Jason McCord, Chief of Surgical Services, did give out orders to Dr. Grady McCord, Resident — more than he had done, or tried to do, as a father warning a son. The next report was of a typed sheet posted on the bulletin board.

The first typed sheet. There were to be three

or four. One of them was torn down and replaced.

I don't know if Grady ever meant to publish anything concerning those bulletins, although he had written them.

Similar bulletins appeared from time to time, Jason told me.

DOCTORS IN FAVOR OF SHORTER SKIRTS
ON NURSES UNDER THIRTY
LONGER ONES ON THOSE OLDER

Grady's . . .

Everyone, Jason said, came up to see Grady's notices. They appeared on the board in the lounge of the surgical floor. Each was headed:

ALL HOSPITALS ARE DIRTY
THIS HOSPITAL IS DIRTY

Then—

DO YOU WANT TO CLEAN IT UP?
IF SO, WATCH THIS SPACE

"Are all hospitals dirty?" I asked Jason. I was thinking of the elaborate rituals of white clothes, sterile gloves, scrubbed floors, turned out rooms . . .

"Oh, yes," said Jason. "In Grady's sense.

Some, of course, are dirtier than others. The patients bring in some of the 'dirt'; some we ourselves incubate."

The second bulletin board notice offered a solution against dirty surgeries.

Jason told me about it, and explained the matter to me. "Grady's so damn smart!" he commented sadly.

It seemed that Grady had described on his bulletin a "tent," a plastic isolator, within which a surgeon could perform his surgery upon highly susceptible or already infected patients. During the operation only sterile air, the doctor's gloved hand and the wound would be in contact. There was an elaborate arrangement for the attending doctors and nurses to slide in and out of the sterile, plastic helmet-jackets attached to the plastic tent.

"Is it practical?" I asked Jason, impressed.

"I think some such things are under experimental use."

"Will the Center . . . ?"

"For now, the reaction has been a few raised eyebrows and very little comment."

"Grady can't get in trouble with that sort of notice, can he?"

My husband only sighed.

Two days later – perhaps the Chief of Surgical Service was regretting the confinement of this resident to quarters – another bulletin, another suggestion, appeared.

"He still asks if our hospital is dirty," Shields told me. He seemed to be enjoying Grady's "stunts."

"Explain it to me."

"I'll try. Or I could make a copy of the notice. . . ."

"Just tell me in your words."

Shields tried. This, he said, had to do with a sterile ward. . . .

I stopped him. "Aren't hospital wards already sterile, Shields?"

He laughed and shook his head. "Clean, Mother. We mop 'em, we use Lysol and stuff — but our warm bodies, the patients' warm bodies, the cleaning orderly's mop, the nurse's hair-do — No, we are not sterile."

"All right, tell me."

"Well, Grady described a ward such as certainly would be desirable for the care of highly susceptible cases. The staff would have to enter through a changing room after a complete washdown — there's time involved there, Mother. Air conditioners would filter out particles down to one-half micron —"

"Whatever that is."

He was patient. "Supplies would be made sterile and brought in through hatches. Used stuff removed."

"Is that all?"

190

He laughed. "That's all."

"How did the hospital people react to this?"

"Well, Dad shrugged."

"I see."

Jason brought home to me a duplicator copy of Grady's next bulletin. "They are being circulated throughout the hospital," he growled. I looked at the sheet of paper in my hand. Yes, it began:

ARE YOU A SHEDDER?

I looked up. "What's a shedder?"

"Read it."

I read it.

ARE YOU A SHEDDER?
IF YOU WANT TO BE, SIGN HERE.
IF YOU DO NOT WANT TO BE,
SIGN HERE AND BE TESTED.

That was all. "What's a shedder?" I asked again.

Jason told me. A shedder, he said, was a sort of Typhoid Mary, a person who carried in his body — usually his nose — staph germs which could cause terrific epidemics, or the death of a patient, in the hospital.

Surgical teams, he said, were apt to contain shedders.

191

"Because we are most subjected to staph infections."

"But that's terrible, Jason."

"It's bad, yes."

I lifted the sheet of paper. "What will this do?"

"We'll test our teams more carefully. But, the primary reaction was — well — explosive, Helen. I do wish Grady wouldn't."

"He'll stop if you tell him to."

"I know that. Just as he knows I won't tell him."

Jason was right; there were explosions. Our doctors exploded — in their own homes and in each other's homes. There were, as well, scenes of all sorts and dimensions in the hospital. The Staff seemed agreed that Grady — McCord, or no — should be disciplined.

This declaration brought on a full-scale family conference, which began one late afternoon on the parkway where Taylor Falk was helping Joe's little boy ride his pony. Joe came up the street to see what the trouble was. Jason went out. Bishop joined them — the matter of the tightly held rein and the possession of a whip was settled; the men came back to the sidewalk, to stand talking. Lucian saw them there, and came down. A.B. did, and they all came into our house together, all talking busily. I offered coffee; they said they would prefer beer. I

192

followed Orlie and his tray — the men talked as if there were no interruptions or listeners. Shields came downstairs.

The family doctors, I thought, were ready to agree with the Staff decision. Grady must be disciplined.

How? I asked myself silently.

It was Joe who asked softly if the charges made in Grady's bulletins were not true. He held his beer glass up to the light, and turned it to make the bubbles swirl.

His question had silenced everyone.

"It's a matter that needs looking into, of course," said Lucian — uncomfortably, unhappily. "If what he charges is not true, the boy's been making pure mischief. But if they are true . . ."

Bishop got to his feet. "Of course they are true," he said brusquely. "We know they are true, and to what extent. For instance, how strictly do we enforce the rule that all surgical gloves and gowns are to be removed, and kept within, surgery? I'll say that such true charges of our being dirty should be corrected and not quarreled with."

There was quite a bit more talk. I went upstairs to change my dress, but I could hear the rumble of the men's voices rising, falling. After half an hour things became quiet, and I decided that everyone had gone home. I came downstairs and found that Bishop still sat with Jason, and they were still talking.

They glanced at me and rose when I entered the room. They knew that I was there and could hear. I wanted to point out to them that they had not accomplished much by confining Grady to the hospital, nor by their efforts to "divert" him into an interest in girls. I kept still. But I did quite a bit of thinking.

Sometimes the two men spoke of other things — the vestry of the church wanted to do some remodeling; Joe didn't think his boy would ever learn to ride. Bishop thought he would, with time and patience.

"Joe hasn't learned that it takes a lot of both to raise a son," said Jason wearily.

His bachelor brother laughed. A little. "Tell me, Jase," he asked, "is Grady doing these things, these days, to devil his elders?"

Jason shook his head. "Not within the hospital," he said. "I am sure he is not so motivated."

I sighed in relief, and turned the wool in my hands.

"Oh," my husband was continuing, "Grady likes to stir things up. He enjoys it. He really does. And this past week he has been going about with a lot of cream on his whiskers."

"I've seen it," said Bish. "That riles the staff, too."

"I know it does. Grady knows it. But, Bish, I

truly think he believes that these shocking truths, brought out where they'll be noticed, are a way to help the sick. And, whether we like his methods or not — I often do not! — I am beginning to suspect that my son is a true physician."

I felt pleasure sweep over me in a warm wave. I did so need to be pleased with Grady — after the past month. "He is a physician," I said firmly, "by nature and by inheritance."

The men turned to look at me. "What do you think we should do about him, Helen?" Bishop asked.

"You could try letting him alone."

"We can't have him plastering the bulletin boards with his scare headlines."

"No, I suppose you can't. And I think there orders should be passed out."

"This matter of shedding," said Jason, "the hospital knows about that danger. But what we're afraid of is that his stuff will get into public print. That shedder bulletin could drive patients away in droves — patients who need care. If they'd read that sort of thing, if a newspaper would get hold of a bulletin —"

"A lot of stuff does get into print, Jason. Vinegar and apples for rheumatism, copper bracelets for arthritis . . ."

"The trouble is, Grady isn't a quack."

"No," I agreed.

"When you said to let him alone," said Bishop, "you were thinking of his personal life, too, weren't you?"

"Yes," I agreed. "Of course I was."

"Well, I am ready to agree with you there."

"If we try it," said Jason, "what will he do next?"

I folded my knitting. "Don't you think it will be interesting to see?"

Perhaps it was the next thing; certainly it was a significant development. In any case, within a day or two David told us that he and Isabelle were moving to Arizona — for the climate. "We've talked about it, Mother."

Yes, there had been some discussion, inconclusively. I was not prepared to have it happen so suddenly, and perhaps they had not planned it that way, either.

David said he had been working on it. He had, with Schmitt's help, been learning to drive a hand-operated car. Yes, they were driving out. They had bought a home — on ground level. Grady was going to drive out with them, to help move some of their gear — take the second car for Isabelle's use. Then, there was the wheelchair, books . . .

I listened to David, then I went in search of Grady. "Have you known they were planning this?" I asked him.

"Yes. I was told a week ago."

"Grady . . . ?"

He patted my cheek.

"Is that why . . ."

He smiled. "It takes quite a jolt to make David remember he's a man. And he should get away, Mother."

"And . . . ?"

"It seems that David, now that he can earn his living, wants to have his own house, his own car —"

"And his own wife?" I asked sharply.

Grady only looked at me, still half smiling.

"She's found she can't get you," I said crossly. I didn't like being left out of my family's planning.

Again Grady's fingers patted my cheek. "Take it easy, Lady Vere de Vere," he said softly.

"Grady . . ."

He nodded to me and walked away. Well, he was right, of course. Certain things could not be talked about.

Jason was upset about Grady's plan to drive out with David. "You'll take the time out of your annual vacation!" he told his son.

"Sir!" said Grady.

He was gone for five days, and came home with pictures of the new house. "I think they'll get along fine," he told us.

I studied the pictures of the low, pink adobe

house; a wall enclosed a garden; the roof was of tile. Beyond the house, mountains rolled up along the horizon. "Its very far away," I said sadly.

"You can fly out there in a few hours, and go twice a month," Grady told me. "What's new around here?"

There was always something "new" around Southshire Place and the McCord family. That same evening various members of the family came to our house to see Grady, to see the pictures of David's home — and to talk about June and Dodie Mulvihill.

In a big, old house like ours there are numerous rooms built supposedly for one purpose, then converted to more modern uses and ways. Such a room is what we call the children's dining room. It is a small, square room adjoining the kitchen. The large windows are bordered by small squares of stained glass; these windows look out upon the back lawn, the blooming trees, and, that evening, the cold rain. When my boys had been small, and their table manners uncertain, they had been fed at the big, round, pedestal oak table. A high-chair still stood in one corner, against visiting little ones or hoped-for grandchildren. The oak side chairs had been painted a bright lemon yellow to match the walls and one of the window colors. A couple of yellow pottery tureens stood on the shelves of the old "press." A Boston fern flourished in a brass jardinière on an oak plant stand. It was an old-fashioned room, but pleasant. Lately Jason and I had been eating our breakfasts there, or our Sunday evening suppers.

We were eating such a meal, with Grady, on that Sunday evening when the brothers began to drop in — Bishop in time to get, and enjoy, a popover and orange marmalade, Lucian and Joe to share a cup of coffee with us.

They welcomed Grady, asked about his trip. How had David managed with the new car?

"Fine. Schmitt had seen to it that he learned to drive it before they started."

"Is Schmitt going to stay with them?"

"I hope so. David needs someone."

There was a little more talk, renewed and repeated with each arrival, then Jason repeated Grady's request to be told "what was new in Southshire."

"Did you tell him?" asked Lucian dryly.

Grady looked at him over the rim of his coffee cup. "June again?" he asked.

"Who else?"

"Oh — it could be others. An engagement announced — one of the kids could break his leg — But you're right. With me out of town, it would be June. What's happened now? That

Mulvihill thing was petering out. . . ."

"We thought so, but June didn't," said Jason. "He never knows when to quit."

I played with the fringe of the yellow mat under my blue plate.

"Don't tell me," laughed Grady, "that he finally came to blows with Mulvihill!"

"No," said his father. "Not that, thank God."

"Jason . . ." I protested.

He turned to me. "I am not being profane, Helen! I do thank God. All we needed —"

"What did happen?" Grady asked his Uncle Bishop.

"She pitched him out," said Bish bluntly. "He hung around until she got a chance to throw him out and tell him that he'd better grow up."

Grady laughed and shook his head. "That's fair enough," he said. "June needs to do just that."

"At his age, I would think so," growled Jason.

"What are you going to do with him now?" Lucian asked.

"You don't *do* things with boys that age, Lucian," said Jason.

"I plan to if my boys require it."

"And I'll sit back and watch you try."

"June still is at the seminary?" said Joe with the lift of a question in his voice.

"So far as I know. He's stopped wearing that

damn collar." Jason glanced at me. "That time I was swearing," he told me.

Grady laughed. "You men," he said, shaking his head.

"We don't manage things right, do we?" Lucian asked him.

"No, sir. Or — well, yes, I suppose you do. The fault I find is that you attempt to manage at all. Once your sons are grown — educated — I think you'd be happier, and they would be, if you'd just relax and let them be the men you've been trying to raise."

"But, Grady . . ."

"I know, I know." His bright gaze went around the table. "We make jackasses of ourselves. Didn't you, ever, when you were young?"

Nobody said anything. "Did anybody," Grady persisted, "force you to be jackasses? All right. You did it yourselves, and it took doing. Then why should you try to force us to be sensible and creditable and all of those things? You can't do it by force."

I thought he was right.

"Sure, said Grady. "Dad should stop financing June. If he doesn't go through with this church thing, tell him to get a job. But don't have any idea that you can force him to find the right job and do good work at it. Give him some rope, let him plunge about, skinning his own legs and banging his own head. Sooner or later, just as the rest of us have, June will do all right, going along on the momentum you've given us."

"Yes, but with June, that going along isn't always good going."

"No, it is not," Grady agreed. "June's got more than his share of jackass blood. But he still has to learn to run the course for himself, Dad. David's just learned that. I've had some rough times. All of us — you, too, if you'll look back clearly and honestly — we have to make our mistakes, run into the barbed wire, and then learn to watch that we don't do it again — or at least not too often. We know how to run a straight course. We've been taught — trained — to know what the right thing is."

"Even June?"

Grady shrugged. "Even me." He held his coffee cup out to me, and his gaze reassured me.

"In our home —" he said, settling back, "and that includes Uncle Lucian's home, and Uncle Joe's — we have known such discipline. . . ."

"All right!" cried his Uncle Lucian, bending toward him. "Since you acknowledge that discipline — what good is it going to do me — or us — to tell you to let doctoring alone!"

I was surprised, and I thought Grady would be. But he just laughed. "You don't want me

202

to do that," he said.

"I do too want it!" Lucian insisted. "What good does it do you, or the rest of us, for you to publish that article of yours coming out in next week's *Post?* Telling the AMA that it needs socialized medicine."

I sighed. I had not heard of the article, but Lucian was ready to tell us about it. And Grady was ready to defend himself. The argument got pretty heated before they were through; I thought Grady made a good thing of his side, but the men also showed up well.

The AMA, said the young man, *was* too powerful. No other country in the world allowed a medical association such power.

"They've made good use of it."

"They have not. The record of their use is — is extraordinary."

"They have advanced reforms, changes —"

"Ah-huh!" said Grady. *"Ah-huh.* First they fight advances, then they claim credit for their accomplishment. That's how they advance. Take group medicine — That's been the biggest fight of all. Why, Uncle Lucian, the AMA opposed Mayo's as group practice. Later, of course, they reversed themselves and elected the brothers as presidents of AMA."

"That's one instance," said Joe. "And I think you will find, Grady, that, over the years, and judging its entire history, the AMA must be called one of the significant and progressive factors in American medicine."

Grady nodded, "You're right, but I wish they had stayed with medicine. Lately they've spilled over into political, economic, and social fields. . . ."

"The people . . ."

"I know it. The people in this country do not look after their own interests. The Federal Government, though timidly, is the only force ever to oppose the power of AMA."

I thought the men were quarreling. A woman — this woman — never learns that men can argue on a plane above bickering and personalities.

"Arrogance," Grady was saying. "There's your big fault with our doctors. From the time he begins his internship, a doctor is told he will be all-powerful, that no one will question him or his decision — nurses, patients — nobody. And that is heady stuff, sirs. A man gets to believe in his godlike powers and status. He is infuriated when the Government, or business, or the community at large dares question his judgment and behavior."

"You're making trouble for yourself, my boy," drawled Bishop, tilting back in his chair.

"I know it," Grady conceded. "I like to be in a position of total command. There's a bit of Hitler in all of us. But he was wrong, and we can be."

Joe, his eyes squinted, was studying this nephew of his. Grady was very much in earnest. His face, all around his eye patch, was flushed scarlet.

"Tell me, Jase," said Joe. "Is this boy of yours a good doctor?"

Grady glanced at him, relaxed, and sat back in his chair.

Jason considered his reply, and I saw a sparkle come into Grady's eye. Now was his father's chance!

He should have known that, on such a subject, Jason would give a considered, impartial answer. "Grady is a very good surgeon," he said slowly. "I've missed him this past week — or month. And I'm glad he'll have to keep his nose to the grindstone for a while, paying back all the covering that's been done for him. Yes, he is good."

Joe shook his head. "I don't know if that helps or not."

"I don't either," said Jason dryly.

I looked again at Grady; his face was entirely sober. He could value the praise which his father had given.

"I do regret," Jason continued, "that the youngest doctor in the family has undertaken to instruct us as to what we are, and are not, in the profession."

"I don't do that, Dad," said Grady quickly.

"You do it — whatever your purpose and reason."

"If there are faults — I have enormous respect for doctors as a group."

"You should," said Lucian, and somehow I wished he had kept still. This was the closest I'd known of the men, and Grady, coming to a discussion or an agreement on these matters. Lucian pontificating —

"The medical profession," he declared. "The doctors, if you like, is an educated group, and a courteous one. We do, perhaps, react more slowly to change, but this can mean, and usually does mean, that we execute judgment."

"I agree with you, sir," said Grady soberly. "But I also think the people, as a whole, have two rights. In the things I publish I try to speak for them."

"What are your two rights, Grade?" asked Bishop.

"Oh! They're simple, you'll agree. I think the people have a right to question, and I think they have a right to a reasonable answer."

"Don't they get it? Your answer?"

"Not without personal vilification; no, sir, they do not. Not always."

I sighed. The men seemed to understand what he was saying. I did not, completely. But that rainy evening I thought I saw a closeness between Grady and his father, a mutual respect and admiration. I thought about this, rather than listening closely to the talk that continued. Lively talk it was, not too heated. Voices were raised, and there was laughter.

Finally Lucian asked Grady, in some exasperation, if he really believed all the things he said.

Grady shrugged. "I do like to argue," he admitted.

"You like to make trouble!"

Grady considered this charge. "Well, yes," he finally conceded. "That, too, I suppose. It's a good – maybe the best – mental catharsis. You get a lot of things thought about and solved."

"You certainly do!" cried his father. "For instance, David's affairs. June . . . Oh, get out! I've had all I can take. And you're needed at the hospital."

207

Chapter 8

The air had been cleared. There was no more talk, to my knowledge, of deciding what to "do" with Grady. The uncles seemed to have listened to his plea that the young be allowed to make their own, though stumbling, way.

Or perhaps it was just a matter of Grady's being busy. He was, that winter. He was finishing his residency in surgery, and, he complained, the Chief, his father, was pouring it on him. He was at home only occasionally, and irregularly, and when he was there, he and Jason did a lot of talking about "Grady's cases." He was preparing to take his Board examinations that next summer; his father had withdrawn from the Board, and Grady was relieved. "He's too tough on me, Mother."

"Doesn't that make you learn more?"

Grady groaned. "Must you see good in everything?" he demanded.

"It isn't always easy."

When the weather turned warm, he went off

— to Chicago, as I remember, and was gone for three weeks. "Does it take that long?" I asked Shields.

"No, but he's going to do some intensive book swatting. We all get away from the books during our residencies."

"Will he pass?"

"Grade? Sure he'll pass. And probably be lecturing to the examining doctors."

"Do things come too easily to Grady, Shields?"

He looked at me in surprise. "Why, they don't come easily to him at all, Mother. That guy agonizes."

"I've never seen him."

"You'd better watch."

I thought about it, and certainly I agonized while he was away. He came home as quietly, unobtrusively, as he always came in and out of the house. He was not there, then he was there. Yes, he had passed. He was now a Diplomate in the College of Surgeons — which was a very fine thing to be for so young a man, so new a doctor.

The family expressed itself as being very proud of Grady, and his father said I should give a family dinner to celebrate. I did, and the family told him that they were proud.

He looked proud, too, though he told us that he'd taken the Boards only to show he could pass them.

"Next," he added, his blue eyes sparking, "I'm going to try to qualify as a G.P."

His uncles thought he was making a joke, but I saw his father looking hard at Grady. "The passion for learning . . ." I murmured.

Jason glanced at me. "What do you know about being an internist?" he asked his son.

"What I learned as an intern. Nothing. But I said G.P., sir."

His father stared at him, then he made a gesture with his hand that showed exasperation and an acknowledgment of defeat. "You had better settle down," he growled, "and get to work."

"I am working."

And of course he was. He was given staff status at the hospital. His name was on the surgery schedules; he had some sort of supervisory position in making those schedules. And he worked regularly in the o.r.'s. I'd check the lists when I could, doing my volunteer work. I was glad and reassured to see his name. The other McCords — one just expected Shields, and Jason, even Bishop — especially Bishop! — to do their jobs. But Grady —

He went to the hospital with the other men in the morning, he was frequently called out at odd hours — because he was a new staff surgeon, Jason explained to me. He seemed to

be working steadily and enjoying it. Our meal-
times became pretty clinical, what with
Shields' enthusiasm for his expanded burn center, and the cases which Grady and Jason
worked on together.

Grady still did not have an office or any
private practice. "That will come," Jason assured me. "I want him in my office. . . ."

"Have you said so?"

"I told him there would be room when he
was ready."

"He's settling down, don't you think?"

My husband smiled at me. "With Grady, that
can be a bad sign."

It could be. It was — because before the year
was up, Grady had written, and published, a
book. He called it *Your Hospital.* It was a fairly
thick book, with an eye-attracting blue and
white jacket. One morning, that boy took a
stack of them and went from house to house on
Southshire Place distributing his books among
the family. He left one of them at Jason's place
in the small dining room of our house.

He went down the street and through the
gate to Joe's house. He gave his book to
Walther, Joe's Teutonic houseman. "Put this
beside my uncle's egg," he told the erect white-
haired servant.

"Yes, Mr. Grady." Walther turned the book

end over end and looked questioningly at the early caller.

"You do what I say," said Grady. "Uncle Joe will understand."

He went in under the arches of A.B.'s house — the maid invited him for breakfast. "Haven't time," said Grady. "I have these others to pass out."

"What are they, Mr. Grady?"

"Books. I wrote 'em. It." And Grady was away, down to Bishop's house.

"Does my uncle eat breakfast?" he asked Raymond, who is older than our Orlie.

"Of course he eats breakfast," said Raymond, affronted.

"Wouldn't dare not to, eh?" said Grady. "Well, put this with his cornflakes, will you?"

And he was off again, running, the tail of his short blue coat flying.

Surely he had some temerity about going to Lucian's house that early in the morning, on such a mission. But not enough to stop him. Lucian, too, found his book and probably glanced through it, as Jason did.

"That's a good way to ruin my breakfast and spoil the day," Jason told me, pushing the volume away from him. "Where is Grady?"

I looked at Orlie.

"He says he's got an early schedule, ma'am,"

Orlie answered, looking worried. "He took off —"

I nodded and reached for the book. It still thrilled me to see my son's name in print. And this book — the pages were thick, creamy, the binding of dull blue cloth, gilt-trimmed. There was a caduceus midcenter of the front cover. The jacket —

"What's it about?" I asked Jason.

Shields had come in and I handed the book to him. We both waited for Jason to answer.

"I've only glanced at it," he told us. "The jacket says it will tell us what is wrong with hospitals and medical practice."

"Oh, dear," I sighed. "When his uncles find out . . ."

It was then that Orlie told us of the distribution. I dreaded to see the men start for work, and I felt sure Jason dreaded facing his brothers.

But I saw him walk down the street with Bishop; they looked much as usual. Late that afternoon the brothers gathered behind our house to discuss the layout of a croquet court. We had a large enough stretch of ground; it would mean leveling and the removal of some shrubbery. The men thought the work could be done during the winter. They paced off distances and gestured. Finally Bishop came up to the house to ask me to come outside to help them decide what bushes should go.

The court as staked out was on the south side of our corner property; the wrought-iron fence which separated us from the sidewalk of the Boulevard was only ten feet away. The fence was old, but sound; one of the big tree trunks had grown about the top railing, a burl or knot had formed.

"It's a wonder the tree hasn't died," said Lucian.

"That burl was there when I was a little girl," I told him.

He smiled at me. "It should be well established then," he said gently.

"If your court is to go this close to the street, shouldn't you plant some shrubbery here for privacy? If you don't, you'll have patients leaning across the fence to consult you."

"Provided we have any patients," growled Joe. "Or hospital!"

The book. I knew it would be discussed. If this was the time, I wanted to go — run — back to the house. But Jason held me to the matter of shrubbery. I thought he also wanted me to hear what the men would say about the book.

"There was a real blowup earlier," he told me. "I don't blame them. I am very angry at Grady."

The men talked. The gist of what they said was that they could not tolerate these things!

214

Grady must be stopped. This matter had come to a place where the whole McCord family was tinged — tainted — smeared.

"How could he be on the Staff and continue to do these things?" asked Joe.

"I asked him that," said Jason.

His brothers turned to face him. "What did he say?" asked A.B.

Jason shrugged. "He laughed and suggested changing his name."

"*Aggggh!*"

"Of course he can't change his name," I agreed.

"Helen — don't you have any influence?"

"He loves me. He wouldn't want to hurt me. But he loves you, too. This book — What does he say in it?"

They answered me, all at once. Evidently some rapid reading had been done during the day. Grady, they told me, had said everything.

"Everything he shouldn't," growled Lucian.

"Did he write about your hospital? The Center?" Though I was almost afraid to ask.

"Oh, no," said Bishop. "Not specifically. Except that all hospitals are indicted."

"I don't think he often had us in mind," Jason defended his son. "The faults and dangers he lists are not frequent with us. We have a right to be honest about that."

"We have a right to be honest and to know

that," said Lucian. "But outsiders — the patients — won't know it. Rival hospitals will take advantage of the possibility that Grady gathered his material while working with us. And they will take advantage of the publicity he will get. . . ."

"The damn thing is sure to be a best seller," growled Bishop.

"He'll do a lot of damage," Joe agreed. "Loss of confidence. It's too big a price to pay. The patients have to trust us!"

I pulled at Jason's sleeve. "What did he say?" I asked again.

"You'll have to read it," he told me.

"It's an interesting book," said A.B. "The boy can write — and really, he takes the reader on a tour of the hospital. Our hospital. Any hospital. He begins with emergency and goes through to the autopsy rooms. O.b., o.r. — the works. I even get scorched in my lab. There is too much science, he says, not enough humanity in the hospital today."

"Is that true?" I asked anxiously.

"Too true to be comfortable," A.B. told me.

That night I took Grady's book and began to read. It was fascinating — and the style made it read fast. I forgot that this was my son's book; I became eager to find out what was wrong with our hospitals. And there seemed to be plenty wrong, according to Grady's book.

He did begin with the emergency room. We had one at the Center. I knew it; I had worked at the desk there, and Jason was right. There was a similarity between our hospital and the ones Grady told about in his book.

I was interested in his pointing out that the hospital e.r. had, since World War II, come to take the place of family physician, house calls, and even private doctors' offices. "If your town knows the habit of doctors' taking Wednesday afternoon off, that will be the busiest day in your town hospitals' emergency rooms. And that isn't good, because with the doctors out on the golf course, or out of town, e.r. will be manned, at the best, by learning interns, at the worst, and most commonly, by nurses and orderlies."

He said that a patient, coming into e.r., should see a *doctor* within fifteen minutes. And that this did not often happen.

He said that e.r. should be open and easily accessible to the street. (Ours was.) He said an e.r. should be quiet, efficient, and with proper personal attention available to each patient. Our hospital would not qualify there. E.r. was a hurly-burly.

He told about the great number of "doctor-less" hospitals in the country — hospitals where doctors were not continuously present. That again did not apply to the Center, but I was not

217

sure how qualified the doctors in our e.r. were, or on what basis those doctors served. I began to think of questions to ask poor Jason.

Grady gave some heart-rending examples of mistreatment, lack of treatment, callousness, in e.r. There was, he said, too much paper work involved in caring for and admitting patients to and through e.r.

There were too many patients, too few personnel – manners were brusque, examinations hurried – radiology too often was not available in e.r.

He told the faults, and he suggested the ideal; there should be, he said, sufficient medical personnel to examine the patient quickly. These should be backed up by enough medical strength to care for serious illnesses and accidents. He described the ideal e.r., with plenty of doctors there, or on call if needed. The department should be open twenty-four hours a day, be on the ground floor, with adequate waiting room for relatives and friends, adequate X-ray and diagnostic facilities, and the best of all instruments used. I still remember his saying that a dull needle hurts just as much in e.r. as it does in a pavilion private room.

He concluded that chapter by stating unequivocally, "If emergency room care in your hospital is good, the hospital care may be."

Just "may be." I read on.

I believed Grady was right in most of the things he told about hospitals. When I asked Jason, he too said the boy was right – often – but he shouldn't have said them.

"Why not? If it means better care for the patients?"

"That won't – that hasn't been – the first result, my dear."

"Can you talk to him?"

"I've tried. Like you, he thinks shock treatment may do some good."

Bishop had been right. Grady's book did become a best-seller, a sensation. Newspapers and magazines quoted from it, wrote articles about it.

When a reporter came to our front door, late one afternoon, to ask for a statement from Jason about the book – he would be glad to do a feature, he said, agreeing with Grady's book, or not; either way it would make a pip of an article – Jason told the man to leave, and slammed the door behind him.

Within that week, Grady moved out of our home. What hurt his father and me was that he did not discuss the move with us – which would have been courteous, at least, said Jason.

"I have my rights in this house," he stated, "but so does Grady."

Henry Tibbs tried to protest the move. He had been calling Grady "Shedder" ever since

Grady had posted his bulletins about dirty hospitals. "You shouldn't do this, Shedder," he told the young man.

"Yes," said Grady. "Its time."

"But where are you going? You can't live here with me. I couldn't stand that."

"Nobody can stand me. I'm fixing up some rooms over the carriage house at Baggie's."

He meant the carriage house behind Lizzie Paradis' home. He had long called her by the name of the Korean woman.

I hated the original Baggie, and Grady's use of that name made me dislike poor Lizzie. That she would let Grady . . .

Lizzie Paradis was a foolish woman; no one on the Place really liked her. Until now we had made an effort to conceal that dislike. Some of us even made an effort to be kind to her. But this thing of Grady –

I was deeply hurt, and I showed my hurt to Grady, when he finally said something to me about the move.

"I hoped you would understand," he told me, jiggling from one foot to the other.

"I don't understand your making such a move. You're one of the family, and our house . . ."

"I want to be one of the family," he assured me. "That's why I'm staying on Southshire. I can't afford to buy a *house*. This seemed to be a solution. I'll be here, among all of you, but not so much in your hair."

"You have never bothered me, Grady!"

"I have, Dad."

"I'm sorry, Grady."

"So am I. You know, Lady Vere de Vere, I seem to spend my life being sorry for something."

"It's because you keep doing things to make yourself sorry."

He touched my cheek. "I can't stop doing them."

I sighed. "All right, Grady."

Jason saw that I had abandoned any effort to make Grady reconsider, and he also saw that I was hurt. He asked his son to have dinner with us on an evening early the next week, and Grady showed up, kissing me, eating with good appetite, telling a few stories about the hospital. Shields watched him, and I did. Grady was marking time, as was Jason. I knew both men very well.

With the dessert, Jason laid his napkin beside his plate and leaned toward Grady. "You know that your mother is hurt by your leaving our home?" he asked.

Grady flushed. "I've talked to Mother about that."

"I understand that you have. But she is still

hurt, and I feel that you are doing this thing, Grady, to hurt her."

"Sir!" said Grady, stiffly.

"Oh, Jason," I protested. "I don't think Grady had any such thing in mind. He has a right to live where he pleases."

"Little birds from the nest must fly," said Shields dryly.

Grady glanced at him and laughed. "I hadn't thought of it just that way, brother buzzard."

Jason snorted. "If you're flying away from the nest," he rasped, "why don't you go to the hotel? Or to the Club? Why move in with the spiders and old trunks up in Lizzie Paradis' carriage house?"

Grady laughed. "You know the place, don't you?"

"I know all old carriage houses. Our own is a depository for junk, and a haven for spiders."

"Yes, sir. But you know? I like Baggie's carriage house. There's room — a bath. Why don't you come down and see it? I'm not settled. I've only just got the old junk swamped out. . . ."

"And only part of the new junk moved in," drawled Shields.

"Well," laughed Grady. "Something like that. Come on. We'll go look at it."

Jason said he didn't want to go, but I could persuade him, since he was only being stubborn. "I won't talk to Lizzie," he assured me, as we walked down the street. There was a cold east wind blowing; I wrapped a scarf around my head, and the men laughed at the idea that there could be both warmth and protection in chiffon.

"You could try it on," I suggested. Their way of protecting their heads was to hunch their shoulders up about their ears.

There was only a dim light in Lizzie's home. We went up along the drive, and Grady unlocked the door to the carriage house. Originally there had been two bedrooms on the second floor, and a bath. The coachman and a groom had been quartered there. As we went up the steep flight of stairs, Grady again explained that he had done little more than clean up the place.

We looked about, and he explained his ideas. "I thought I would use one of the rooms for a bedroom; I've already got up some shelves. And the other would be a living room. I'll have a closet-kitchen in one corner. You know? A small stove, a few utensils and dishes. I suppose a refrigerator somewhere. And I'll want a fireplace. I'll get a free-standing one. There will have to be painting done."

I was gazing at the far wall. In the exact center above where Grady had scribbled "fireplace" he had hung the old fencing foils from the tack room in our carriage house. All those years . . . and Grady was still fifteen, still lonely.

"D'you have a phone?" Jason asked him sternly.

"Yes, sir. First thing I did."

"All right." Jason followed me down the stairs.

"The place isn't too bad," I murmured as we walked back toward home.

"I'll tell the others that Henry Tibbs is not helping him in this."

I stopped. "Did they think he was?"

"He enjoys seeing one of us out on a limb."

"Henry is very fond of you."

Jason didn't really answer that. "I'd not cry," he said, "if, this time, Grady was the one out on Henry's perch."

"Oh, Jason. That boy —"

"That *boy* is thirty-five years old. It is time he was settling down!"

That was a busy autumn. Grady was furnishing and furbishing his apartment. He didn't ask for any help from me, so I became occupied with other things. Taking a semester away from college, Taylor Falk was making her debut, and so were Joe's twin girls. I told Jason we should give a party for them.

"All right. Give one. Here at home?"

I shook my head. "I understand old houses

can't take modern parties."

"Then the club – Country or University?"

I chose the Country Club, and when the time came close, I began to worry about the weather.

Grady came bringing his invitation to me. "Joe's girls and Taylor aren't old enough for this kind of party, are they, Mother?" he asked, his face concerned.

"Do you get any younger?"

He laughed. "But Taylor . . ."

"I told you a year ago that she was growing up."

"I guess you did. She's a cute girl, too. Pretty. Do you know if she still jumps rope?"

"Why don't you ask her?"

"I shall."

At the party, Taylor told me that he had asked, and she had demonstrated. "Is he coming tonight?" she asked, looking about.

"With Grady, I can't commit myself."

"I hope he will come. It is a lovely party, Mrs. McCord."

It was a lovely party; the weather was perfect. There were two orchestras, a marquee on the lawn for the rock and roll dancers, delicious food eaten at small tables covered with gold cloths. Garlands of golden flowers and ivy against the walls – three pretty girls. Joe's twins are pretty, one blonde and luscious like

225

her mother, the other dark and slender like Joe. Taylor was beautiful in pale yellow net, with an orchid tucked behind her ear. It was green to match her eyes. "Grady sent it," she whispered to me. He was late coming, but when he did arrive, he danced all night, mostly with Taylor, his cheek down against her burnished auburn hair.

Like any normal mother, I began to daydream, though there were many things to disrupt my dreams, as well as my life.

A book is published, it must be read, talked about, read again. . . . It took a few weeks for the full impact of Grady's book to be felt at the hospital Center. But before Christmas the staff was so aware of it that a rather large staff conference added itself to the many, many family conferences it had occasioned.

Jason told me about the staff meeting.

Everyone kept saying that something should be done about Grady and his writing, which was called everything from impudent and outrageous, to subversive and dangerous. So the staff held a meeting. Not a formal one, Jason explained. In that case, Grady would have had to be notified.

"You men just wanted to get together to talk about him."

Jason nodded. "There's Grady's charm," he said thoughtfully. "His smile, and his eye patch. He disarms us very quickly."

I turned my knitting. We were sitting in the Palladian room, alone on a snowy night. Through the windows I could see the street lights haloed, and under each one a circle of pink lamplight on the snow. Everything was quiet, stilled. Cars went up and down the Boulevard, but not as many as usual. We could not hear them. Shields had gone off somewhere, perhaps down to Grady's. Jason had stacked magazines beside his chair, to catch up on his journal reading.

I waited for him to continue about Grady. He picked up a journal, flipped its pages, then sat staring at me, but not seeing me. The little birds in the big cage stirred and murmured sleepily.

"There was a lot of talk," Jason said slowly. "Various ones covered the whole book — Grady's book — and they were ready to argue each point. Various ones thought he should be asked to leave the staff, and that a statement should be given — publicized."

"And the McCords?" I asked. "Was Shields there?"

"No. He had a new case. . . ."

"I expect he was glad. Shields believes Grady should be allowed to say, and write, what he thinks."

"So does the rest of the family."

I looked up in surprise. "You agree with him?"

"With Grady? By no means. Not always. And we don't think Grady always agrees with himself. We suspect that he is writing sensationally to attract attention."

"He isn't an exhibitionist, Jason. Not in other things."

"That point has worried me. I've about decided that he feels sensationalism is the only way to attract attention to his nuggets of truth."

I smiled. That sounded like Grady. "There are nuggets, then?"

"Oh, indeed, yes — so far as conditions in the hospital and in medical practice are concerned. It *is* absurd for all the doctors to take Wednesday afternoons off. There *is* too little clinical training for resident and interning doctors." Jason leaned toward me.

"It's his ideas, his recommendations, that rub a lot of the men raw, Helen."

"They aren't good?"

Jason sighed. "Again, every adjective was used — half-baked, irresponsible, radical. And the worst of all still, I am afraid, socialistic."

I shook my head.

Jason laughed a little. "The talk was wilder than anything Grady has ever written. And they kept coming back to dismissal. Finally one of the men — Tony Witt, I think it was — he's

228

in Orthopedics — he put it straight to Lucian. Asked him if he didn't think the staff should kick 'your nephew' out."

"Oh, dear," I breathed.

"Best thing that could happen," said Jason, straightening in his chair, and looking more animated. "Nobody tells Lucian what he should think or do."

No. No one did. Besides . . .

"The McCords rallied round, I suppose," I said innocently.

"Yes, of course they did. I did. Joe spoke up. He was the best one to do it. He said that we had a suggestion in which the staff might be interested. He waited until he got everyone's attention, then he said that it might challenge Grady to keep him on the hospital staff, expected to put his own ideas into use. Joe felt — we felt — that in such a way he would learn first hand what the problems were. He said he thought Grady could be expected to write fairly about his findings."

"What did the men say?"

"Well, there was a lot of arguing about it. Someone — the head of thoracic surgery — pointed out that Grady would need to be given authority. I told him he already had it — or enough. He already was supervising surgery scheduling."

"And doing his own surgery, isn't he?"

"Oh, yes," said Jason. "Definitely yes. Then Bishop spoke and said we could put Grady in charge of resident and intern training. He's barked up a lot of those trees."

"Are they going to let him . . . ?"

"Yes. They've agreed to try giving him every opportunity to stub his toes."

"Hoping that he will?"

"We didn't expect much charity to come out of that meeting, Helen. But, yes, there was some evidence of hope. The older men said they would be watchful. And one of the emeriti commented that young doctors needed their noses bruised. He reminded us that we'd all been through that experience."

"Did they all agree?"

"Oh, no. Not all of them, and not all at once. In fact, I think most of the men thought that there should be some sort of discipline meted out to Grady. There were some who, categorically, said to kick him out! He'd learn that way."

"Oh, dear."

"Don't worry. They won't do it. I'd be the first to advise against it, though no one gets angrier when one of his things comes out in print."

"But, Jason, if he shouldn't write them . . ."

"I'm not saying he shouldn't. I just wish he wouldn't. He tears things up. . . ."

The way he had done for David and Isabelle.

We had had a letter a week ago, asking our approval of their adopting a child.

"Are you men . . . ? Don't misunderstand me, Jason. But are the staff men afraid to kick Grady out?"

He smiled grimly. "I suppose it amounts to that. He knows too much, and he's found a way, a place, to tell about it in an authoritative manner. Personally, I don't think he'd be any worse if we'd kick him out. But, yes, there are those who do think so."

"Would you pitch him out?"

"Helen." He laid his magazine back on the stack. "Look at me. Way back — years ago — when one of the boys did something we didn't like, I told you that nothing — absolutely nothing — would ever make me disown a son of mine."

He had been sorely tried. June, Abe — Grady — but he had said that, and meant it.

"If Grady disrupts . . ."

"He won't disrupt the hospital. He doesn't fight that way. He thinks always, and first, of the hospital. At the meeting, one of the men pointed that out to us, and it is true, Helen. It is true."

I felt relief sweep warmly into me. Grady! Of course he was doing the right thing — and I was glad.

"And someone else — he got agreement,

too – thinks that what Grady has been doing, that his behavior will have a cleansing effect. He called it a purge."

I laughed. "Was one needed?"

Jason reached for his magazine again. "I believe one could be used."

"You're saying that Grady is right?"

"No, I am not. Because he isn't right. Not always."

I knitted a row and let the heap of red wool fall into my lap. "Jason?" I said then. I could feel him look up. "Tell me," I urged. "What do you, personally, individually, suggest? Forgetting your responsibilities as Grady's father. Or even as Chief of the Surgical Staff. Can you so detach yourself?"

"Hmmmmmn," said my husband. Then I glanced across at him. He was deeply thoughtful. "That isn't an easy one," he told me.

I waited.

"Well . . ." he said finally. "I think we should stop giving him things to write about. I think, each one of us doctors, or all of us, should open our eyes, do some evaluating of our practices, and clean our houses. Then – and maybe only then – Grady could settle down to his doctoring."

"Is he a good doctor, Jason?"

"I remember answering that question a short while ago. Grady was right there with us. My

232

answer still is: Yes! He is very good."

I suppose he offered his suggestion to his fellow staff men. For a time I heard little about the hospital. I was busy at other things. Once Shields said something about Grady being given every dirty surgical job that came along. "And he does 'em, Mother."

I asked him if this was routine for a young staff surgeon. Or was it discipline?

Shields smiled at me. "He does 'em," he said again.

Then, just as I thought things might have settled down, one, two, he came out in print. There was an article in a very popular magazine, with Grady's picture and a brief summary of his life, who he was, what he had done.

And he was featured in a drug company's magazine, again with his picture, this time on the front cover — a good picture, eye patch, crooked smile, his crest of brown hair.

The magazine article had to do with anesthesia. It was a plea for the recognition and an increased respect for the doctor-anesthetist. I got the idea that these doctors were held on the level of a technician. He had things to say about leaving routine cases to the nurse-anesthetist, while the doctor officiated only at major surgical problems. He cited instances where a routine bit of work could result in serious complications due to the anesthesia itself. He offered suggestions as to ways to correct the bad aspects of anesthesia administration – a close determination that the patient had no temperature, a more comfortable atmosphere where anesthesia was to be administered, both preoperative and postoperative watchfulness . . .

And again, a plea for the anesthetist. "The danger is not in the anesthesia," he said, "but in who administers it. We should train the best people for this delicate, vital job, and train enough of them that they can follow through with the postanesthetized patient."

I overheard Bishop and Joe talking to Jason about this article. The magazine, with its glossy pictures, lay on practically everyone's coffee table. "The guy's so damn right!" said Bishop.

And the other article. Jason gave me the professional magazine. I gazed at Grady's face on the cover. "Read it," said my husband.

"I can't help but be proud of the boy," I told Grady's father.

"All right. Be proud. But read the article."

"Won't I still be proud?"

He smiled at me and went away.

So I read the article. In the popular magazine, Grady had dealt with technical facts. In this magazine for professionals, he made a plea for the doctor as a man, as a human being.

He said that a new image of doctors was needed — that the profession had overemphasized professionalism, the data and science side of doctoring. Patients were puzzled, he said, and hurt by the impersonalism encountered when they took their most precious possession, the health of their own bodies, to a doctor — any doctor — to be met by a page of two hundred questions to be answered. Their blood was tested in a machine that could do eleven tests at a time; they were talked to, a little, by technicians and X-ray men; and only finally were they to be admitted to the august presence of the doctor at his desk, with an array of reports before him, a man who could even say to that same patient, "Don't tell me. These test reports tell me the whole story. And now *I'll* tell *you*."

"All right," the article continued. "That is the modern, high-powered, and for the sake of argument, highly proficient doctor.

"Does he always get the best results?

"Per patient tested and interviewed?

"No, he does not. Because a good percentage of his patients walk out and take up faith healing, or hunt for a less proficient doctor whose fingers feel the lump in his side, whose ears listen to his story, and who even offers a little sympathy and reassurance.

"What has happened to our doctors?" the

article asked. "Do we like the image we now present, or should we seek a new one? Can we not, profitably — in every sense of *that* word — renew the image of friendship plus, and over, the scientific approach?

"Why can we not produce a two-ply service to the people for whom we exist? We plea for more doctors, for new young doctors to train. Could we start with them, and make them *men?* Not machines, not reports, but men with knowing hands, and good, trained minds?"

He urged as full an education as possible for doctors. But, he said, let them come out learned men, not intellectual giants. Or at least not that, first and foremost. He said the medical profession needed to recover some lost talents, compassion being an important one. He urged the return of idealism. "Then," said my son, "we can think about the doctor's intellectualism."

I put the magazine down. I still have it. I was proud of his article then; I am still proud of it. His uncles were proud, too.

"I didn't like that picture he drew of me behind my desk," admitted Lucian.

Lucian!

Truly Grady had achieved what he wanted to achieve.

I don't believe there were any staff conferences because of those two articles. How could there be? I wanted to talk to Grady about them. And I planned to do it. But just that day, the best I could think of to do was to gather up a bundle of sheets and towels and take them down to his apartment. He had built a frame in one corner of his bedroom. On this was a good box spring and a foam mattress. I put my offering on top of the green blanket, with a note that said only, "I love you. Come to dinner tonight. Mother."

He came. Shields and Jason were there, and Bishop, whose cook was sick. We had a roast loin of pork; the men ate heartily and talked.

I listened.

"You and your hyperactive pen and pencil," Grady's Uncle Bishop chided him. "You have the patients pretty darn restive and hard to handle."

Grady put jewel-red currant jelly beside his slice of meat, "Tell 'em the things I write are not true," he advised.

"I've tried that, but they keep after me."

"Who," asked Shields, "do you have in mind to change things, Grade? The law?"

"Oh, no," said Grady. "The doctors will have to make any changes. We surgeons must police ourselves. . . ."

"Why not include the internists?" asked Jason. "Most of our work starts with them."

"You're right, Dad, and they can change

things. Diagnosis is a powerful club to wield. But, to the patient's mind, the surgeon is the final, the extreme of a hospital experience."

"Is that why you are tearing up my surgical department?"

Shields and Bishop lifted their heads and sat up straight.

"He's trying to," Jason told them.

"Can he?"

"Well — he's proven that he is a surgeon. Even the men lined up against him agree on that."

"Could you please elucidate?" asked Bishop, speaking delicately.

"Shall I tell them, or do you want to?" Jason asked Grady.

"Whoever heard of the McCords talking one at a time?"

Jason chuckled and looked around at Orlie. "Fill up our plates," he said, "then let us alone. This will take a little time."

I was prepared for anything. Shields and Bishop waited, bright-eyed. The meat and the vegetables went around the table; hot rolls were brought in.

"Now!" said Jason. "This boy —" He caught the glint in Grady's eye. "All right, this proven surgeon has come up with an idea. . . ."

Shields made a faint, moaning sound.

"His ideas have always been dangerous," Jason agreed. "And this one – I believe Grady would headline it to read, 'If a man says he is a surgeon, make him prove it.' "

Bishop put his fork down on his plate.

"No more trial and error?" asked Shields innocently.

Grady laughed. "That is the precise idea!" he declared. "I dumped this thing on Dad the other day."

"He has a way of putting a thing so you can't argue with him without seeming a rascal, a charlatan, or a quack." Jason's tone was plaintive.

"But you said some of the men are opposing it," Bishop reminded him.

"And they sound like rascals, charlatans, and quacks," agreed Jason.

I could only sit there and look at the men and try to follow what was being said. It was not my first attempt at such a thing.

"Tell 'em, Grady," said Jason, reaching for a roll.

Grady finished eating his meat. Then he sat back a little in his chair and looked at us – even at me. "I hope I can make you understand this on my first try," he said. "It's a big idea, but once started, it should go of its own momentum. My idea is this: To require that any new surgeon coming to a hospital should operate under the critical observation of other surgeons before gaining full privileges."

Bishop whistled again. "That is an idea!"

"Credentials no good?" asked Shields.

"They can be as good as gold. But alone they should not be enough. If the new man has to prove himself . . ."

"Let me get this straight," said Bishop. "Any new man on the surgical staff, wanting to operate, must . . ."

"He must be assigned to a group of older doctors for a period of probation. He can operate only under his senior's supervision for a specified time."

"Mhmmmn. We have a new hospital starting up in the county . . ."

"Yes. My idea is to offer the services of our staff surgeons to supervise their new men. And in the future, to offer that service for any new surgeon coming into the city who wants surgical accreditation and staff position."

"You mean, Jase is going around, his lab coattails flying . . ."

"Yes, and my Uncle Bishop," Grady agreed. "Don't you see, Bish?"

"I see a whale of a lot of problems. For instance, will the new hospital agree to this sort of thing? Will County, or Mercy, or . . . ?"

"They don't have to agree. We can offer the service and tell who has accepted."

"But that's holy blackmail!" cried Shields.

"It is not!" said Grady. "And if it is, people have a right to be able to judge the kind of doctors available." He hitched himself closer to the table and leaned forward. "Look! There were those who said my recent articles have frightened the public. This sort of program should do much to counteract any fears I instilled. If the public, which needs education, learns that we are trying to give them the very best surgical service possible . . ."

"Do these surgeons need to be supervised, Grady?" I ventured to ask.

The three men answered me in chorus. Yes, they could use it. Some surgeons were quite bad — very bad — bunglers, exhibitionists. . . .

I sat appalled.

Then the men cited cases to each other. And I sat, still appalled.

"Well," said Grady, "public acceptance seems to be the least of our problems."

"I can think of one problem," said Jason. "Young surgical squirts — like you, Grady — usually think themselves better-trained than their seniors."

"Make 'em prove it," said Grady cheerfully. "If they are, they can."

"You, too?"

"Sure, me, too."

"But you're Board-accredited!" Bishop pointed out.

"I should be able to prove the Board was right."

"I see." Bishop sat thoughtful. Then he looked up. "Can't we — Can't the supervision requirements be used by us old hands to block out competition?"

"Yeah," drawled Shields. "And who says who has the legal responsibility in a supervised operation? Who gets what fee? Who's in charge of the patient?"

Grady tipped his head back and looked at the ceiling. "Once I heard it said that Grady McCord was the trouble maker of this family," he mused aloud.

"After thinking this over," said Jason, ignoring the boys' interchange, "I honestly believe that if Grady's idea should be accepted, and put to work, we older men could be instrumental in insuring high standards of patient care — and without creating any, or many, problems of monopoly, liability, *or* money."

"I hope you're right, Dad," said Grady quietly.

"Who would be called your older, more capable men?" asked Shields.

"At first, they would be selected on some basis of experience, longevity — position. In time, the younger men would join or replace us, having proved their own qualifications."

"You mean Grady?"

"I'm getting older all the time," Grady assured his brother.

"Tell me how it will work?" asked Bishop.

"All right," Grady agreed. "First you have a new man come into the city. Or maybe we take on a new staff man at the Center. We do, you know."

"Thoroughly accredited and qualified."

"Ah-huh. He comes in. He at once gets minor surgical privileges. His credentials are verified. But he can do major surgery only under the supervision of a surgeon who has already earned the privileges he is seeking."

"For how long?"

"Probation could be based on the number of procedures. Six to twelve I think would be a good number. A busy surgeon could qualify much sooner than the other sort."

"But to be busy he has to have hospital affiliations."

"He'll get 'em, if he qualifies."

"I can think of some men, including me, who would balk at your observation routine."

"If we get a pretty good appliance of the rule, balking would do him little good."

"As staff head, Jase," asked Bishop, "do you really approve of this scheme?"

"It sounds rather good to me," said Jason.

"For an open staff hospital," Bishop agreed. "Yes, it does. Perhaps all should have such a system. What about liability, Grade?"

"Oh! The new man is put squarely in charge of the surgery, and there is no fee for the observer, ever."

"Fair enough. Would you like this entry into your surgical life?"

Grady answered him seriously. "It's a lonely feeling," he said, "the first time you are on your own with full responsibility in the operating room. I don't know how other young doctors will feel. . . ."

"They'll feel that privilege should come automatically with Board certification," Bishop told him.

"Let 'em," said Jason. "But with the courts holding the hospitals legally liable for the negligence of attendings, it is unlikely that the hospitals can safely accept Boards alone as evidence of competency. Besides, this system takes the matter away from the control of the mortality, morbidity, and pathology committees."

"G.P.'s," said Bishop. "All of 'em."

"That's right. The young men will find it better to be reviewed by a surgeon."

"You say some of the staff men oppose this idea?" Shields asked.

"Yes. They won't let me call Board certification a piece of paper. They claim it is a standard with which to start, and if there is any doubt, the newcomer should be supervised by the Chief of Surgical Service." Jason made a wry face. Then he said thoughtfully, "I'm on the examining boards. I know how greatly an applicant's training and qualification can vary. Board certification is fine. But direct observation is the only way to judge surgical techniques. I do think it should continue. . . ."

"I'll work on that, sir," said Grady, and the men laughed. I rang for Orlie and the dessert.

I was glad to see Grady and his father in accord, and for some time I leaned on that comforting thought.

The brothers still held their conferences on Grady. I heard them talking about him. That winter the croquet court was the family interest. Professionals did the real work, the bulldozing, the plowing, and leveling. Eventually, the sodding. Each evening the brothers surveyed what had been done, and often came into our house to talk about their project.

And about Grady.

The men talked about consultations. I didn't listen closely. Of course doctors held consultations! Then I caught Grady's name. "He's insisting on one hundred per cent consultation, and at the bedside!"

"Well, for radical sections . . ."

"If the patient asks for it, he gets it."

That was not enough. Grady thought

245

the patient should be protected, and by the hospital rules. The men seemed to come to an agreement with him.

"Are things now better for Grady with the other men?" I asked Jason.

"Oh, Helen – he's a gadfly. Maybe we're just getting used to having his buzzing in our ears."

"But is he a good doctor?"

"Yes. Yes, he is."

"Is he making some money?"

Jason smiled. "Grady claims that any graduate doctor can make fifty thousand dollars a year just by hanging out his shingle."

"But –"

"He isn't entirely right – what with group practice and other things. But it is too true for comfort. Of course that sum is deceptive. I will say that few beginning doctors starve these days, though it still takes a surgeon longer to get himself established."

"You once said you hoped to take Grady into your office."

"I've asked him. He says he probably will come someday."

"Why not now?"

"He isn't sure he'll continue to specialize in surgery. Just now he's hipped on the subject of introgenic diseases, and spends all his spare time going about investigating that situation."

I put my hand on Jason's arm. "What is introgenic disease?" I asked.

He smiled at me. "Sickness the doctors cause."

"I'm serious, Jason."

"So am I. And what's more important, so is Grady. He's off on a hot trail just now, determining how much trouble withdrawal of tranquilizers is causing us in the hospital."

"But — tranquilizers —"

"Mhmmmmn. Harmless — if taken as prescribed. If taken as prescribed by *one* doctor for a specific situation. Not duplicated, not continued. You see, Grady had a woman stand talking to him — she was a candidate for surgery of some sort. And she fell flat on the floor in a true *mal* . . ."

"Jason!"

"A seizure, dear, convulsion, fit. Like in epilepsy. *Grand mal,* you know?"

"Slightly. A bowing acquaintance."

My husband patted my shoulder. "That's enough. But Grady may have something in this thing. His woman had had some psychiatric trouble. She had been given meprobamate — by four different doctors — and she kept four bottles of the stuff in her purse. She managed to dislocate her shoulder in the fall, and Grady had a difficult surgical case on his hands due to her withdrawal symptoms. That was enough to send him whoofing and yelping along the trail."

I laughed, but I protested with Jason, too. Grady seemed to me to be, if anything, only overly conscientious.

"He is that," Jason agreed.

He had walked down to A.B.'s house to fetch me home for dinner. Christine was going to be married in the early spring. She and A.B. had asked me to sit in on their planning as substitute mother. I loved doing it. That afternoon we had wistfully considered a home wedding. It seemed a shame not to make full use of their gorgeous staircase.

Now, walking along beside him, I tucked my hand into the warmth of Jason's elbow. It was a cold day, with snow on the ground. He was cautious of where we stepped, so our progress was slow.

"I've been thinking, this fall and winter," I told Jason, "that Grady was getting along better with you men. Of course I don't know about his situation in the hospital."

"It's practically the same as it is in the family, Helen. We admire him as a doctor, and we all think he had better learn to work with the staff; that applies to everything from what he teaches the students to the way he puts on his surgery cap."

"I don't suppose," I said slowly, "that anyone ever considers that the staff might learn to work with him."

I could feel Jason stiffen. "By George, Helen!" he cried loudly. "Would you suggest that we let a man his age, and of his experience, call the turns at the Center?"

"I suppose not," I agreed. "But I'll have to remind, you, Jason, that we've had to let him do it in the family."

"Now, what do you mean by that?"

"Oh, his getting David to go to school, to marry . . ."

"A proper mess he almost made of that!"

"But he did not make one. He forced David to get out on his own. And he and Isabelle seem very happy." I had just returned from a week's visit with them and my first grandchild, their adopted baby. They *were* happy!

"He's put us over the barrel a time or two," Jason growled.

"Yes, he has. When he ran away from home, when he moved out of our house — but that's working out, too, Jason. He should be on his own. I hope A.B. is ready to let Christine set up her own home. . . ."

"What will he do with that big house?"

"She'll come back to it someday. Especially if she has a family. But for now . . ."

We talked no more then about Grady.

In fact, I think the next family discussion of him was held at the post-mortem gathering of the McCords after Christine's wedding reception. We were tired and happy. I still felt myself to be A.B.'s hostess, and stayed on. The brothers were staying around to bolster A.B.

"We won't abandon him too soon," Jason told me.

"I'm going to take off my shoes, and you'll have to carry me home."

"We'll get you there," Grady promised me. "It was a beautiful wedding, Lady Vere de Vere."

It had been beautiful. I could relax in the corner of the couch and look at the flowers — pale yellow roses and white stock in golden vases. I could see through to the dining room where things were being cleared away by the caterers who had come in to help A.B.'s servants.

I felt, as A.B. must have, to have his family there together, a couple of the men smoking, all of them ready to loosen their cravats and talk to each other amicably. A bridesmaid had left her bouquet on a chair.

Shields came over to where I sat, bent over and kissed me. "It was a good wedding, Mom," he said. "No fights. Now I'm going home and change out of these striped pants and go to the hospital. Grady?" He turned. "You want to go with me?"

Grady sat in a fragile-looking Hepplewhite chair; against it he stretched his length, propping his heels on the rug, his neck on the chair back. "I'd better stay here," he said. "There are always fights at the hospital."

"There can be," Shields agreed, walking toward the dining room. He came back with his left hand filled with puff pastries and little sandwiches. "Dinner," he told us, going toward the front door.

"It will be a lucky girl who'll marry him," said A.B.

"He'll do the marrying," Grady said. "If ever."

"He's certainly doing a fine job with his burn center," Jason said. "His only trouble is to get more money and more space. The things they do with the badly burned! You wouldn't believe it, Helen."

"I'd believe anything of Shields," I said contentedly. "He does things with silver, doesn't he? New dressings, new techniques — he explained it to me one time."

"And he does it without fighting, too," drawled Joe.

Grady laughed. "I'll agree there should be more men like him," he said languidly. "How'd we ever get him in the family?"

"The big question is," said his Uncle Joe, "how were we lucky enough to get *you?*"

Grady laughed again and sat up. "Now, you know . . ."

"I know this," said Joe rather truculently, I

thought, "that we have a right to say almost anything to you, Grady. Because of the fact that when people – the public, yes, and the profession, too – read the stuff you write, and hear the things you say, they decide at once that you are pointing your finger at your family."

"Oh, but . . ." objected Grady, then he sat thoughtful. "You wouldn't want them to think, I suppose, that the McCord family was pointing its finger?"

"You suppose right," said Lucian firmly.

Grady nodded. "I guess some people do think, when I offer constructive criticism . . ." His father snorted, and Grady's lips quirked. "I guess they do think, or may think, that I am pointing at the family. But the hospital knows different. Look." He sat forward on the edge of his chair. "I go to the big health centers in New York, Washington – I look at dozens of hospitals. I take many, many trips. You know that I do, and our colleagues at the Center know it."

We did know it, and the hospital knew it. Of course.

I ran a finger along the pattern of lace over my knee. "But the things you say can still embarrass the family, Grady."

"I don't see that, Mother. I mean, I don't see why they should."

"If the patients think you are writing about your family . . ."

"But there's no need for them to think so. Patients, you see, generally are not fools. That's a point I have difficulty selling a lot of the time. But I firmly believe they are not idiots. They read, yes. They read the stuff I get published. They note the things I object to, but if they do not see the things I object to happening in our hospital, if they don't see Dad letting a nurse do a doctor's work, if the p.g.'s hear Joe and Bish caution against the introduction of any new drug during their pregnancies – just as I write about, and they read about – they don't think I am writing about the McCords."

"I hope we can keep doing the things you think we should do," said Lucian sourly.

"Sir," said Grady, "I am not worried one bit about the things you do. So, just go on keeping your noses clean, and stop worrying about me."

"You'll worry yourself when your first lawsuit falls on you," said his father.

"Oh, Jason . . ." I protested.

"I expect to be sued," said Grady. "That's why I've made friends with Henry Tibbs."

"I suppose you know you're joking," said A.B. "Nobody makes friends with Tibbs. Not in that sense."

I thought he was wrong. I believed, of all the people on the earth, Henry loved Grady.

But then I thought, too, that Grady probably would never need the friendship of a lawyer like Henry.

It is dangerous to have such positive thoughts. In any big family, a mother should learn not to overvalue a period of calm. She should never say, "Things should settle down now. There's nothing about to happen." Because it always does happens and sooner than later, usually.

It was not long at all after Christine's wedding that Grady found himself needing Henry — or some lawyer.

It was not really hot weather on the afternoon that Grady came back to his rooms in the Paradis carriage house and found Sammy Bacquillon sitting in his long chair, a can of beer in his hand, and evidence that he had prepared some sort of meal and eaten it. He was well established. He wore one of Grady's knit shirts, he had his shoes off and was watching TV.

Grady stopped at the stair head. "What the devil . . . ?" he cried. "How did you get in here?"

The slender man smiled. "I am Sammy Bacquillon, captain," he said, his voice oily, the words sliding greasily from his tongue.

"I know damn well who you are!" cried Grady. "What I want to know . . ."

"Why I am here? Oh, that is simple, captain. My mother saved your life one time. I helped her. We know you are doing well — as we are not. We see your name in the newspapers, the magazines; we know your brother. Oh, yes! We know *him* very well!"

Grady frowned. His brother. Which . . . ? Abe in New York? David in Tucson? June — June, for a year, had been going about, following causes. Humphrey was on a ship in the Pacific. . . .

"Get out!" said Grady.

"Oh, captain. You have forgotten my mother?"

Grady would never forget this young man's mother.

"She did many things for you," said Sammy. "Things I too know about and could tell. . . ."

"Don't threaten me, you little . . ." He stopped short from using the word. This Sammy. He had been a thin little boy. He was a thin, small man, built on wire. His skin was the color of used leather, his black hair hung down the back of his neck. His eyes were — mean. He had a large mouth, with a square, undercut jaw.

"I don't want to dirty my hands," said Grady, "but if you don't leave, I'm going to throw you out. And I mean that, don't doubt me." He must have towered, there in the low-ceilinged room, above that small man.

But the small man only smiled at him.

255

"Assault, too," he said thoughtfully.

Afterwards, Grady said that was when he began to be afraid. He picked up the telephone, then he put it down. He would go in person. Sammy already had, probably, explored every inch of the apartment and stolen what he wanted to steal.

Grady ran the length of the street and burst into our house. "Shields still upstairs?" he asked me as he went through the hall. He and his brother had come home from the hospital together.

I could only watch him as he raced up the stairs.

They came down again, at once. "Don't worry, Mother," Grady told me as he passed me.

"I'll tell you all about it," Shields promised.

And they were out through the front door. "Don't run," I heard Shields say. "You can tell me as we go down the street."

Their heads disappeared beyond the hedge at Bishop's. I could only stand and clasp my hands, gone icy-cold. I had not seen Grady so frightened since David's polio attack.

I wanted to follow the boys. When Jason came in and I told him, I said that I wanted to follow them. Something had happened — or was happening!

Jason would not let me go. "You know you

can trust Shields. If Grady had the sense to come get him — Probably Lizzie's had an attack or something —"

"He'd phone; he wouldn't leave her."

Jason agreed, but he still said we couldn't go down to Grady's apartment.

I could only sit tensely, or walk about the house tensely, until someone would tell me what was going on.

Shields too saw at once that his brother was frightened. "I never thought I'd see the day," he told us afterward.

Grady told Shields that he had found Sammy there; he reminded Shields who he was. His mother, Kim Bacquillon — Baggy — had effected Grady's escape from North Korea. It was Sammy who had found him on the mountain top. Sammy was a worm, he told his brother. "And there he was. He'd made himself at home."

"Why did he go to the apartment?"

"My name and address is in the phone book. Lizzie told him he could wait. I suppose he had no trouble forcing the lock. He must have been there an hour or more. He had eaten crackers, cheese — stuff. He indicated that he could blackmail me through one of my brothers. . . ."

"Which one? June?"

"He didn't say. I don't know where he came

from. But I'm going to beat him up, Shields. And I wanted to have a witness that I was justified."

"Me?" asked Shields.

"I'll let you see him and talk to him. Maybe you'll do the beating."

"What you need is a lawyer," said Shields. "Let's stop and get Tibbs."

"Oh, now, look. Henry couldn't even get up the stairs. He's old, with a bad heart."

"Yes," said Shields. "But I wish you'd told me to bring my lead pipe and brass knuckles."

Later, Shields told us what happened, and there was fear in his face, too. And I had *never* seen Shields frightened before.

Sammy, he told us, was a really awful man. He really was. "Somehow, to come up into Grady's rooms. There was a bowl of popcorn on the table, and a checker game half played – somehow that sticks in my mind. And to have this slimy little man – he can't weigh a hundred and twenty five. He's like a piece of old string. Or no! He's like one of those fishing worms that come out after a rain – the sun catches them on the sidewalk, and they dry up. That's what Sammy is like. Except for his eyes. They are big and wet-looking. Dark, of course.

"He had on this yellow shirt – too big for him. And he just sat there and grinned at us. And told us what he wanted.

"It was blackmail, of course, of the rawest kind. He would tell things. He said he could prove things. What Grady had done while staying at his mother's brothel, his traitorous acts, and then – This really got to us. He brought up old Hump's name."

Old Hump is Humphrey, a year older than June. From the time he was an enchanting three, he has been "old Hump" to his brothers.

It seemed that Kim Bacquillon was now running a different sort of brothel in Tokyo. This was an establishment for homosexuals. Sammy told that she had been very kind to Humphrey because of Grady, that he had made it his headquarters, and brought other officers to the place. Sammy had pictures; he would give them to Grady for a price, of course. "A man has to live," he explained.

The boys insisted that they had not laid hands on him, but they finally persuaded him to leave.

"Then Grady tore into things, cleaning up. You'd have thought a septic section had just contaminated the place. I talked to him the best I could. For one thing, I knew we'd have to talk to you folks. And to Tibbs. So I wanted to get things straight."

Shields questioned Grady, and we questioned Shields. Was any part of what Sammy said true?

Grady had told again of how Kim Bacquillon had taken him in and had kept him — clinging to him, threatening him, using him. But no! The things Sammy said were not true. The things he suggested . . .

"Why did he come here at this time?" asked Jason. We were very troubled.

"He said that his mother had sent him. She was old and sick, and they needed money. Grady, he said, had money. He argued that Grady should share with the Bacquillons —"

I went all to pieces. I had always known, and said, that that woman meant trouble!

"But, Humphrey . . ." said Jason, worried.

"He says he has pictures of old Hump and his friends in the place this Baggy runs. Grady denied categorically that they could have pictures. He said old Hump would never have gone to such a place. . . . Only I stopped him cold by pointing out that they could have got to old Hump through Grady himself. And then he did collapse."

"Where is he now, Shields?"

"I left him sitting there at the table, moving checker counters around, and looking scared. I don't remember Grady ever looking that scared!"

"I'm going down there," said Jason.

"I'll go with you," I said quickly.

But the men wouldn't let me go. They

would do all they could to bring Grady back to our house. Let Sammy Bacquillon break in here! They would insist that Grady talk to Henry Tibbs. Yes, they thought that they could persuade him.

And they started off. I don't remember that we ate dinner at all that night. I do remember how frightened I was, because I was remembering how Grady, all his life, had done terrible things when he was scared — ridiculous things.

Like killing this Sammy Bacquillon.

Chapter 9

The men did something. I never knew exactly what. I suppose they brought Henry Tibbs in — and in some way they got rid of Sammy, if only temporarily. I asked if this meant they had given him money, and Jason shouted "No!"

"We are buying time," Shields told me. "We want some facts on this matter."

"What kind of facts?"

"Well, where old Hump is, or has been. . . ."

"I've had letters."

"We are using that."

"Did you see the pictures?"

"No. We'd like to set something up to catch him in the act of blackmail."

"Is Grady cooperating?"

I remember the way Jason and Shields looked at each other.

"I'm worried for fear Grady —" I began.

"We're worried, too," Jason told me. "And we managed to show Grady that we were. He agrees he could do something violent. . . ."

"Tell him it would kill me."

"We are using some delicate blackmail on him," said Jason, and that was about all they would say about what they were doing.

It had to be that same week that June came home. The first thing his father said to him was to have his hair cut. "And get a shave."

June looked at me. I nodded. "You'd better, dear," I said.

And June did. I was glad to have him at home, but we had enough things to upset us just then, without June —

He got himself into something like an acceptable appearance and dress. He was thin. Whatever he had been doing this past year, he'd been making his own way. We'd had a post card or two. He had wired me flowers at Christmas and on Mother's Day.

We managed to eat Saturday lunch together without any unpleasantness. No mention was made to June of Grady's worries. He had asked for Grady, and was surprised to know where he was living.

"I'll go down and see him."

He did go, midafternoon, and found Grady writing a letter to Humphrey.

This part, you will understand, I have to piece out from things Grady and June told me afterward.

June came up into the apartment, and Grady was surprised to see him. "I thought you were

263

peace corpsing or something. Expected you to come home with a beard."

"Dad made me shave it off."

This made Grady laugh. "Make yourself at home," he told June. "I want to finish this letter, get it down to the hotel box so it will go out by evening."

June wandered around the apartment; Grady had done a good job with the old place and the oddments of furniture. Paint was his chief implement; the place was gay with red-painted floors, and walls done in shades of dusty pink, dull blue – even green behind the shelves in the bedroom. His stuff was a hodgepodge. His one good chair was the black leather recliner and footrest where he had found Sammy sitting. But an old sofa, reupholstered, a couple of piano stools at the table, even a couple of camp stools and pillows made to fit the tops of some sturdy boxes – He had his fireplace, a free-standing one, with an aluminum pipe through a hole cut in the roof. Of course, that afternoon, no fire was desirable.

When Grady finished his letter, June suggested that he go along to the hotel to post it. Could they jog?

He rather expected Grady to object, but Grady fell into pace with him. They jogged to the hotel, and they jogged back, circling the entire course of Southshire, picking up an assortment of small boys, a few dogs, and two girls wearing Institute blazers.

Grady looked back over his shoulder at these. "I thought one might be Taylor," he told June.

"Taylor Falk? Are you crazy? She graduated from the Institute years ago. She must be in college, or married, or something."

Grady slowed his step, shaking his head. "I remember," he said, "but I don't realize. I went to her debut party — and she was Christine's maid of honor. Golly, she's a pretty girl! Let's go up to my place again. This old man needs a drink, and I'll give you one, just to be sociable."

They went up to the apartment, and Grady opened beer. June took over the long chair, and Grady let him stay there. "Since you're company." He sprawled on the couch, closing a couple of books to get them out of his way.

He looked at June. "What are you doing?" he asked.

"Oh, a bit of charity office work, some urban renewal jobs . . ."

"Get paid?"

"Enough to eat and sleep. Not well, I'm afraid."

"June . . ."

"I know. I should settle down. That's what I came home for. To talk to you about it."

"Me?" Grady sat up straight.

"Well, as I say, we've been in the

265

same boat a time or two."

"I can't remember," said his brother.

June ignored this. He'd had enough knocks that his shell was tough. "You'll recognize similarities in this idea I have," he said. "Because, you see, I came home to ask your advice about what I would need to do to get into medical school."

Grady groaned. He stared at his brother June, and he groaned again. "Not that, June," he begged. "Please not that!"

"But," said June, "I think it will please Dad, don't you?"

He talked quite a bit about his idea, and Grady sat looking at him in dismay. He got up once to get two more cans of beer, and he came back, still dismayed. This June — He listened. He recognized that he was feeling about this idea of June's exactly as the whole family would feel.

June would fail, as sure as God made little green apples.

He had the brains, but not the stick-to-itiveness which the study of medicine required. And if he failed — if he made one of his famous bloopers — he would embarrass everyone — including Grady. That's when the thing hit him. He, Grady — the don't-give-a-damn boy, was ready to prevent such embarrassment at any cost. Oh, no! June must not do this!

"That's when I joined the older generation," Grady told us later. "And the responsibility of it scared me half to death. There I sat, with my second can of beer, and June kept on talking. He felt he owed it to the family, he said. 'I've been a pretty terrible creep. I've worried the family. I know that. And I should start as soon as I can, and the best way I can, to come back into the family pattern.' "

"But you don't have to — Look, you've already gone to school longer than is normal, June. The study of medicine — it's *work* — hard work."

"You did it — when you were older than is customary."

"The reasons were different. Besides, I'm me, June. I love medicine. I had always planned to study it. It was what I could do, and did do. But you —" He could only sit and shake his head.

"And feel a hundred years old," he told us.

"I'd stick with this," June insisted.

"I'll bet you would . . ." said Grady sadly.

"But — don't you want me to do this, Grady?"

"No!" Grady shouted. "The thought of your starting scares me to death. And if you stick with it — There are enough poor doctors in the world. Don't do this, June. Don't *do* it!" He *was* scared.

"When you did it," said June, "everyone thought it was wonderful."

Everyone had not. There had been doubts there, too — doubts which Grady had only this minute begun to comprehend. "This would be different," he said slowly.

"How?" asked June, beginning to look stubborn.

"Well, we're different — you and I. When I said I wanted to study medicine, there was not any loud applause. But the family accepted it because, whatever mistakes I've made, I always knew where I was going. You, June — your plans go nowhere."

And June, in his naive way, said, "You really disapprove of the plan, don't you?"

Grady shook his head. "Sometimes I run out of words," he murmured. He drained his beer can, then leaned toward his brother. "Look, June," he said, "isn't there something else you could do? Isn't there something you really want to do?"

"I thought I wanted to study medicine."

"But you're not fired up about it. And medicine is a long, hard row to plow, June." He could see June committing every error, tragic and comic, which had been invented by all the student and novice doctors before him, Grady McCord among their numbers. Only — "This project would take years and years. I don't know if you even could qualify to enter medical school."

"I could try. And if I once started, Grady, I'll promise you to stay with it."

"Isn't there something else?" Grady asked again.

"Well, yes," said June. "As a matter of fact, there is. Though I don't know how the family would react to one of us in show business. . . ."

Grady stiffened. "Show business? What kind of shows?"

"I thought," he said afterward, "of medicine shows, and I'm glad I didn't say *that!*"

He didn't, and June went on to tell of some auditions he had done for TV. When he'd been doing his city-renewal work, he'd often been on local newscasts. He had a resonant speaking voice; someone mentioned that, and suggested that he do these auditions.

Grady looked at him obliquely. "For a doctor part?" he asked dubiously. "Ben Casey? Dr. Kildare?"

June took it as a joke. "No-o," he said. "That wasn't the part offered. Someday I might make it, however."

"Would you like TV work? Would you be good at it?"

"I think so. This thing requires some singing, and I can sing."

"You sure can. Then — why the devil all this

talk about medical school?"

"I was thinking of the family."

Grady looked at him. "And you thought . . ."

"I *didn't* think they'd want a McCord in show business."

"Why not? If you'd be good, they'd be proud of you."

June looked more cheerful.

"Are you good?" Grady asked him.

"I told you. I can sing —"

"Yes," Grady agreed. "And you have a dimple. So I'd say, take the job, June. And be good at it!"

Both boys told me about their conversation, with different coloring to the experience, of course. Grady was right. June did seem relieved not to have to study medicine in order to please the McCords. At the time, I didn't think too much about Grady's surprise at his newly discovered family conscience. At the time I was realizing that our house again would contain but one son. And Shields is so quiet, keeps so busy, that even I can forget he is here.

Though I never truly do forget. Shields is a great rock on which to lean. And we needed him those days. Jason, Shields, and I — and especially Grady — were all living under the shadow of Sammy Bacquillon.

He would give us a week, he had said. But

Shields and Grady had very little idea of what to do in that week.

"Are you afraid that what he said about Humphrey is true?" I asked them.

"He's been away from home; we never know. . . ."

For some reason, Jason had not talked to his brothers about this development. I expected him to. But he did not.

He didn't tell the rest of us not to mention it. It was just one of those situations where you are so disturbed, so frightened, really, that you don't talk about the matter — not even to one another.

We were glad that June didn't stay very long; he was gone by the first of the week. June was just naturally a well-meaning bungler. And he would have thought he could do something; he couldn't, and we were relieved to see him depart before we had to handle Sammy.

Shields drove him to the airport and came back to say he was sure that at least three of us had given June money.

"Four," I said.

The men looked at me, then at each other, and laughed.

"He needs clothes," I excused myself.

"I hope, for your sake, he makes good at this."

"I believe he will. June has always lived in a world of make-believe. If he can find that sort of job . . ."

"Fair enough," said Shields. "Grady was right. He would not have made a good medic."

"He thought he might — because Grady did."

"Oh, but he isn't Grady!"

"Now what do you mean by that?"

"Just what I said. Grady's going to be the most brilliant of the Doctors McCord. Isn't he, Dad?"

"I suspect you're right, Shields."

I was puzzled. "Any of you —"

"Any of us could be, Mother. But Grady has a faculty born into him. We might acquire it. I'm trying. But Grady, of himself, thinks only, and first, of the patient. Not the comfort or efficiency of the doctor, not the easy way for the hospital personnel to conduct things, but the new bed, the new way of serving meals, the new hospital shirt — will the patient like it, be comfortable with it, and get well? The heck with the laundry and what it thinks of hospital shirts! You have to iron the wrinkles out because of the *patient!* Isn't that right, Dad?"

Jason was smiling. "It's right," he said. "And I sit in staff meetings and seek to mollify the chief of nursing services, and the administrator — and I talk to them, listen to their ideas — and all the time I know. Grady is right. There should be no wrinkles in a hospital shirt. Literally and figuratively.

"If a technique or a procedure makes things easier for the doctor, that's good. But it is not to be used unless it makes things better for the patient, too!"

"Grady argues that?"

"He says that. And who dares argue with him? Oh, Helen, Helen — that boy. He's taking science right out of the hospital and putting the human being back! Shields is right. It takes a brilliant man to move mountains."

"But he still won't have an office," said Shields.

Jason chuckled. "Except for that little glass cubicle overlooking one of the operating rooms. He might as well still be a resident. I've offered him a place in my office. He and Shields could open one in the Tower."

"Do you have an office?" I asked Shields.

He smiled at me. "I have a cubby, too, up on the floor near the burn center. But since I do, and can do, other sorts of skin disorders, grafting, things like that — burns of all sorts, initial treatment and subsequent — I probably should go into something like a practice."

"Every doctor on the staff would welcome you."

"They would welcome Grady," Shields answered his father.

"I'd think Grady would belong in an office with his father," I decided. "They are both surgeons. . . ."

"Did you ever talk to your son," Jason asked me, "on the subject of doctors' offices?"

Like any father, he hands his sons to me when he is in disagreement with them or about them. I waited for him to expand the subject.

"He sounds off," Shields told me. "Where do we start, Dad?"

"Answering services," said Jason. We were sitting out on the terrace after dinner. We didn't have any lights, but the city streets beyond the hedge a hundred feet or so away gave us illumination.

"Yes," Shields agreed. "Answering services. Grady won't have one. If he had an office, he'd have to have one or be on twenty-four-hour call."

"Oh, he couldn't do that," I said quickly.

"He couldn't," Jason agreed. "But he'd think he should try. He gave me hell a week or so ago —"

"Jason . . ."

"He did, Helen."

"And you took it?"

"Well, Grady has this maddening way of being enough right — let me tell you. You see, I had this patient. She's not young — a woman in her seventies. I operated on her. No matter for what. It was abdominal. I sent her home and talked to her daughter about things to do

274

and to expect. I said that if difficulties seemed to go beyond that, she could get in touch with me or bring her mother back to the hospital; that's routine. Well, of course, a complication did arise. At night, naturally. The daughter called my office number — they live in the suburbs, by the way — the answering service told her that I was unavailable, that my office hours were so and so —"

"Grade calls it letting the telephone get between the doctor and the patient," said Shields quietly.

"What did the poor woman do? The daughter."

"Well, she tried to get other doctors. She said she knew she couldn't get a house call, but if she could just talk to someone . . ."

"I think Grady's right."

"Of course he's right. That's what we're telling you. He's too often right, though the possibilities of what he thinks must be done . . . Anyway, the daughter finally got an ambulance and brought her mother in. Grady handled the matter the next morning and gave me hell at noon. He thought both women should have had their fears allayed the night before."

"Was it something serious?"

"Not really. But —"

"The disaster was to the patient-doctor relationship."

"I'm afraid you're right," said my husband. "Though I am not an unfeeling man."

Of course he was not. But he was a good surgeon, and time and strength were both exhausted before he could answer all the calls made upon him during a long day.

"Does Grady make house calls?"

"He'd answer emergencies if he had an office. Now, within the hospital, he does assigned surgery and clinic referrals."

"What would he consider good office practice in his line?" I asked.

"Oh, he sounds off on that, too. At least six doctors in offices together. Common recourse to files and records. After-hour calls rotated among the six, and cared for."

"But that does sound possible."

"It is possible for some men," said Jason. "I could join such a group if I were not Chief of Surgery at the Center."

"I see."

"I don't give up my individual patients, and I do the best I can for them."

"Grady knows that."

"Humph!" said Grady's father.

"Then," said Shields brightly, "I think Mother would like to hear his opinion of the God-complex which we doctors acquire."

"He once wrote something about that," I said. "Lucian said it hit home."

"It does hit home. We doctors do patronize our patients. Sometimes it is, again, a matter of time. We simply cannot sit down and carefully explain to an unsophisticated person the intricacies of — say — leukemia or meningitis or — But it is true that we should make one good honest attempt to explain. We should *talk* to our patients. Instead of being arrogant upon our pedestals of degrees and Board certifications, hospital appointments and plush offices, we should give that patient understanding, sympathy, and a right to participate in the treatment which we are advising."

"Grady says frustration keeps some patients from getting well," said Shields.

"I suppose it could," I agreed. "Why do the doctors . . . ?"

"Oh, there are reasons. Some men are naturally secretive and draw their godlike power about them. Some men are just inarticulate, Helen. Others don't respect the patient's intelligence."

"What does Grady suggest?"

"Well, he thinks our hospital staff doctors must be impressed — he begins with the interns and ends up with me — must be impressed with our duty. . . ."

"Absolute duty," put in Shields.

"That's right," said Jason. "Our *absolute* duty to get the facts, to analyze them, make our decisions, and *then* to communicate the situation to the patient in a way which he can understand. After that, *he* has the absolute duty to decide what is to be done with his body."

"But —"

"Ideally, yes, that is what happens. Actually, not always. I myself have heard doctors say — again from interns to staff chiefs — 'Don't question me. I know more than you do on the subject.'

"Grady says he writes his articles and books to prove to the patient that he can know a few things, too. He encourages that."

"He does seem to be right a lot of the time, Jason," I murmured.

"Of course he seems to be. Because he is right! Damnably right. We doctors *are* losing the human aspect of medicine — which we should not do."

"Is there a solution?"

"Watch Grady," said my husband. "He's full of ideas."

"I hope he comes up with something for Sammy Bacquillon," Shields grumbled.

"Has he heard from him again, Shields?"

"Not yet. But he will."

"I hope Grady tells us."

"I think he will, Dad, but I'm keeping in touch."

"Good. You do that. Has he any plans?"

"Beyond wringing Sammy's neck, I don't think so."

That night a full moon was overhead, and little breezes blew. Two nights later it was stormy. Lightning slashed the sky, thunder roared and rolled, and rain fell in sheets.

Grady had spent the evening with us; Bishop had dropped in from next door. Shields was reading while we played bridge. If Bishop had been brought in on the matter of Sammy, we might have discussed it. The week's grace was all but expired.

But it was just a cozy, domestic scene, lamp-light and safety, with the elements tearing up things beyond the walls of our house.

We all groaned when Orlie came to tell Grady that there was a telephone call for him. "Did you bring your car with you?" Shields asked. "That's a doctor summons, if I ever heard one."

"He always leaves his number," said Jason. "It's sure to be a hospital call."

The call had indeed come through the hospital. We all listened frankly while Grady talked into the phone in the hall.

"It's a patient . . ." Shields confirmed.

We listened.

"Just where do you live?" we heard Grady say.

His hand over the receiver, he came to the

doorway. "Where's Auburn? Nine thirty-five?"

"North of there," said his father. "Six blocks or ten. It's come to be the worst slum in town."

If you live in a large city in these times, the slums quickly encroach. I could remember when Auburn was a pleasant little street off the Boulevard, with trees, flower boxes on the window sills. Lately it was littered and rundown, with few attempts at neatness and decency.

"What's your problem?" Bishop asked Grady. He dealt the cards with the sure dexterity of a surgeon using his hands.

"A girl — a woman. I removed an ovarian cyst from her a while ago. She seems to be hemorrhaging."

"Don't go," said Bishop and Grady's father in one breath.

"I have to go," said Grady.

"Not to the house. Tell her to go to the hospital emergency room."

"Sammy could be up to tricks," Shields murmured in his father's ear. I shivered. I don't know why he connected the two things, but I was ready to accept his doing so.

Grady had taken the phone back into the hall. Bishop stood up. "I'll get Joe," he said.

"And a policeman," advised Shields.

Bishop's eyes flared. "What goes on here?"

"Let's go out the side door. I'll tell

you. I'll be back, Mom."

"Not if —"

"They'll take care of things," Jason told me.

Grady came to the doorway. He was getting into his raincoat. "I'm going to the hospital," he said.

"Take my car," I offered.

"I'll get mine," said Grady. "There can't be all that hurry."

Jason's warning hand on my knee made me keep still.

"Will you call the police, Dad?" Grady was asking. "Tell them to go to nine thirty-five Auburn. A bleeding woman to be taken to e.r. I'll meet 'em."

"It will work out," Shields told us when he came back. "I told Bish about Sammy, and he thinks this is a setup of some kind." He shook his wet head. "Of course we haven't yet figured how Sammy would get hold of this woman. Grady said she was a former patient."

"Could we give a little to luck and coincidence there?" Jason asked. "If Sammy has been staying in this district. Grady had something of his quoted in the newspaper yesterday. Perhaps this girl was in a bar, or at a gathering, and said Oh, she knew that Dr. McCord. Sammy saw his chance and set the thing up. She — or someone — called. Grady's home phone didn't answer. So he called the hospital, and —"

"He's after a lawsuit," said Shields. "Malpractice. If Grady had refused to go, he'd have an abandonment. If he would go to her home, abortion. Sammy may still think he can get that, even if Grady meets the girl in e.r."

"He's going to meet her there."

"Yeah, but Uncle Bish and Uncle Joe will, too."

And that's the way it was. Grady got his car and drove it to the hospital. He parked and ran to e.r., getting there just as the police cruise car came up with the young woman. But before he could meet the stretcher, two tall men, grave-faced, stern-faced, stepped ahead of him. "Allow me, doctor," said Bishop McCord.

"Will you hold the door, doctor?" said Joseph McCord.

Grady's jaw dropped. Then — "I can handle this!" he cried.

"We are handling it."

They did handle it — with plenty of witnesses, including the driver of the police car. Grady was there; a resident on duty examined the patient; it was decided that the hemorrhaging was superficial and could await clinical decision the next day.

There was no sign of Sammy Bacquillon.

"But we could smell the guy," a subdued Grady told us when he came back to the house.

"Where are Bish and Uncle Joe?"

"Home, we suppose. It's after ten."

Grady sat down heavily in a chair. "I'm not half as smart as I sometimes think I am," he told us.

"No," agreed his father.

"They knew what to do. How'd Bish guess?"

"*I* guessed, Grady. I have been expecting something of this sort. You should have expected it. And on the medical side."

"I've been expecting a mugging – something like that."

"You're most vulnerable as a doctor," Jason told him soberly.

Grady sighed. "Evidently. Well, I'm glad you caught this."

"It's the sort of thing a doctor learns from experience – to smell a trap."

"You had this one spotted," Grady admitted. "That girl, the patient, met up with Sammy, and –"

"A-hah!" said Jason. "And along that line, I'll give you another tip. In these setups, women are most often involved."

"We feel sorry for 'em." Grady sat thoughtful. He accepted the drink which Shields brought to him, but he did not taste it. "Those two," he said thoughtfully, wonderingly. "There. Stepping in. Uncle Joe and Bish. Their faces were as calm, their manners perfect. Everything ethical. 'Will you hold the door, doctor?' " He roused and sat erect. "You can't get your head in a noose holding a hospital door! At least ten people watched me do it. Whereas, if I'd gone to that house . . ."

"We wouldn't have let you go."

Grady looked at his father, then he nodded. "I guess not. But I did admire those two – No. Respect is the word. I couldn't have been so calm. I would have got mad. In fact, I did get mad."

"You were frightened."

Grady drank some of the highball. "Yeah," he said. "Scared. I'm still scared, Dad."

"We'll handle this."

"How can we? If old Hump is involved – There's his career in the Navy."

"That's true. If Humphrey were involved."

"Sammy said he was. And now. . ."

"Now he can't touch us through Humphrey. He doesn't have any authentic pictures, Grady. He couldn't have."

"He claims he does. He says he'll show them to me. . . ."

"When he sells them to you?"

"Yes, I suppose."

"Remember, you had a witness to that conversation. He mentioned certain dates?"

"In a general way, yes, he did."

"Mhmmmn. Well, Humphrey could not

284

possibly be involved, Grady."

"How do you know?"

"Would you take the Pentagon's word?"

Grady laughed. "You guys . . ."

"Yes. We did get in touch. Dates, times, places. Your brother . . ."

"Tell him," said Shields. "Tell him his brother is in the Navy. His name has been appearing on certain lists, news items, fleet newspapers. But not on those dates, actually. You see, Grade, we learned today that old Hump has been doing some highly secret, electronic investigative work. He moves about."

Grady put up his hand. "Don't tell me. I'm shook up enough. Maybe Sammy — Could he think we'd tell him this?"

"I don't know how clever, or devious, your Sammy is. I think it will be enough just to say you are not interested in his pictures. After tonight —"

"Yeah," said Grady. "After tonight."

He said he was shaken, and he looked shaken. We all were sorry for him. "I'll have the guy picked up," he said at last, "if he ever comes around me again."

"And gives you legal justification," his father agreed.

I was not inclined to let him go this time. It was Grady who persuaded me. "The only reason I was so damned scared," he told us, "was because of the family — what the things he threatened could do to them. I didn't think straight because of that fear. It paralyzed me."

His family.

"I was afraid . . ." I began.

He glanced at me. "I know, Lady Vere de Vere. But again I was stopped cold by the thought, the realization, of what it would do to all of you if I would kill that slimy snake."

I never loved my son Grady so much as I did that night.

Grady called his Uncles Bishop and Joe to thank them for coming to his aid that evening. Joe said he thought Lucian and A.B. should know what had been going on.

"I'll tell them."

"Maybe we could get them all over at your house. . . ."

They all came, and the men talked until midnight — a real family conference.

When Jason came up to bed — I'd arranged for sandwiches, fruit, coffee, drinks, and taken my leave — I asked my husband if he thought Grady would now settle down.

"Settle down to what?" asked Jason, checking on the next day's clothes which I had set out for him.

"Well — respectability, I suppose, would be a word."

Jason chuckled. "Of course he won't, Helen.

And I for one hope he doesn't. Respectable people aren't much fun." He went into the bathroom and the shower roared.

"Is Grady fun?" I asked when he came out again.

He looked at me as if I'd lost my senses. "You said —"

"Oh, yes. Well, no, Grady isn't always fun. For one thing, he too often kicks my shins."

"Oh, Jason."

"I have the scars to prove it."

"But he shouldn't. . . ."

"Well, now maybe he should."

"I am sure he admires you. And he must know that he has so much to learn from you."

"I often think he is the teacher, Helen." He opened a window; the air smelled fresh from the rain. He turned off the lamp and got into bed, groaning as he always did when he stretched out. "He's good, Helen," he said. "A good doctor. Better than I am."

"Oh, no!" I protested quickly.

My husband chuckled. "Well, yes, he is," he told me. "Now, listen to me. He is not the experienced technician that I am. Maybe he's not. That is something which takes years to acquire, and it is my chief quality. But Grady is a *good* doctor — in every sense of the word. He thinks always and first of the patient. The patient is his main interest. Technique, new drugs — new approaches to a disease — everything is considered from its application to the patient and his welfare. That is his preoccupation, along with the teaching of good young doctors. There is Grady's campaign. He really cracks down on the youngsters, Helen. Beginning in medical school, and intensified through intern and resident training, he insists on their learning and doing."

"How do the young men . . . ?"

"Oh, they respect him. Not at first, of course. They try all the old tricks — but he's young enough, and good enough, that they come to accept his rules, and before we know it, we have a class of glittering stars. Or as near to that as the teachers can produce. Grady has come pretty near, at that, because the other teaching doctors don't dare set their sights much lower than his. They complain that he makes 'em work harder."

"Does he?"

"Not in the long run. Eventually the students, the interns, the residents are doing so much better work themselves — it balances out."

"What does the staff itself think of him? I know, for a while there —"

"Yes. And they still think he is a gadfly — which he is. He sticks his buzzer into everything, and attacks everything, from the smell of

288

food in the halls to the whole medical system."

I let Jason talk. The evening had him keyed up. Talking to me let him unwind. Within half an hour he would sleep.

"He attacks the hospitals," Jason was saying. "He throws our men the sop of agreeing that the university-affiliated, the voluntary hospitals are better, then he accuses us of freezing out the G.P. and driving patients to the proprietary, private hospitals. Distance does this, too, he claims. When people move to the suburbs, they find themselves a long way from the Medical Center, so private hospitals are set up in the suburbs, and used."

"I suppose Grady has some solution . . ."

"Oh, yes. We should educate the public to the need for proper accreditation and supervision of all hospitals. We should make them want, and support, voluntary hospitals, not giving a group of doctors the excuse to set up a private institution."

"Aren't there laws on accreditation?"

"Not enough laws, not good enough laws, not strictly enforced laws. Grady has a great deal to say on what *is* a ridiculous phrase. Which is *minimal standards for accreditation.* He claims there should be no *minimal* anything in the care of patients. He says accreditation is only the beginning of the change in hospitals necessary if the best possible care and safety are to be provided."

"Don't get excited, dear . . ." I murmured.

"No, I won't. But Grady gets excited – on that and other subjects. He is particularly talkative on the subject of individual doctors, and what they do and do not do for the patients."

"I don't see how he has any friends."

For a minute or two Jason was silent. I hoped he would go to sleep.

"Grady has admirers," he said then, speaking slowly. "But friends . . . among the doctors – well, that would come with some agreement, I suppose. He is so – so dedicated, Helen."

"Yes, dear."

"The other day, at a staff meeting, old Harry Sanders – he's older than I am, and that's *old* – attempted a fatherly protest to Grady, pointing out that, as a young doctor, he could go far. And do you know what Grady said to him?"

I was afraid to ask.

"He said, 'Sir, I *have* gone far.' "

I worried about Grady, though I was proud of him. What Jason had said about his having admirers – I too wished he had more friends, in the sense that a young man should operate in a group. But some of my worry was through my wish that he would act more *young* – that he would even do some foolish things. Certainly he could be gay. Of course he did have friends, of a sort. He and Bishop were friends. He and Shields got along wonderfully well, which was good for him. He and Taylor Falk were friends. I didn't know exactly how much they saw of each other. But a word or two was said; I'd even seen them together. One night at the Symphony in the outdoor arena, once in Grady's car — that was a Sunday afternoon. I'd seen them talking; the girl would come over to play croquet. And she and Grady would squabble in a way that had to be protected by friendship.

Maybe I could do something . . .

When I was asked to be a sponsor for the Royal Ballet troupe, I had what I considered to be a fine idea. I talked about it to Taylor and to Bishop. Oh, yes, they agreed, that would be fun.

"I thought Grady might enjoy it," I explained.

"If he comes . . ." said Bishop.

"Wouldn't he want to?"

"I'm sure he would want to. The thing is —"

I knew what the thing was. If something required his presence at the hospital, he would not be with us. I urged Taylor to entice him to think our affair would be at least as important.

She laughed at me. "I'm not an enticer, Mrs. McCord."

"You are better than you think," I assured

her. "Who else ever got Grady to jump rope with him?"

"All right, then, I'll try. Are your dancers coming?"

"They are. And a good list of interested guests. In fact, people are asking me for invitations."

"I'm glad I am included."

"As an enticer," I teased her.

She was better at that than she would admit. She was a lovely young woman. Her mother and father said they were happy to have her at home; she was doing some work at a psychiatric clinic. She enjoyed tennis and golf. She went to some parties, and she told Grady that she very much wanted to come to mine. "Imagine your mother entertaining those wonderful dancers! What is she planning?"

"Mother likes people," said Grady. "And she just gets a bunch of them together, she'll have food, and vases filled with pretty flowers, and she'll clear some of the stuff out of the lower floor so that those who want to can dance, but she'll leave enough chairs so that they can sit and talk. You'll see."

"I hope I do. Will you take me?"

"You don't have to be *taken* to our house!"

"I do when the Royal Ballet is there."

He laughed. "I'll take you," he promised. "To the performance, too, if you like."

She told me that it was as easy as that. But I wasn't sure until they came into the seats beyond ours at the opera house, and until they showed up at the house afterward. Taylor was wearing a lovely dress of thin silk, the color of her green eyes, with little Jade pins holding her thick auburn hair behind her ears.

"Golly, she's pretty," Shields told me. "If Grady doesn't make time, I'm going to."

But Grady did "make time." Taylor glowed with pleasure.

The Ballet members enjoyed themselves. They ate enormously; they sat flat on the floor with their valuable legs extended before them. They danced with each other, and with the young guests. The modern, silly dances – the frug, or the – well, the names change so fast I can't name those they danced on that particular night. The two biggest-name stars sat in low, comfortable chairs and watched everything. They talked to me for a few minutes, the fine-drawn English woman wrapped in a chinchilla coat, and her fire-filled Russian partner. He wore tight black trousers, a silk brocade jacket, and a huge medallion hung on a thin chain about his neck. Jason asked them anatomical questions about their art, and I told the dark-haired woman how to make the tiny lemon tarts which she found delicious.

We watched the dancers in the wide hall. I

identified other McCord doctors. Bishop, Joe – his daughters – my son Shields, my son Grady . . .

"The beautiful one with the eye patch," said the star. "How was he hurt?"

"Being a hero," growled Grady's father.

"Oh, but that is tragic!"

"Not for Grady."

"No," said her partner. "See – the ladies notice him."

The ladies did. The young people did. The professional dancers were gay, nice people. Everyone was having a wonderful time.

Especially Grady. I was glad I had found a way –

Of course, not starting until after eleven, the party ran late. And I marveled at the endurance of the Ballet members. The women were all as thin as strings, their hair smooth, their eyes enormous – their legs not pretty, but certainly strong. The men were muscular, with slim hips, their hair a little long, their manners good.

"They have to be nice people," A.B. told me. "The discipline of their profession weeds out the other kind. They – *Oh, oh!*"

I glanced up, then followed his pointing finger.

And I too said, "Oh, oh!" For, coming up from the front door, her gray hair frizzled and wild upon her head, her scarfs fluttering, her embroidered silk shawl clutched closely about her, her feet stumbling in her foolish slippers, was Lizzie Paradis.

"Did you invite her?" A.B. asked me.

"No. Something's wrong."

Orlie was trying to take care of the woman. But, while it is difficult to upset Orlie's aplomb, he was really glad when A.B. and I came up behind him. "Madame . . ." he said helplessly.

"Thank you, Orlie. Lizzie! How nice to see you."

She looked at me, wild-eyed — vague-eyed. She looked at A.B. "Oh, Dr. McCord!" she breathed. "You're not Grady . . ."

"Let's take her into the cardroom," I murmured.

We tried to guide her. She couldn't see without her glasses. "I knew you were giving a party," she told me. "But the watchman said — Is Grady here?"

A.B. looked around for Orlie. "Get Grady," he said quietly.

We had got Lizzie into a quiet corner by the time Grady was found; he came quickly, sliding the last few feet on the waxed floor.

"What's up?" he asked, straightening his coat. His face was flushed and his hair tumbled. "Oh, hello, Baggie! I didn't know you were here."

"Something's wrong," A.B. told him.

Grady glanced at him, then back at Lizzie. Behind us the orchestra played, the young people danced and laughed and talked. The pink carnations and the daisies, the —

Grady put his hand on Lizzie's shoulder. "What's wrong, sweetheart?" he asked, his voice kind.

She looked up at him. *"You're* Grady!" she declared.

"Yes, sure. Did you want to see me?"

"Oh, yes," she said. "There was something . . ." Her poor old face wrinkled with her effort to remember.

"Something about the watchman," A.B. reminded her.

She smiled sunnily. "Yes!" she cried. "The watchman came for Grady — then he told me to find Grady — and —" she faltered — "and tell him to go to Mr. Tibbs' house," she concluded triumphantly.

Henry. Well, for years we had lived expecting word of that sort.

"Take care of Baggie," Grady told me, and he was out through the front door, running up the street in the windy moonlight.

He found the old man very ill, and said at once that he must go to the hospital. "I'll get an ambulance — have everything ready —"

"Can't," gasped poor Henry. "Lucian — Europe —"

Lucian was indeed in Europe.

"There are other doctors," Grady reminded him.

"I won't go," said Henry firmly — in time for Bishop to hear him say it. He had followed Grady as closely as he could. But no one could run as fast as Grady.

"What'll I do?" the younger man asked him.

"You'll take him to the hospital," said Bishop.

"Well, of course. The phone's across the hall."

They did take Henry to the hospital. The poor old man was so very sick. And Grady stayed with him. Bishop came back to tell us.

"He isn't going to make it this time."

"Now, Bish . . ."

"Henry knows he won't. Riding to the hospital, he asked Grady to empty his house."

"Did Grady . . . ?"

"He told him he'd burn it down."

"Now what sort of thing is that to say . . . ?"

"It's the way Grady has always talked to Henry. Of course it was the right thing."

I looked at Bishop in his handsome black-blue coat and his spotless linen. I thought of the way Grady had looked that evening.

"You must have made a stir in the hospital emergency room," I said foolishly. Grieving, one says foolish things.

Bishop knew that. "The nurses liked us," he said, kissing my cheeks. "Good night, Helen. It was a lovely party. You didn't have any leftover dancers, did you?"

"Weren't they lovely?"

By morning, Henry was dead.

It was a sad time. Grady took it rather strangely, we all thought. He kept asking why he should have died.

He'd had a bad heart for years, we reminded him; only the pacemaker had let him live so long.

"But why just *now?* Why didn't it go on letting him live?"

He'd ask that, and be answered by any one of the doctors to whom he was talking. Then he would ask it again.

Henry had left a will, remembering various "children" on the Place with money bequests. Shields was so remembered, and called a child. That shook him. To Grady went his residual estate, and the specific task of disposing of Henry's possessions. This prospect dismayed Grady.

For the first time he must set foot on the stairs of Henry's home and go fearfully up into the unknown territory above. And what he found . . . He walked, unbelieving, through the echoing, empty rooms. There was not a thing up there! His own footprints on the dusty floors showed that no one had been there for months or years!

Feeling very strange — "As if I were undressing poor old Henry," he told us later. "Taking off his high collar and the brown silk tie he wore, unbuttoning his shirt. That's no way for a guy like me to treat an old man I've always respected."

Feeling this way, he drove at once out to Henry's house in the country. This was a truly beautiful home, built of rock. Henry must have arranged for someone to keep the grounds in order. But inside —

The rooms were beautifully furnished. But no one had been in there for years. Carpet beetles had riddled the rugs, the upholstery was as fragile as tissue paper, the draperies rotted at the windows. No one, Grady thought, had ever lived in that house. No one had slept in the beds, or put food upon the dishes. Mice had even eaten the insulation from the oven of the stove in the kitchen. There was nothing of worth in the house except a safe — a sturdy, large safe, its door painted with a scene of mountains and a lake. It still showed the name of a "Mercantile Company."

Grady came back and went again through Henry's papers, searching for the combination of the lock. The attorney for the estate made a search. Eventually the safe had to be blown open.

"He'd been in there not too long ago," Grady told us. "Maybe twenty years. . . . There was tear gas between the inner and outer doors. That guy didn't trust anybody!"

"Was there anything in the safe?" his father asked.

"Yes, sir," said Grady, "there sure was. Diamonds — unset diamonds. The first estimate is that they are worth about sixty thousand dollars."

Jason whistled. "You're rich!"

"Not too very," said Grady. "There are the two houses. But only a very small bank account. He left bequests to a dozen kids — Shields, Taylor Falk, Joe's boy. You know about the will. Once those are paid . . ."

"But what happened to his money?" I asked. "I thought he made a good income."

"He should have," said Jason. "On retainers alone."

"We know where it went," said Grady. "For years and years and years he has been sending bank checks to a P.O. address in California."

"Could you trace them?"

"If we wanted to."

"Did he have a wife?" I asked wonderingly. Henry had never mentioned a wife.

"It couldn't be a wife," said Shields. "She would have a claim on the estate — if she was notified."

"A notice was sent to the post office address," said Grady. "But you do wonder . . ."

He wondered. He talked about Henry and the things about his life at which his death hinted. The country house, built, furnished, and never lived in.

"Could old Tibbs have had a romance?" he asked one evening.

"Yes," I said confidently. "I truly believe he did."

Grady smiled and shook his head. "Who'd think that old goat . . . ?"

"He wasn't always an old goat, Grady," said his father testily. "That's a thing you brash kids don't take into your consideration — or your calculations. That a man grows older, and sometimes wiser."

Grady nodded. "Yes, sir," he said. He sat thoughtful. "Those dusty, empty rooms in his house here," he mused. "They got to me. I decided that it was not good for a guy to be alone that way." He glanced up. "Like Bishop, even. Or me, with my silly old piano stools for chairs."

When we felt it safe, Jason and I exchanged raised eyebrows. If Grady had learned that lesson . . .

He kept wondering about Henry Tibbs. The old man's death and its revelations had shaken him in a way he thought strange, considering Grady's own brushes with death, and the fact that, as a doctor —

"Do you think," he asked us, "that old Henry committed suicide?"

"Oh, Grady!" I protested.

"Nonsense!" said his father.

"But how do you *know?*" Grady persisted.

"He died in the hospital. An autopsy was done. His heart just failed and stopped."

"Could it have been the pacemaker that failed?" asked Grady.

"It could have," Jason agreed. "Involuntarily, however."

"How do you know *that?*" Grady persisted. "How do you know it was involuntary?"

Jason looked at me. "Do you understand why the staff men at the hospital call this boy of yours a gadfly, Helen?"

I laughed. "He's been one since he could talk at all. The first word he ever said was 'why.' "

"I know. Followed by 'what,' 'where,' and 'when.' "

"Okay, okay," said Grady impatiently. "I still want to know if it is not possible, or reasonable, to think that Henry prevented the operation of the pacemaker?"

"And how would *you* know that?"

demanded his father.

Grady nodded. "That's right," he agreed. "I don't know it."

Shields got up from his chair. "I'm going to bed," he told us. "But first I have a word of advice for my younger brother."

I laughed.

"You never can tell, Mother," Shields said to me. "It may do some good."

"Try it and see," Grady urged him.

"Well, it's a simple thing. But you could try it. I just feel you'd do better to keep still on this whole matter of how Henry Tibbs died, and why."

Grady looked up. "Me?" he asked in innocent surprise. "Why, I wouldn't . . ."

"You would if you thought it could stir up some trouble," said Shields bluntly, "or cause a little excitement."

Grady started to say something — then his bright face crumpled before our unbelieving eyes. "Henry . . ." he said gruffly. "He used to chortle — you remember how he did — down in his Adam's apple. And he would shake his head and say, 'Think of a McCord a rebel!' "

"You think of it," said Shields. "I want to get some sleep."

Chapter 10

This was the day, the month, the year of medical Houdinis, of great daring, and even greater publicity about that daring. I would hear the men talk about transplants, and the wonder of rebuilding the human body, the marvels of prolonging life. They discussed the moral aspects of "playing God." They spent hours on the subject of the ethical values of euthanasia. They would follow some newspaper report of a "miracle" – monkey kidneys transplanted into a young girl. Then they would read and discuss the same matter as written up in their medical journals.

That year they did a lot of this sort of talk. Mary and I would knit, speak softly to each other, and hear only the rumble of the men's voices in another part of the room.

Eve, if present, always resented shop talk, and either she forced the men, unhappily, to speak of other things, or I, with Mary's help, would entice her out of earshot. We could do that by announcing the purchase of a new coat to be inspected, or the redecoration of a room.

I suppose the men discussed the publicity attendant on those miracle operations. I didn't particularly remember any such discussion, but I was well aware of the McCords' adherence to the code of keeping their names out of print concerning professional matters.

But one could not always control the patient, or the patient's family. And it was in that way the "thing" descended on us like a canopy of some sort that hovered over us, threatening, and then fell upon us, enveloping us. For what seemed like a long time, we could only dread, struggle, fight, and find no way of escape.

By "us," of course, I mean the McCord family — all of us. The doctors and their families — even some friends — were caught into the smothering, inescapable blanket of outrage and helpless anger.

The "thing" began, at first unnoticed, with a rush of business in Joe's office. He was, he would say, ruefully, incredibly busy. "Women all over the place," he told.

As the days went by, this busyness increased, and his amazement did, too. He was always busy. But these women — those who came to his office, those who wanted to come, either by direct petition or referred by some doctor, were women wanting an abortion, for various reasons. Now Joe did specialize in that field, but there were laws and ethics. . . .

"It's a nightmare," he told his brothers.

His nightmare was still building when Shields' began. Since he had no private practice, since he operated completely within the structure of the hospital Center, approach to him was a little more complicated, and it had to be made through the hospital. He was in charge of what was called the "burn center." Here Shields used what he felt to be the latest techniques in the treatment of people suffering from third-degree burns over enough of the body to make their recovery hazardous. He had teams of co-workers, he attempted always to get more space, more beds, more help. He worked very hard himself.

Always he was being forced to turn away cases for lack of time, or space, or both. And then the flood washed in upon him. His desk was piled with mail, with telephone messages. . . . "Call Dr. So-and-so, at such and such number in such and such town. Urgent!"

"Some of them are urgent, too," he would tell us. "Immediate attention is needed. Some are older burns, and the request is for plastic surgery, grafting — treatment of secondary symptoms." He ran his hands through his hair. "I don't understand the whole mess. The Administrator doesn't understand it, nor the Chief of Medical Services."

"You must have been advertising," drawled Bishop. "And Joe, too."

Joe's eye corners crinkled. "How do you suppose he figured that out, Shields?" he asked.

They were closer than they knew to an answer. Not a solution to their problems, however. But they could have looked up and seen the parachute floating down upon them.

It was only a day or two later that Bishop brought a small, pocket-sized magazine to the house. "Here's where Shields does his advertising," he told Jason. His face was grave.

Jason picked up the little book. It was one not familiar to us. Its pages fell open to a bold headline.

TO ME THEY ARE GOD

Jason began to read. I saw his face get red. He glanced up at Bishop, who nodded. "Bad, isn't it?" he asked.

"Its incredible!" Jason flipped the pages. "Who wrote this, who publishes this . . . ?" He was angry.

"What is it?" I asked Bishop.

"Oh, some writer — from the style, she was trained, I think, with the movie magazines — is doing a series on miracle men. She has now reached the field of medicine. And the Mc-

Cords are to be the miracle men about whom she writes. Joe got it two weeks ago for the abortions he has performed, the mothers' lives saved, the crippled babies. This week it's Shields. The miracles he does for the badly burned."

"I think we should talk about this," said Jason tightly.

It was the signal for the first of many family conferences. All of them together, two or three coming together – the McCord brothers would gather and talk. As the articles appeared – there were four of them – they tried to trace the source, and place blame. The stories were basically true; the treatment distorted these facts into sensational claims.

The third article told of a colostomy which Jason had performed twenty years before, and of a recent, new operation restoring the ascending colon to function. As a matter of fact, Jason told me, Grady had performed the second bit of surgery.

"Was it a miracle?"

"It was a good piece of surgery, Helen. No more and no less."

"Why don't some of you say so?"

He didn't answer me. The brothers were saying plenty to each other, and, I suspected, to their colleagues.

The fat really went into the fire when A.B.

was singled out for his miracle in chemistry. He had done certain things connecting mental disturbances to the chemistry of the human body; his work had been revolutionary, and good. The radio, TV, the newspapers and then other magazines took up the matter. Articles appeared under titles like "Are They Miracle Men?"

The hospital did not like the situation one bit better than did the McCords. In as many ways as possible, it objected. Staff meetings, impassioned conferences between the Administrator and a single Dr. McCord. . . . There was a Board meeting called on the subject.

Things were said about theatrical braggadocio and unwarranted clinical claims.

Jason was not sure, telling me about this, which phrase made the McCords madder.

"What did you say?"

"Well, various things, besides pointing out our innocence and lack of connection with the original articles."

"Did the Board believe you?"

"I don't know, and I don't much care. A.B. gave a nice little talk on the overexcited publicity which had become precedent. Some asked if doctors, especially in research, didn't really like publicity."

"And . . . ?" I asked.

"Well, A.B. can get pretty darn smooth.

Suave. He said something to the effect he tried to cooperate with reporters — those who came to him on legitimate business. His main concern, he said, was to be sure he was quoted accurately, if at all. Then, of course, someone brought up the matter of transplants. Lucian closed that off with the opinion that publicity had gone far to dilute scientific discretion in these matters."

"Did they know what he meant?"

"He made it clear."

But the Board, the staff, and the hospital were still upset. You would have thought criminal acts had been brought to light rather than notable achievements. Some of the men, the doctors, became vicious in their attacks and their protests.

"Could be they were jealous," suggested Shields.

"Do they make a connection between this and Grady's articles?" I asked Grady's brother.

"Oh, sure. But Grady didn't do this. He signs his stuff. And he's as upset as the rest of us. In fact, he admits that the printed word has backfired on him. And he's just about the angriest of all the McCords. He mentioned the braggadocio bit — and pointed out that his writing has not been colored that way."

"Then what?" I persisted.

"Well, the uncles, and Dad, listened to him

and looked at each other."

"I've *not* done that sort of thing!" Grady insisted. And they agreed. No, he had not.

But, said the McCords, if this publicity had backfired on Grady, it also had backfired on them. They should have stopped him. And long ago.

Efforts were made to discover how the author of the articles had got her material. It had to be from someone connected with the hospital. Grady thought not. He asked Joe who the first patient told about would be. He himself could identify the colostomy.

It was Shields who suggested sunroom gossip. "I hear the patients, especially women, spreading their doctor-worship like — like shaving foam. Not scientifically — but those articles were not scientific. No doctor would say, 'After twenty years, Dr. Jason McCord put my mother's plumbing back into normal operation.' These women, patients, or family, meet, they compare notes, they strive to outdo each other in their dramatic experiences. Someone could have passed along this information to a writer. If the magazine did any tracing, it would find enough truth in the claims. . . . Of course, the florid style is their own contribution and we can't do anything about it."

They all accepted this solution, but still were being disturbed and resentful when the parachute, the smothering canopy, collapsed completely upon us, and no escape seemed possible. The hospital became the object of a lawsuit, with Jason named. A patient had asked that a secondary colostomy be performed, and had been refused.

"Great guns!" cried my husband. "I've had a dozen patients come to me since that damned article was published and ask me to do that. I couldn't agree. Only one case in a hundred qualifies. And why should they sue me? Why not Joe for refusing an abortion? Why not A.B. for his failure to discover the cause of infant hyaline membrane suffocation? Why not . . . ?"

"Don't get so excited, Jason," I told him.

"*Get* excited? I *am* excited. I do not *like* lawsuits! They interfere with my work."

We were at Joe's. After dinner that evening, Jason had asked me if I wanted to walk down there with him. On the way, he told me of the lawsuit. I knew the family would join us.

When Eve welcomed us, she suggested that I might want to sit upstairs with her away from "all this doctor-talk."

I looked pleadingly at Jason. "Let her stay," he growled. "She's in on this as much as I am."

"How could that be?" Eve asked me.

"I'm not as clever a wife as you are, dear," I told her.

This must have puzzled her if she got beyond the surface of the words. She excused herself.

She did not understand all the talk that had been going on lately. She was glad Joseph did not involve his family in his profession. If I grew tired, "Come upstairs, Helen, darling."

I said I would, and I found myself a chair in the corner of the parlor where the men were going to sit. All but Jason. He paced the Oriental rug all evening.

The men came, they found seats – the big wingback chair, the handsome needlepoint chairs that flanked the fireplace, the couch. Grady sat on the footstool.

The men discussed the lawsuit. Had Jason refused such a case?

He would, he said stiffly, continue to give his opinion honestly. The case in point would not be a fit subject for further surgery. He'd say the same thing to a man wanting his leg sewed back on, one he'd lost through cancer ten years ago. He –

"If you're firm in your position," said Lucian, "we'll have to fight this with expert testimony. Did you see the case, Grady?"

"Dad says I did, sir."

"And you did the repair on the publicized case?"

"I did, but the article gives Dad the credit. I might says he's welcome to it."

"That's all very well," said the "head of the family," "and I'll accept your statement that you

313

had nothing to do with writing these articles. But do you think that you could be, perhaps, the ultimate object of this attack on us?"

This was a new idea, and a strange one. Lucian was asked to elaborate. And in doing so he mentioned Sammy Bacquillon.

Grady glanced at his father, at Shields — finally at me. And he laughed. "That's pretty far-out thinking," he said. "But Sammy is not involved. He's out of the country, and, I understand, under surveillance."

Jason nodded. "He is. The Navy is taking care of that."

"All right, then," said Lucian. "But I do wish Henry Tibbs was available to get this thing cleared up for us."

"I'm glad he's dead," said Bishop. "If he weren't, this would have killed him. He was a great believer in the McCord family."

"He could still believe in us!" snapped Jason. "Don't talk as if I were guilty."

Bishop laughed. "In malpractice," he told us, "the accused is guilty even after the case has been tried and the verdict of innocent given."

Grady sat on his footstool, one knee lifted and held in his clasped hands. "I'm stymied," he said musingly. "D'you think Henry could have seen something of the sort coming, and — "

"He foretold your comeuppance," Joe told his

nephew. "That was his term. But I do not think he committed suicide, or would have, just to avoid a fight of this sort."

"He could have stopped that pacer," said Grady. "I'm not convinced he didn't."

"And you never expect to be convinced," agreed Bishop.

"But you're right, Uncle Joe," Grady continued. "He wouldn't have walked out with this row in prospect. He loved the McCords, but he loved a fight better. And he'd have won this one for us, too. Do you suppose, without him . . . ?"

"We are not," said Jason firmly, "going into court to fight this sort of charge. And we are not going to sue that damn magazine! Win or not, all malpractice suits are a threat to good medical procedure. I am sure Henry would be telling us the same thing. As for myself, this will be my stand before the staff and the Board."

The brothers were instantly agreed on this. Shields and Grady looked at each other. Then Grady shrugged. "I guess so," he said reluctantly.

"What makes you so sure he committed suicide?" A.B. asked Grady. "Henry, I mean."

"I'm not sure," said Grady quickly. "I just like to speculate about such things. It would be the perfect, undetectable way. . . ."

"I think you sound grisly," said his Uncle Joe reprovingly.

"I don't mean to." Grady spoke quickly. "I was fond of the old boy. And he — one thing you can be sure of, Herry Tibbs *cared* what happened to us."

"I suppose he cared what happened to all his clients."

Grady thought about that. "Yes," he agreed. "He must have. He's dead, isn't he?"

"If that means," cried Lucian, "what it appears to me to mean, why do you want us, as doctors, to care more for our patients? You propagandize constantly on the subject. . . ."

"Sure I do," Grady agreed. "Its what I meant about Henry, too. Every bit of what you read into my words. Now, look at it this way, Uncle Lucian. I know all your arguments, as a heart specialist, for moderation. You say to live moderately, to love moderately, care moderately. Bring moderation to one's work. Do it, then leave it behind one. I know the whole routine.

"But, listen to this, will you, sir? And look at life — yours, for instance — this way: You are alive. You were given life. Then you studied and trained to help people. If asked, I am sure you would say something about giving your life to medicine. Giving your *life*, remember! All right, then. *Do* it! A long life, or a short one, what difference does it make? You will have done your allotted job."

The room was very silent. Lucian took out a cigar and lit it. Jason finally sat down in the chair beside me. His eyes sought mine.

Bishop cleared his throat. "Grady," he said huskily, "I'll bet you live to be a hundred."

Grady tipped his head to one side, thinking about this. "Because I have no conscience?" he asked.

"That is exactly what I mean!" said Bishop crisply.

"All right," said Grady cheerfully. "One hundred. Hmmmmn."

Jason sat shaking his head. "But I won't," he told the others. "I can feel my allotted years drop away from me like leaves from an artichoke."

Grady sat looking at him. He said nothing.

Later, as we walked home, Jason said to me, "I think that boy loves me, Helen. I think he does."

Chapter 11

The next shock, and to date, perhaps it was the last one, the latest one, came about a year later. It was winter. I remember that I was watching TV. June's program would come on at nine o'clock. Jason was sitting with me, though he was not watching the screen. He would, when June appeared, though even then he would pretend to be sorting fish lures and straightening lines. He never had come out and said that he was proud of June. I was. Under the name of Jackson McCord, he had made good in TV. Within a year he had progressed from a small-part player to a leading character. The truth was, when he first appeared in the popular series, he had been a hit. His smile, his voice, his — manner — the audience response to him was great. And in TV, audience response is essential. By popular demand, he was put into every one of the series' stories. Parts were written in for him. I read all this in the TV news and the trade magazines. At the beginning of the second year, his name was listed as one of the stars.

He had found his medium and seemed happy in it. He had come home, I had visited him, and June was in his element. He drove a good car, he had a nice home in California, he was planning to be married. I had met the girl and was relieved to find her not another Dodie.

June told me, incidentally, that he had heard from Dodie.

"Did you . . . ?"

"I'm pretty busy, Mother."

For half of the year he worked long, hard hours. For the rest of the year he was in demand for guest appearances, night club acts . . .

"Busy enough to stay out of trouble," said Grady.

I thought that was the solution, but I defended my son —

As I defended Grady when Jason told me about his latest. That night he waited until June's program was over, then he asked me, almost indifferently, if I knew what Grady was up to those days.

"Oh, dear . . ." I said.

Jason chuckled. "Our wayward sons."

"Not *wayward*, Jason!"

"What do you call 'em?"

"Individuals — nonconformists, perhaps."

"I'd say so. Certainly."

"What's Grady been doing now?"

"Nonconforming."

I got up and turned off the TV. "Tell me," I said firmly.

"It's bedtime."

"After you've told me."

"I can't go into detail . . ."

I reached for one of his heaps of string, or thread. He gave me a pasteboard reel. "Wind it on that. Straight, Helen, not twisted."

I nodded and began to work.

"Well," said my husband, "of his own accord, your son has decided he can be a G.P. and live on twenty-two thousand a year instead of the fifty or seventy-five he could earn as a surgeon."

"Is he a G.P.?" I asked.

"Oh, yes. He's kept to his idea of qualifying as an internist. Hasn't passed the Boards yet, but he will."

"And what will he do to earn twenty-two thousand?" I asked. Somehow, this time, I was not frightened of what Jason was going to tell me.

"He's given up surgery; his name's gone down from the board; he is organizing and will head the Center's emergency room service."

My hands stopped. I had heard Grady say things about the importance of e.r. These later days, years. . . .

"You know that City Hospital Number Two

was closed earlier this year," Jason continued. "For lack of funds. Actually its closing has overburdened all the emergency rooms in the city. Especially ours."

I began to work again.

"And Grady had this idea."

"Tell me."

"Well, simply — he outlined it in the book he wrote a couple of years ago. And when the staff repeatedly challenged him to follow some of his own prescriptions — I think that is behind this — I guess I can be thankful he did not computerize my o.r.'s. Though this is — " He smiled at me. "You know, Helen, that e.r. is ordinarily staffed by interns and residents on a rotating basis. Grady thinks it should be an important part of the hospital setup, equal with surgery, internal medicine, and so on. He calls it the weakest link in the hospital's chain of service."

"I've heard him say — and he's right — that it's the center of chaos."

"He's right in the weak-link bit, too. Though I hate to lose a bang-up surgeon."

"Is Grady thinking again of the people?"

"He is. His scheme, Helen, is to establish e.r. as a unit. He will head and administer the operation. He says he will, and can, get eight G.P.'s as his staff."

"Why G.P.'s?"

"Because you get every class of patient in

through e.r. Their treatment begins with diagnosis. If what they need is beyond the G.P., he can call in a specialist, either resident or staff. Grady thinks the sometimes life-or-death decisions made in e.r. should not be left to nurses and interns."

"Should they be?"

"Grady asked just that question in staff meeting. And of course there is no choice of answer."

"And you think he is going to do this?"

"He's already started. I heard him brief his staff, Helen. He made quite a thing of telling the men that they had staff status, and not to answer the telephone like a resident."

I laughed.

"I say men," said Jason, "though one of his doctors is a woman. And she's a good one. Grady's first choice, I hear."

My interest quickened. "What is she like?"

"Mmmmn," said Jason. "She's attractive. Young. Thirty, I'd guess. Slender, dark, very sure of herself."

"And Grady must think she's a capable doctor."

"I suppose."

"Where did Grady get her?"

"Where he got all his doctors. He surveyed the G.P.'s we had on the staff and as attendings. He chose those who had less responsibilities in

322

the way of family, home, and so on. He put his proposition to ten of them. The regular hours, the assured pay — the staff position they would have, the recognized position of the e.r. committee at all hospital conferences. And he got eight doctors."

"Through his own personality."

"Perhaps. He appeals to the patients on that basis, too."

"As a surgeon . . ."

"He isn't going to serve as a surgeon. The things done in emergency are limited. For instance, e.r. doctors do not apply plaster or care for torn ligaments. Specialists are still to be on call to come in on cases diagnosed as needing their service. Grady estimates about forty out of one hundred e.r. patients do need a specialist."

"The patients don't all stay in the hospital, of course."

"Oh, no. And Grady is working out a system by which return visits can be regulated. The patients who need additional care are given a choice of doctors. Their own, or some doctor other than the e.r. men. Though on a trial basis, a lot of patients are saying they want the e.r. men to dress a burn or take out stitches."

"Personality again."

"That, and performance. These doctors will not be on duty for a week or a day. They will be permanently on this job, they will care about the work they do. Of course there are drawbacks to the idea. One is the personal closeness of doctor and patient. You never know the background of a patient in e.r., and you don't often follow up a case. From the hospital's — not the patient's — viewpoint, this situation causes the e.r. doctor to order more tests and X-rays, to be sure he is covering the situation, you see. I call this a drawback, though Grady has convinced the administration that the full examination is a protection to the hospital should there be medico-legal complications."

I realized that Jason was talking with great interest in this thing which Grady was doing.

"Practically all e.r. patients have insurance of some sort," he was saying. "Workmen's compensation, automobile collision, liability. Grady thinks his plan will give the hospital better representation in court than the testimony of an intern or nurse."

"Wouldn't it?"

"Sure it would."

"Is this going to work, Jason?"

"It will take time to establish it. At first, of course, it may be difficult to get — keep — his staff doctors. The administration is going to have a ticklish job seeing that prestige is maintained. We have had this problem with our pathologists and radiologists."

"Then, I suppose doctors like the freedom of private practice."

"They do. But they realize to start one means long hours and high expenses."

"Do all Grady's men get twenty-two thousand?"

"Yes. With the promise of a two thousand raise at the end of eighteen months, should they contract to stay on."

"Will they stay on? Are they all young?"

"Not beginners. The girl is. But Grady has men who have been in practice for ten years; one man is fifty. He likes the forty-four-hour week."

Jason was beginning to pack up his fishing gear. By then it was much more than bedtime.

"Grady could live on the twenty-two thousand," I said. "Unless he marries."

"There's that woman doctor," Jason teased me.

I had other plans, and he knew it.

"And if he does marry," I went on, "he can earn what more he needs by his writing."

My husband groaned.

"And he can do research," I continued. "He calls it that when he travels about to see what else you and your hospitals need. You say he has already started this project, Jason?"

"It's to be announced in staff meeting tomorrow as an accomplished fact."

"Oh, dear."

"Now what does that mean?"

"That you McCords will be having family conferences all over the place. Should I invite everyone for dinner?"

That night he laughed at me and said I'd better invite the staff. They were going to be stunned, too.

I suppose they were. In my volunteer work during the next week I had several men protest with me. Grady was too good a surgeon, they said, to bury himself. . . .

On Sunday afternoon the brothers gathered for a full discussion. Jason told them at once that they would do better to talk to Grady rather than about him.

"Can you get him up here?"

"I can try."

Grady said, yes, of course he would come. And he did. I can see him now as he stood leaning against the fireplace, his hands in the pockets of his dark trousers, his laughing face above the roll of his white, heavy-knit sweater. He let his uncles say all the things they had to say.

This project was a mistake, they said.

"Sir, I'll be the first to know that."

"You're too promising a surgeon."

"I'll need everything my father has taught

me. We are set up like a miniature operating room, you know. Techniques, procedures . . . Uncle Joe, if you get called on a case in e.r., you come running. You'll like working there."

"We'll see," said Joe.

"Won't you need a rather comprehensive ambulance service?" Bish asked him.

"Ambulance service is a weak spot in medical care," Grady agreed. "Walking cases, and cases where the family is functioning, can be brought where they want to be. But if I'd go down to the Boulevard, get struck by a car, with the Center only a couple of blocks away, I'd probably land in the City General e.r. three miles away."

"Then what?"

"Well, I have two plans there."

The men looked at each other and burst into laughter. Grady waited for them to settle down.

"To start," he said, "we could have better private, franchised ambulance service, with trained attendants. Second, the city should give us a modernized, centralized system, with a trained, centralized communications board. Attendants must have more training, and the ambulances must be better-equipped."

"You'll never get it."

"Don't *say* things like that!" Jason urged. "Like as not, he'll have you driving one of his meat wagons."

"Why not?" asked Shields. "I think I'd like it."

"You got any more puppies in your basket?" Joe asked Grady suspiciously.

"Yes, sir," said Grady at once. "I am going to work through the city medical society, through the city health bureau, and certainly through publicity, to force every e.r. in the city and county to be as good as ours is going to be."

"I'll bank on the publicity," growled Lucian. "I suppose you'll have a reporter follow cases through. . . ."

"That's a good way," said Grady. "He'll find it interesting."

"I'd find it interesting, myself," said Bishop. "May I take the tour?"

We thought he was joking, and the talk went on to other things. The men got back to Grady's reasons for thinking *he* was the one to effect all these changes.

He liked the word "reform" better.

"All right, reform. I suppose e.r. does need some improvement. . . ."

"Don't get hit by that car," Grady advised.

"I'll try not. But this bucking City Hall — "

"He's probably ready to run for alderman," said Jason wryly.

"Or mayor," suggested Shields. "Don't put it beyond him. Then Mother would be first lady of the city, and — "

"Let Grady answer his own questions," Lucian reproved the young man.

"Sir!" said Shields meekly. And the men laughed again.

"Pick one," his father advised Grady. "Tell us why you wage this war for the patient and against all the rest of us."

"I'm not *against* anything," said Grady. "Except maybe stodgy self-satisfaction where it isn't justified. There are individual doctors who do not come up to the best standards in behavior and proficiency. And medical emergencies do have to be handled. They should be handled in the best way possible, too.

"I suppose my chief aim is to have medical care *available*. For instance — who was it that was going to be hit by a car?"

"You volunteered," said Shields.

"O.K. I'm going to be hit by a car. But as things are now, I'd damn well better not do it on Wednesday afternoon, had I? — with every specialist in town out on the golf course, or otherwise luxuriating. I'd better not let it happen at night, or on the week end —"

"He'll get to house calls any minute," said Lucian behind his hand.

"I'd certainly like to," Grady assured him.

"Are your doctors in e.r. going to work nights and week ends?" Jason asked.

"Yes, sir. They are."

"You, too?"

"Me, too."

"This I *have* to see!" said Bishop.

Lucian came over to sit on the couch beside me. "Helen," he said, "do you understand what this son of yours is doing?"

"I think so, Lucian. Without knowing anything about the technical part of Jason's profession, I have tried to keep in touch with his environment."

"I know you have. But – I don't think he'll tell you, but just maybe –" He looked across at Grady. "Maybe he'll tell you, Helen, dear. So will you please ask your son *why* he is doing this?"

I looked at "my son." "Can you tell us?" I asked softly.

Grady rocked back and forth on his heels. "Yes," he answered readily. "I can tell you." He paused and we all waited tensely.

"There's been a lot of talk," he said then. "Mainly by me. But once, I think it was Uncle Lucian who said I should be forced to test one or some of my ideas. Well, simply, I am doing just that."

"I should bite my tongue!" cried Lucian in wry dismay.

"Isn't it a good idea, Lucian?" I asked, not needing to look at Jason. He had guessed.

330

"It appears to be an excellent idea, Helen. But — you realize that the boy is a fine surgeon?"

"Yes. I know that."

"And this can break his career into splinters?"

The rest of the family was listening to us and watching us. Grady, too.

I clasped my hands together on my knees. The diamond which Jason had given me forty years ago blazed on my finger. "The first time I saw Grady jump from the carriage house roof," I said, "into the gingko tree — he was about five — I knew he could break himself into pieces. I could have stopped him that one time. I didn't. He's broken himself into chunks a few times since. And he may this time. But I think I'll be proud of him."

"He could go on, be another McCord, in the family tradition."

"Yes." I could see him in a shadow-plaid gray suit going down the street. "And I'd be proud of him then, too."

Lucian took a deep breath. "This thing is a shock," he said.

"It could be the biggest one Grady has put us through," I agreed.

"Yes," said the "head of the family," "it could be. Because I have an idea, disturbing as it is, that Grady is not going to be the only McCord making these changes."

Grady and his emergency room got publicity, and it stirred the city from end to end. The next day the new regime was announced in staff meeting, and reporters were present. In that night's paper, his picture was on the front page — a new, posed, studio photograph. He was giving the patient a break, the headline said. Next day, in the morning paper, the news was repeated, with a challenging statement from the city's health director. For the taxes paid, as good emergency service as possible was being given in the city-owned institutions. The doctors themselves were to blame if e.r.'s were overcrowded and understaffed.

Next day, Grady was interviewed and photographed. This time he was in his whites. He said the city health director was right. He carefully outlined the new routine established at the Medical Center. He said, yes, he expected the system to be a success. He was sure his own hospital and others who might adopt it would thank him for instituting it.

"Why did you give up being a specialist, Dr. McCord?"

"I am still a specialist. My specialty now is to be that of emergency room physician."

"Haven't you gone institutional?"

"That isn't a dirty word to me. I shall be

working in a place where patients come to me, many of them in critical condition and needing a good, trained doctor to attend them."

"But you will have fixed hours and income."

"Yes. Your men in private practice arrange to have fixed hours, too. My income will be less than theirs, but it will be sufficient."

"The Hospital Center will pay you?"

"It makes us a guarantee of income. Yes. We are not salaried."

"Are you head of this operation?"

"I have been named Chief of Emergency Room Service. I shall have my duties as supervisor of the project. But I intend to take my turn working in e.r. as well as supervising and instructing the interns and residents assigned to the service."

"Will your e.r. operate on a twenty-four-hour basis?"

"Oh, yes. And may I say that the doctors on duty will see more of the glamor of medicine than do doctors in private practice? The blood and guts, life and death cases. Those patients come to us. We care for them. And isn't that what medicine is all about?"

That evening, Taylor Falk came across, asking to see Grady.

"He isn't here, my dear," I told her. "He lives in his own apartment, you know."

"Yes, but I don't think Dad and Mother feel

I should go there."

"Not alone," I agreed. "Is there something special?"

"Well, of course there is something special, Mrs. McCord. All these stories in the newspaper. Don't you and Dr. Jason think he is wonderful?"

"Not only lately, dear."

"Well, of course not." She looked around. "I thought perhaps he'd be coming here for dinner."

"He would, if I'd ask him."

"Would you, Mrs. McCord?" She spoke eagerly. "Tell him about my old-fashioned parents, tell him that I want to talk to him."

"And tell him," growled Jason amiably from behind his newspaper, "that you have roast beef for dinner."

Grady came up the street for dinner, and he and Taylor talked about his work. They talked during dinner and after the meal, they talked for an hour or more in the corner of the parlor, then Grady agreed to walk her home, and I suppose they talked some more. I know they stood for a long, long time on the front steps of her home. I saw them there under the lights at the front door when I went upstairs to bed.

"The next picture will be of Dr. Grady McCord under an oxygen tent, for pneumonia," said Jason dryly at my shoulder.

"Oh, Jason, don't you remember — though we lived next door to each other — how we used to stand out on the sidewalk and talk and talk?"

"Mhmmmn. And now you're still talking." But he put his hand through my arm and drew me close to his side. "D'you think Grady and Taylor . . . ?"

"She's a lovely girl."

"She is all of that. But she's younger . . ."

"I couldn't ask for a better match. She knows him, she understands him . . ."

"Good Lord, Helen!" exploded my husband. "Don't tell me *she's* a genius!"

The city's Medical Society's weekly newspaper gave a whole issue to a discussion of Grady's ideas on emergency room management and service. It was announced that he would be present at an open forum at the upcoming meeting, where members could ask questions and state their own views.

Jason came home very late, and tired, from that meeting.

"Did the doctors give Grady a hard time?" I asked him.

Jason snorted. "That kid's got all the answers," he told me.

Jason showed me the articles about Grady

and his weakest-link e.r. philosophy in various medical journals. I myself saw his smiling face in the current-events magazines. I was not one bit surprised when Taylor came across to ask me, "Did you know Grady is to be on a TV talk-show, Mrs. McCord?"

"I knew he was going on a short trip."

"That's where he is going. To New York! Oh, Mrs. *Mac* . . ."

"Come over, and we'll watch it together."

"It comes on late."

"The whole family will be here."

She smiled. "I wish I could go with him," she said wistfully.

"Now, I don't believe your parents . . ."

She giggled. "June phoned and asked him if he knew what to wear."

"Oh, my."

"Yes. And Grady really had answers for him."

I quoted Jason on the subject of Grady's answers. Taylor laughed about that.

"Do you know what he plans to wear?" I asked the girl.

"I wouldn't suggest a thing. He may ask me. . . ."

"You're seeing him, then?"

She blushed. "I don't know that I'm managing *that* — but he does drop in — and we've gone some places. Oh, Mrs. Mac, he is wonderful!"

I continued with what I was doing – planning the next week's menus, as I remember. Anyway, I was doing something at my desk. The girl in her dark green slacks and white blouse was curled up in Jason's big chair, her shining hair back against the blue cushion.

"He's a gentle person," she said thoughtfully. "A gentle man."

"But he's always fighting for something, Taylor."

"Yes, I know. And I recognize his great strength. But that's necessary for a man to be gentle, Mrs. Mac."

I made a mental note to tell Jason that Taylor was not nearly as young as he thought.

On the night scheduled for the broadcast, which was widely advertised, the main part of the program was to be given to this war hero, this young doctor with his radical ideas about patient care. I invited Taylor to come over for dinner. She and Shields, Jason and I, would play bridge afterward until –

"The uncles will come 'round," Shields reminded me.

"I expect them to. I've ordered some midnight food."

Early in the evening, Taylor asked Shields if he knew what Grady was going to wear.

He rearranged his cards. "He said he had a

new brown suit."

Brown! Taylor and I looked at each other in dismay. But of course it was too late to do anything.

Jason was jittery. He said he hoped the big TV was working.

By nine-thirty the brothers began to drop in. Lucian made a feeble excuse; the others frankly said they'd come to watch Grady together. By ten-thirty, we were seated in a tense semi-circle before the set. Some of the men held drinks. There was sandwich material, crackers, cheese, a coffeepot on the table against the wall.

And after a preliminary fifteen minutes, there was Grady!

"Oh . . ." gasped Taylor.

"I told you it was brown," said Shields.

"It" was brown, and the color was exactly right — Grady's suit. Oh, you couldn't call it a *suit*. His Tuxedo jacket was of a rich brown velvet. He wore it over a pleated-front white shirt. The trousers were of fine brown worsted, the same tone as the coat, but they looked lighter because of the texture of the wool. A brown silk handkerchief was tucked into his breast pocket, and silk made that still another shade. His head was high, his smile ready. His eye patch . . .

"He's wearing brown all right," I said, sniffling. To think that June had wanted to advise

338

him what to wear!

"Watch it, Helen," said Jason. "And listen."

Grady was introduced. A few explanatory words were said about his ideas, and his writings, on the present status of medical care. And then the matter of the emergency room project was introduced. Grady said some of the things – a lot of the things – we had all heard him say. But I suppose they sounded different to the huge audience he had that night. The master of ceremonies, or director, or whatever the big star was called, acted as if he had never heard of some of his facts. The interview was very well done.

Grady talked about the change in the e.r. status since the war – patients not able to get doctors, the rising incidence of accidents, and disaster illnesses. He talked about the common hospital practice of rotating e.r. service among the attending staff doctors. Interns, nurses and orderlies did most of the work. These people found themselves acting as family physicians for the indigent. Forty per cent of e.r. cases were the indigent who brought in everything from a head cold to childbirth, from a mashed finger to a completely mashed-up body. Grady was specific and sometimes amusing.

Rotating the attending physicians, he said, was not an effective service to e.r. Yes, one idea was to have a paid man, but a salaried physician posed problems. For one thing, the hospital could not collect professional fees from insurance companies and other third-party payers.

Another solution, he said, would be to have a large group — say thirty doctors who would rotate their services in e.r., working one twenty-four-hour tour of duty a month, the fees collected to be divided among the thirty men.

There was a little discussion of those fees.

Then the matter of Grady's solution for the problem was brought forward. He'd already spoken of part-time emergency rooms.

He said his solution was to have a small group of doctors that would keep close to the emergency room situation, who would be interested in preventing problems as well as solving those which came up, who would have a big stake in the success of the venture.

He described his own group of men who had completely given up their private practices. He named them, and described his woman doctor as "a most attractive girl." He told that they devoted their full time to patient care, around the clock. He said that they, under him as chief, would have full charge of the operation.

What did Grady do as chief?

He acknowledged that he put in a few extra hours. But he could; he was unmarried.

"Oh, oh!" groaned Shields. "He's dead!"

Grady was saying that he arranged schedules, planned meetings to take care of administrative and professional matters, and also planned for a continuing education program to maintain liaison with the medical staff and the hospital administration. The hospital provided facilities, equipment, supplies and personnel to run the place. Yes, by personnel he did mean nurses, orderlies, interns, maids, attendants.

He discussed fees. They were mutually agreed upon by the physicians and the hospital administrator, and were separately listed in the hospital accounts.

"At least he didn't go after Medicare and the Viet Nam War," sighed Lucian as the program concluded.

"He hasn't made a study of them," Bishop pointed out.

"And he does of hospitals and doctors, I suppose?"

"Doesn't he?"

"I wish he'd taken up botany!"

"You don't wish any such thing," said Jason.

"And he was wonderful tonight," I insisted.

"But he didn't tell us anything new," said Bishop.

"He wasn't talking to doctors," Shields reminded him. "He was talking to patients. Now they know what they should be getting."

"They'll want doctors who look like him,"

said Taylor, and the men laughed.

"He was a smash, all right," said Bishop, going over to the table to replenish his drink. "I wonder where he got that outfit."

We talked for another hour. Jason and the other men told how popular Grady was with the patients. They weren't sure if his eye patch was to blame.

"Oh, one forgets he has an eye patch," Taylor assured us.

"Do you?" asked Joe curiously. "Do other women?"

"What other women?" Taylor asked pertly. And of course we laughed.

I was the one to ask the men how much comment there was among patients about the things Grady was doing.

They asked questions, I was told. "And then they all say — the women do — he's *so* handsome!"

Well, he was. Even with his scarred face. And Taylor was right. One did forget the eye patch. That night, the program announcer had sighed and wondered if all men should not wear one.

"I'll bet he gets offers for other TV appearances," said Taylor. "Maybe he could do a series."

The doctors all groaned. "Don't suggest it," said Bishop.

She looked surprised. "We need him," Jason told her.

And she smiled sunnily. "I'll tell Grady you said that."

"He knows it," said Grady's father. "He knows it."

Grady came home and listened to what we had to say. I suppose he listened in the same way to the things which everyone else had to say. He told our men where he'd got his clothes. He said, yes, he was getting a heavy mail. Could he borrow their secretaries to answer it?

And he went back to work. Now and then he would be announced as speaker at some meeting in the city — the Noonday Club, the Ambassadors. Sometimes he would be quoted at length in the newspapers. He told about liking the work he and his colleagues were doing in e.r. They were using their hands, he said. And he went on to detail the limits put upon emergency room care.

He told about the trauma clinics the hospital had set up. He gave credit for this development to the Surgical Service.

"You?" I asked Jason.

"I thought it would work," he said, as if ashamed of what he had done. "Surgeons — and Shields in his burn center — are overburdened with follow-up jobs — removing sutures, second dressings, things like that. Grady's e.r. men staff our trauma clinic; it is held three times a week. And by the way, tell Taylor she should watch things. That girl doctor of Grady's is darn good-looking."

"I've seen her," I said. She was a dark-haired young woman, her smooth hair drawn back from a widow's peak and tied loosely at the crown of her head for a swinging, shining little tail. She was tall, her white lab coat was well fitting, she had a fresh and interested manner. I had told Taylor about her.

"The big job Grady's done for the whole Center," Jason told me, "is to stress the good care given in our e.r. He never fails to mention that such proficient care should eliminate the malpractice suits so often filed against hospitals which do not provide this sort of good initial care. In his talks, he serves a warning to the patients and to the ambulance chasers as well."

"But the care is good!"

"Of course it's good. Grady's just saying so wouldn't be enough."

I wasn't so sure, but I took Jason's opinion as valuable. One day I asked Bishop if he had ever taken his tour through Grady's e.r. He said no, but he meant to — and he would then tell me about it.

"Will you go as a patient?"

He laughed. "No. I've sacrificed enough

344

for my profession. But I can go along, just another white coat, and see what is done to a particular patient."

"What sort will you pick?"

"I won't pick any sort. I'll just go in and follow one."

This he did, and he afterward told me about it.

He selected a Wednesday afternoon, which he thought was significant. Grady had done a lot of talking about the way many of the doctors in the city — in the *country* — took Wednesday afternoons off.

Bishop, doing o.b. work, could not count on having any one afternoon free. He did not hold office hours on Wednesday, but the day he had selected for his tour found him too busy to make it until six-thirty in the evening. He told me that he had rather hoped to get there when Grady was on duty, but he did not.

The doctor in charge was the woman doctor. Bishop, too, thought she was good-looking. Her name — Fannie — amused him.

"Girls just aren't called Fannie these days, Helen!"

"She's called Dr. Hudson at the hospital, isn't she?"

"Not always. And she doesn't mind being called Fannie."

"I see."

"She's good-looking, and she's a good doctor. . . ."

"Did Grady know you were making the tour?"

"Maybe not at that particular time, but he had set the thing up for me. I had asked him to. And of course Fannie started me off in good shape by assuming that I was Grady's brother."

"You didn't tell her different?"

"Oh, no!"

"All right. Tell me."

He chuckled. Bishop had been ten when I married Jason. That night he lay back on the cushions of the wicker couch and looked at the ceiling as he talked.

"I got to e.r.," he said, "at six-thirty. I presented myself to the doctor in charge. . . ."

"Fannie."

"Fannie," he agreed. "At six-thirty, a call came in. A wife said her husband was awful sick, could the hospital send a doctor? I heard the desk girl say she would let the doctor talk to the wife. Fannie did a good thing of calming the woman, getting the facts. She was warmly compassionate and calmly efficient, quick and quiet, all at the same time. Her husband — one John Adolph Mebold — seemed to need help badly. Dr. Hudson said she could send an ambulance at once and bring him to the hospital. The wife could come, but she need not.

Mr. Mebold would be taken care of. Incidentally," said Bishop, "in following this patient, I seldom heard him called anything but Mr. Mebold. The anesthetist – but I'm getting ahead.

"Within two minutes the ambulance was on its way, red light blinking. Dr. Fannie was pre-diagnosing the trouble as an acute appendix, and checked on the availability of an o.r. This was all done quickly – click, click, click – but the other business of the emergency room went on, hardly disturbing its routine at all. There were cases waiting – Dr. Hudson checked on the chart boards of each one, directed intern and resident, looked at two herself – a broken wrist, a man wanting drugs.

"At six-fifty-three, Mr. Mebold was wheeled into a receiving cubicle, with Dr. Hudson, a nurse, and a nurse's aide, ready to go to work on him."

"And you," I murmured.

"And me," said Bishop. "But I stood in the corner behind Fannie. She uses lime toilet water."

"Oh, Bishop!"

"Most pretty women would use a perfume, and that can be a difficulty with some patients."

"I'd think so. Go on. You were about to take Mr. Mebold's history."

"I was not. There was no such nonsense. Later, I suppose it was taken. But not then. No, they took his temperature — 101.6, blood pressure 140/80, pulse rapid. Acute tenderness in the right lower abdomen, extending to left lower abdomen. Spasms of abdominal muscles with resistance to palpitation.

"Tests were made — blood, urine, sensitivity. Dr. Hudson went in and out. She was there when the reports came down from the lab. High white-cell count, infection certain. She made her diagnosis, acute appendicitis, with possible perforation. She decided an operation must be performed on John Adolph Mebold. At eight o'clock he was on his way."

"Did you go with him?"

"Sure. I was the patient. So much so that I had to be reminded to put on a gown and cap, and *then* was jerked back to test my conductivity."

I looked up.

"Oh, that's a little gadget — looks like a box on a post outside the operating suite. You stand on footrests; it tests the chance that you'll foul things up with your static."

"You wear special shoes, don't you?"

"Yes. We do. That made it a little hard for me to feeling like Mr. Mebold, who didn't have any shoes on."

I nodded.

"Well," said Bishop, "wrapped up like a lolli-pop, I joined the operating team already gathered around our patient. Did I say it was eight o'clock?"

"Yes."

"O.K. Well, of course they were ready for us up on the fifth floor. Dressings, gown, instruments, all had been sterilized in the big steel autoclaves. Packages were taken out for this special operation. By the way, a staff surgeon was ready – the whole team. The packages' sealing was inspected. You know, Helen, a broken tape or open packet indicates danger.

"While all this was going on, Mr. Mebold was being prepared. Down in e.r. he had been given pre-surgical medication, and when he came up, he was taken first to the anesthesia room next to o.r."

"Were you there, too?"

"Oh, yes. Got the glucose, saline solution – those hollow steel needles hurt like the dickens, Helen." His black eyes were sparkling.

"You already are half under, at least," I reminded him.

"That's right," he agreed. "And the surgical team was scrubbing, keeping an eye on the clock's second hand as they scrubbed, scrubbed, their hands touching only the soap. Five minutes later, they were through, and ready, the surgeons and nurses, to be gowned in

349

sterile garments. Those packages were opened in the operating room."

"You must have been fascinated!" I murmured.

"Looking on is different from doing," he assured me. "I was an emergency patient, being treated — Where was I?"

"Getting into your sterile gowns."

"The team was. They dressed in o.r., while the anesthetist was giving ether to John Adolph. *She* called him that. She's the sort of girl who can watch ten things at once, gauges, dials, controls, all to regulate and watch Mr. Mebold's respiration throughout the operation.

"Now John Adolph didn't know from nuthin, but he was the exact center of that twenty-foot-square room. There was a huge light directly above him, and practically everything in the room was of stainless steel — anesthesia cart, operating table, racks, and trays — even the kick buckets — "

"The *what?*" I asked.

"Haven't you ever had surgery, Helen?"

"Not with a kick bucket."

"I'll bet you did. That's where the workers drop the used sponges. What did your man do, throw 'em, *splat*, on the floor?"

"Go on, Bishop," I said patiently. I wondered, if Jason should come upstairs, what he would think of our conversation.

"The floor," Bishop was telling me, "is especially constructed to prevent static build-up in the clothing of the operating team, or a spark from a dropped instrument."

"Does Grady know they drop instruments?" I asked innocently.

Bishop chuckled. "Lets see," he said. "We've got the o.r. safe, and there's John Adolph on the table, with the team gathered around the central point of the sterile field. The surgeon faces his first assistant across the table, the second assistant stands by Mr. Mebold's shoulder with the instrument and sponge nurses at stations toward his feet."

"Where were you?"

"Actually, back a few feet. As the *patient*, I was flat on my back, breathing easily. The surgeon took the scalpel, made the first incision, was quickly handed clamps to close off the small blood vessels. He reached the appendix, took a sample of the fluid to be sent to the lab for analysis."

"Why?"

Bishop looked at me and frowned – as if he really *had* been there on that operating table and now had trouble bringing himself back to the Palladian room and me.

"Oh," he said impatiently, "so they'll know the antibiotics best suited to fight the infection."

"I see."

"All right. By now forceps had been applied to the end of John Adolph's appendix, which the surgeon had clamped and divided at the base. When the removal was complete, the infected tissue itself would go down to Pathology for analysis.

"At nine thirty-four, the operation was completed, and Mr. Mebold was removed to the recovery room. He would go to his own bed the next morning – and in three days, having been fed intravenously because of the perforated appendix, he will be deciding if he wants roast leg of lamb for dinner, or boiled tongue. At the end of the week, he'll go home."

"It sounds as if you were satisfied with Grady's emergency room, Bishop."

He nodded. "They treated me good," he said, "and they treated me quick!"

"Did you see Dr. Hudson again?" I asked.

"Fannie? Oh, sure. I told her that I was glad to have gone through her e.r." He sat up. "And I'm taking her to dinner on her next free day."

"Bishop . . ."

"Why not?" he asked. "There are no restrictions on dates between staff doctors. She's the best-looking one I've seen. What's the matter? I thought you'd stopped matchmaking for me."

I shook my head and laughed. What could I say to the man? If this Fannie would seriously interest him, we'd all be glad. There would be still another Dr. McCord, of course. But his big house — and Bishop — needed a woman — one who could be compassionate, calm, quick. . . .

That night when we were getting ready for bed, I asked my husband, "Do you use kick buckets in your operating room, Jason?"

"My . . . ?" He stopped what he was doing — putting cuff links in his shirt — and turned to look at me. "Well, yes," he said. "Of course. They're in o.r."

I didn't say anything.

"Is something wrong, Helen?" he asked me.

"No. No. I just wish you'd tell me things!"

I didn't know myself why I was cross. Certainly Bishop had only praised Grady's new concept. We had all been hoping that Bishop would find a girl. Now, if he had found one — of course I had little to build on. He often had taken other young women to dinner.

I busied myself, as it is not difficult to do in late winter. I took a quick trip to Arizona; then Christine's baby was born — a boy. From the way A.B. acted, this would seem a brand-new miracle. And Lucian stirred up a fuss because he had learned that the family servants were taking care of Grady and his apartment.

I'd known that from the first. Orlie made it a practice to pick up his laundry and return clean clothes and linens to his place. Joe's second maid regularly cleaned the rooms. Lucian's cook, and Joe's — I suppose all the cooks — sent in food. Bishop's housekeeper mended his clothes, working with Orlie on that project.

"This has to stop!" Lucian declared. "If Grady wants to be independent, let him *be* independent! Let him fry his own eggs, and —"

"If you tell your Louise she can't fix his breakfast, have you faced the alternative?" A.B. asked him.

Lucian was cross. Not because the cook — but because this had been going on with only him unaware. "I don't understand," he said coldly to his brother.

The men laughed. "Are you sure Mary can fry you an egg?" asked A.B.

"I wouldn't count on Helen's being able to," said Jason.

Of course I resented that. But I got the message beneath the men's rather silly discussion. Our servant staffs worked together and interchangeably. Grady's apartment was but a temporary annex to the established homes. Lucian should relax and let well enough alone.

He should let Grady alone. I thought, That's what they have decided about Grady. To let him alone. I hoped it was the thing to do.

Chapter 12

Around Easter, Grady evidently stirred up discussion, but no rancor, by an article which he published in one of the newspaperlike medical releases. This had to do with emotional disturbances in physicians.

I heard Joe say something dry about Grady's now setting himself up as a psychiatrist.

"Oh, I don't think so," Shields objected. "It's a problem we all know exists."

"It isn't good for patient relationship to write this sort of thing."

"What patients read it?"

"The doctors do, and I don't think they will react well."

Shields nodded. "I have seen doctors resist, to the point of emotional collapse, any suggestion that they could be suffering from psychopathology and needing treatment."

"Alcoholics, drug users, yes."

"Some of them are," Shields agreed. "Often both."

The demands of a doctor's family, and of

society . . ." said Joe. "Doctors are often men who think they must be all things to all people — patients, colleagues, wife, children, community. They face some pretty rugged realities in the life they lead. Then as an escape they immerse themselves in their profession, with no time for family or vacations."

"How long since you've taken one?" I spoke up to ask.

Joe laughed. "Helen, I am not a candidate for any psycho's couch!"

No, he was not.

"And you already have all the prestige you need," said Shields. "In your case there is no need for aggressive and hostile power drives."

"What happens to these doctors?" I asked. "You say Grady wrote about their emotional imbalance . . ."

The men were working on the croquet court, getting it ready for warm weather. Through the winter, grass and leaves had matted. I had strolled out to oversee what they were doing. Shields offered me a rake.

"The temptation is to punish," Joe told me. "How about setting the wickets to run the other way this summer, Shields?"

"Won't work," Shields told him. "Lay of the land."

"*Lie* of the land?" I asked.

The men both looked up, astonished.

"Go back to talking about Grady's article," Joe advised me.

"I'll be glad to. If you don't punish these mental cases . . ."

"You do have to discipline them," said Joe. "But Grady is right. Compassion and understanding are also required."

"I liked what he said about prevention through early recognition," said Shields, taking off his shirt and giving it to me to hold.

"You'll catch cold," I warned. "How do you recognize psychological tendencies?"

"You begin with vulnerability, Grady says. Just as a doctor recognizes vulnerability of a host to a particular pathogen – he studies a variety of factors, inherent and environmental."

"There is one great difference," said Joe. "A doctor will mention a family history of diabetes mellitus and how it might affect himself. But I never knew one – not *one* – who would willingly confess to certain character traits and personality factors that might create personal problems for him in his practice of medicine. But Grady says no individual can feel that he is immune to mental illness." He turned to look at me. "He urged all physicians, Helen, to feel their obligation to exercise enlightened compassion with regard to mental illness in a fellow physician."

"I like knowing that Grady said that," I told

the men. "But I don't believe he plans to take up psychiatry."

"Oh, no," said Shields, throwing a rock toward the fence. I watched the muscles ripple in his back and arm. "He was just showing us that he plans to keep at this business of being a gadfly."

This pleasant day, that early in the spring, was followed by two weeks of cold and rainy weather. We decided that the spring horse show could never be held. But it was, just the same, though the second day was marked by such changeable weather that Ann wore a whaling-style yellow hat tied under her chin for possible wind, and a sleeveless dress for the sun.

Our so-called Hunt Club and its horse show offered something for everybody. One doesn't have to ride to enjoy the event. In fact, one doesn't have to know much about horses, either.

But each year hundreds of people turn out for that show with the enthusiasm of kids at a Fourth of July picnic. Our Club is one of the larger ones in the Middle West, and the show does afford a chance to see and compete with the top riders and horses from all over the country.

Both Joe and Bishop are proficient, and keep good horses. All of our children are taught to ride. Eve is quite good, and makes a pretty picture with her children mounted well and dressed perfectly. At such times, Joe is proud of his family, and should be. That year they took ribbons riding in the family class and individually.

Joe and Bishop had brought cars — Joe, a bus as well — out to the stables a day early to be sure of a good parking place just outside the ring, and the rest of us knew that in them we would find a home, for they would be as well-stocked with food as a small grocery store.

For Joe, his family, and Bishop, every class was fascinating. Many of us — my riding days had ended at the pony track — attended the horse show for the fun of it, a most pleasant interlude at the end of winter.

Everyone took his family. The McCords showed up in force, with the doctors arranging to be called for emergencies, but interrupting their routine duties to get those two days out in the country and to enjoy the fresh air.

Everyone had fun; the County Police Welfare Fund benefited. That year the weather was tricky, but otherwise things were almost too well-organized. I was ready to agree with Fannie Hudson that it was perfectly thrilling to watch Bishop jump. His chiseled profile, his exactly right clothes, his magnificent horse, lifting, taking a jump of Aiken brush — I could smile at the young woman whom he had brought out and handed over to my care, "While I am busy."

"He's such a good doctor, too," Fannie Hudson told me.

I smoothed the smile from my face. "All the McCords are good doctors," I told her, knowing that I spoke in my best Lady Vere de Vere manner.

I saw Shields grin. And, behind me, Jason snorted mildly.

Taylor Falk came up to our group. Earlier we had watched her ride in what was called the costume class. She still wore the hitched-up long skirt, boots, silk hat and white stock; she was deliciously lovely. Her hair struck fire in the sun; a sprinkle of tiny freckles dusted her pink cheeks.

"I think sidesaddle does more for a girl than these hurdle things," I told her, kissing her.

"I do, too," said Shields, following suit. We were all laughing. I presented Taylor to Dr. Hudson, and I saw Taylor's eyes widen a bit. Fannie was a handsome young woman in a white woolen jacket over a navy blue dress; a blue and white scarf was twisted about her dark brown hair.

"Bishop brought Fannie out," I told Taylor.

"Showing off, as usual," said Shields.

Dr. Hudson would have protested, then had the good sense to wait and see. . . .

"Is Grady here?" Taylor asked, borrowing Shields' glasses to scan the crowd on the opposite side of the ring.

"No," I said. "He came out for a time this morning."

"I missed him then. Did you know?" she asked. "I have decided to marry Grady."

Again Dr. Hudson watched our faces, and they must have been something to see. Jason's, my own — Lucian's — Ann's. . . .

"Do you mean," asked Jason, "that Grady stands a chance of doing something we'll have to approve?"

"Are you going to live in his carriage house?" asked Ann.

"We could," said Taylor.

"Does Grady know about this?" Lucian asked keenly.

Taylor laughed. She is a lovely young woman, and never prettier than on that afternoon. Her face glowed, her eyes sparkled. We had never had a redhead in the family.

"He'll know," she said confidently. "And he'll do it. He's mistaken, but he says I am the only woman in the world so used to him that I never see him."

"Do you?" asked Shields.

"Yes," said Taylor softly.

Shields kicked the bottom rail of the fence. "If he won't marry you, Taylor," he said, "when you tell him about your plans, remember, I'm willing."

"Oh, Shields!" she cried. "One of the nicest things about Grady, you know, is his family."

"A lot of good that'll do us," said Shields gruffly.

"I don't think you're the only girl who doesn't see his face and eye," Jason told her. "A lot of girls — I always thought Isabelle would have married him."

Yes, I told myself. She would have. And that would not be the only reason he would marry Taylor. "You'll make him a good wife," I said.

"Yes, you will," said Jason heartily. "And once you've married him, maybe he'll settle down. . . ."

"Oh, no," said Taylor. "If he'd do that, I'd leave him."

We laughed, but that night, gathered together, a lot of us, in the front and back parlors of Lucian's home, tired and contented, we discussed Fannie Hudson and Bishop. Lucian thought the situation serious enough that he could tell us about the young woman's background. She came from a small city in Ohio, he told us; her father was a building contractor. She had two brothers . . .

Then we discussed Taylor and Grady. Lucian made a point of telling Mary that there still was no engagement.

"But there will be," I said confidently. "That, or the two of them will just come home married someday."

We talked about where they would live. Grady had sold both Tibbs houses. But with Taylor the only child of the Falks . . .

"He won't live with his in-laws," said Joe.

"Nor will Taylor," I predicted. "Though in time — Oh, let's permit them to make their own plans, shall we? She's a darling girl, and she'll make a good daughter-in-law."

"If they marry at all," said Mary.

"Taylor knows how to handle Grady," Shields told her. "They've been seeing a lot of each other lately. And she knows just what to do about that guy's inferiority complex."

Everyone in the room snapped to attention. "What was that?" asked Lucian sharply.

Shields grinned. "I suspect my brother has a very big one. I've suspected it for years. The things he's done — all he's done, in fact — "

A.B. groaned.

"Sure," said Shields, "they've bedeviled us. But he's done them because he's afraid that without them he could not hold up his end. I'm of his generation, and I know that the McCords are a mighty lot for a little boy, a young man, a young doctor, to face."

"But he could always hold his place, and did," said Lucian. I wished Grady could have heard him.

"The McCord doctors," mused Grady's father. "Looking back — we grew up with diphtheria, smallpox, typhoid. Grady, and Shields here — these new doctors, they had polio, measles, and rheumatic fever — I suppose those things do add up fearfully, one generation to another. And then you wonder what things his son will have to do."

"Personally, I can't bear to think of *that!*" said Shields wryly. "And I don't predict that Grady will be able to."

"Takes all the fun out of grandchildren, doesn't it?" chuckled Jason. "But if your theory is correct, Shields . . ."

"I think it is, sir. And Uncle Lucian is right. Going along a straight line, he would have held his own. He proved that in your surgery. But there is one thing you don't realize, and he doesn't. And that is, by working toward all his reforms, and realizing many of them, Grady is going to top all the McCords."

That didn't set too well with Lucian, but the other men were nodding.

"And you are all ready to give up to him," Lucian accused.

"Well," said Jason, "if we can't lick him — and we can't — hadn't we better join him?"

"We?" asked Lucian.

"Well, yes. And haven't we, really? Already? I

don't mean the McCords. I mean medicine itself. And we should not, for any reason, let him give up his fighting."

"That's right," said Shields. "Of course he mustn't let down. Though we could show that we want to join him and help him."

"It's something like Taylor's getting him to marry her," said Jason. "I hope we won't need to tell him right out, in so many words."

"Hell, no!" cried A.B. "I'd certainly hope not. That girl had better be careful, too."

"She will be," I said happily. "Things are going to be very good for Grady."

The next day, I made a point of talking to my son. I went down to his apartment and told him that I felt the place had served its purpose.

"Doesn't it get dreadfully hot up here in the summer?" I asked.

"Yes, it does. . . ."

"You could come back home, no questions asked." I glanced at him. He was grinning.

"Or," I said airily, "it would please me a great deal if you and Taylor —"

He got up and came over to me. "Then be pleased, Lady V. de V.," he said deeply.

"You've *asked* her?" I cried happily.

"Not yet. No. But for a long time that's been one of my projects. A long time." His eye glinted. "Did you know I went into the old tack room at home and practiced jumping rope so I wouldn't make an idiot of myself before that girl? She was only nine then."

"Oh, Grady!" I cried, half-laughing. "Oh, *Grady!* What if she had married someone else?"

"I knew she wouldn't."

"You're very sure of yourself," I told him crossly.

He nodded. "A guy like me," he said, "has to be." And I thought he looked tired.

"When are you going to stop being a guy like you?" I demanded, still cross.

"When I marry Taylor," he told me. "You wait and see! I'll sit back, put my feet up — in carpet slippers, Mom!"

I laughed.

"I will," he insisted. "Real ones. I have 'em already."

And I could only laugh again — happily, helplessly.

THORNDIKE-MAGNA hopes you have enjoyed this Large Print book. All our Large Print titles are designed for easy reading, and all our books are made to last. Other Thorndike Press or Magna Print books are available at your library, through selected bookstores, or directly from the publishers. For more information about current and upcoming titles, please call or mail your name and address to:

THORNDIKE PRESS
P.O. Box 159
Thorndike, Maine 04986
(800) 223-6121
(207) 948-2962 (in Maine and Canada call collect)

or in the United Kingdom:

MAGNA PRINT BOOKS
Long Preston, Near Skipton
North Yorkshire,
England BD23 4ND
(07294) 225

There is no obligation, of course.